THE DUKE'S SECRET CINDERELLA

THE
DUKE'S
SECRET
CINDERELLA

USA TODAY BESTSELLING AUTHOR
EVA DEVON

Entangled Publishing, LLC
644 Shrewsbury Commons Ave., STE 181
Shrewsbury, PA 17361
Visit our website at www.entangledpublishing.com.

Amara is an imprint of Entangled Publishing, LLC.

Edited by Lydia Sharp and Liz Pelletier
Cover design by Bree Archer
Photography by Shirley Green
Stock art by VJ Dunraven/Period Images,
and bonetta/GettyImages
Interior design by Toni Kerr

Print ISBN 978-1-64937-241-3
ebook ISBN 978-1-64937-347-2

Manufactured in the United States of America

First Edition March 2023

AMARA

ALSO BY EVA DEVON

*For Phil, Coochy, and Kelly for always
supporting me and teaching me so much
about myself. My gratitude is unending.*

*And as always for my beautiful boys who
have taught me how deep love truly goes.*

CHAPTER ONE

Rafe Andrew William Henley Dorchester, Duke of Rockford, notched the perfectly crafted arrow to his perfectly made bow, pulled the perfectly woven string taut, and just as he was about to let fly, his mother, the duchess, announced…

"You are getting married."

The arrow flew from his fingertips too soon and quite *im*perfectly arced toward the target butts far across his long, impeccably sculpted gardens.

Instead of striking the central circle of the bull's-eye, the arrow careened off into the air, plummeting downward toward an unsuspecting goose.

The creature honked wildly, shed several feathers, and dashed off with indignant alarm in the direction of the hedgerows imported from Tuscany.

"My dear, I am not in need of feathers for a new hat, and dinner is roast lamb," his mother drawled. "Skewer me if you must, but save the poor bird."

He eyed his mother's hat, which was large, crimson, and be-feathered. Few could get away with the hats his mother donned. Pirates came to mind.

One always knew when the Duchess of Rockford was present from her laugh and from the elaborate structures upon her head.

"I did not know you felt such concern for our feathered friends," he stated calmly, trying to compose himself before the onslaught no doubt began.

She *tsk*ed, gazing upon him with a wounded expression. "I am a friend to all creatures, my darling. Feathered or no."

This did not warrant a reply.

He studied her for signs of more mischief. He saw none.

And his alarm pitched to a new height. Surely, she was not about to produce a bride he must marry, here, in his own garden? He put almost nothing past his mother, such was her recent determination to see him engaged in connubial contract.

After all, it was all dukes said, as she pointed out every time they were together.

And this was what mamas always said; he knew it. He couldn't even begrudge her for it.

It was the grand tradition of ladies. Their main role in life, so to speak.

Once ladies had produced children, raised them, and then reached a certain age—or their sons did—it was their duty by *ton* tradition to ensure the continuation of the line.

And it was the duty of sons, in general, to resist for as long as possible.

However, Rafe was more than cognizant

of the fact that he did have a duty to produce the next duke.

Still, he was in no hurry, nor would he be rushed.

He drove the end of his bow into the almost mathematically trimmed grass. "Mama, we have had this conversation before, and I do not see why you think that I shall change my mind."

"You did seem most alarmed by my tone, though, did you not, my dear?" she said, waggling her brows as she pulled back her own bowstring.

His mother was an excellent markswoman.

Her dark hair was curled over her shoulder to allow for her grand hat and so as not to interfere with her sport.

He eyed her, his unease growing. He'd dueled with men who'd been mentioned in dispatches, faced down puffed-up parliamentarians, and had words with a king who was losing his wits.

None of them gave him pause quite the way his mother did.

The duchess was as beautiful as any woman in the *ton*, and she had been the diamond of her Season. She was capable, skilled, and more accomplished than most of the members, male or female, could ever hope to be.

He adored it about her.

He adored *her*.

But they had a very different line of thinking from each other about the way they should conduct themselves. His mother was, dare he say, perfect.

Nothing ruffled her.

She was an iceberg. It was perhaps the only way to describe her. Oh, she was a wit who could make others laugh, but in the face of emotion? She was implacable. Anything more than a raise of the eyebrow was a case of hysterics, in her opinion. His mother was a formidable general on the field of the *ton*, her domain, maneuvering people as if they were battalions.

This was, of course, a characteristic to be admired by Wellington and his set.

However, it did mean that she sometimes lodged herself into his life with aplomb and determination, forgetting that he was a grown man and that he was not going to be told when and how to marry.

"Mama, I do not have time this Season to look for a wife, and you will not choose mine. Ladies are not hats."

She tilted her head to the side. "Are they not? They are like them. Pick the right one, and everything falls into place. But, my darling boy, you are not looking for a wife."

"A hat?"

"No. A duchess."

And there it was. His mother did not see a

person but a position. It was her great armor, and she was determined that he wear it too.

Unlike the duchess, he did not have a list of specific characteristics he hoped to tick off to achieve or acquire a specific type of person. No, he was hoping for—well, something *more*.

He realized this was a ludicrous thing to think for one of his station.

After all, *ton* marriages were business arrangements, and he was a duke. His marriage would be the ultimate negotiation between two powerful families to ensure the continuation of great lines that had stretched for hundreds of years and would no doubt be stretched for hundreds more.

And yet, he could not help but recall the way his mother had looked at his father when he had been small. The way his father had looked at her. The adoration had softened his father's granite face. And she? She had seemed the picture of happiness.

He snapped his gaze back to the archery butt, and his mother's arrow darted through the air with a slight whistle in the wind. As it landed in its target, he frowned.

She turned to him, her red gloves clutching at her bow, and she cocked her head to the side.

"You have been prevaricating for too long for someone who is so sure and so capable. It is time that I take you in hand."

"I am not a small boy in leading strings, Mama. You cannot take me in hand," he pointed out, determined to recall that she had done her best by him whilst in deep mourning for years she now pretended had not occurred.

"Oh, indeed I can," she countered. "For I have something that you want."

He laughed. "I respect your opinions, of course, but you are far too clever to think you can withhold anything I desire."

She blinked, then stated, "The foundling hospital, my dear."

At first, he was so stunned he could barely comprehend what she was saying. But then her words sank in. "I beg your pardon?"

She cleared her throat, then beckoned for one of the footmen at the small tent that had been set up in the garden for her visit. She thrust the bow at the fellow and swept her hands over her skirts. "The foundling hospital that your grandfather created, Rafe. That you have such high hopes for, that you plan on—"

"What the blazes are you speaking of?" he bit out, his reserve rushing from him.

"I'm going to give it to someone else," she said coolly.

He gaped. "You cannot possibly be serious. You know what I—"

"Indeed, I do know what you hope for, my

dear. But it is time that you wed, and I see that it is now imperative that I take action to ensure you marry a suitable young woman—someone who will fill the role of duchess, which has now been neglected for decades. Someone who will assist you and support you, who will not distract you from the work you need to do."

"Mama," he warned softly, stunned by her audacity. "You are on dangerous ground."

"What a delightful place to be," she replied without flinching. "Your father… I miss him so desperately. But we must do our duty. And I am doing my duty to him by seeing you wed."

He swallowed at those harsh words.

His mother and father had loved each other more powerfully than anyone had ever done in the *ton*. Their love had not been in grand gestures that lasted but a moment. No, their love had been in the small things. The daily things. The image of his father, a duke, silver tray in hand, bringing his mother her cup of hot chocolate every morning without fail, flitted through his mind.

His father had not missed a single day unless they were parted by miles. And they seldom were.

Whether they had fought the night before or even if he was ill, his father had gotten up in the dark hours of the early morn, gone down to the kitchens, and brought the much beloved beverage to his beloved wife *himself*.

He could still see the looks of love on their faces, no matter the circumstance in the moments that he had witnessed.

He wanted that. He wanted someone who recognized that love was in the little things. The consistent things. How could he find that on a list?

He understood why his mother said what she said. But it gutted him nonetheless. It had broken her, his father's death, and he had been but six years of age when his father had collapsed, never to tower over him, strong and kind, again.

The implication that he was not doing his duty galled him. He'd devoted his life to the dukedom—an heir was necessary. But surely not yet? Surely, he'd never be the father his own papa was? Could he ever have the impact that his father had had on his son? Or could he find the great love his mother and father had known? He would settle for nothing less. Anything else would leave him ever bitter with wanting.

He blinked and turned back to the archery butts, drawing in a deep breath. He wouldn't allow the memories to slip in.

If he did, the pain of it would be unimaginable. Well, that was not entirely true. He could imagine it. The darkness, the struggle, his mother's tears, his inability to pull her from her bed with his boyish pleas.

"My dear, I've already begun arrangements."

"What?" he all but yelled, a sound that did not usually come from his being, a being shaped by control under her tutelage in these last years.

She had ensured that in all things, he was completely capable, but in this, he found that he was growing more and more shocked.

His mother was determined—more determined than he had ever seen her.

"Mama, if you wish so heartily to see a marriage in this family, then *you* wed," he declared.

"Never," she retorted. "I have done my duty; there is no need for me to do it again. You have yet to fulfill yours."

He gazed down at her, nearing the end of his rope. "I have fulfilled my duty in every way that counts—"

"Except the one," she cut in, "that matters most. Your father died when he was but thirty-nine. You are thirty. If you do not marry soon, you will be risking a great fissure in the Rockford line, and I cannot bear that. Besides, you are waltzing about life as if you are looking for some young lady who will suddenly take your eye, and that is no way to go about this."

She lifted her chin, causing the feathers on her hat to dance. "No. One must be practical. One must find a partner who does not lead one into…"

The word she searched for? He knew what it was.

"Despair" was the word. There had been such joy once, and the truth was, he wanted that. He wanted to feel that, just once.

But he never had, and he was beginning to think that he never would. Love had never once neared him, though he'd kept his eye open for it.

But he would be damned if he would allow his mother to push him down the path of a practical marriage in which he could barely tolerate his wife.

"I have a list," she said quickly, blinking her dark lashes lest any moisture pool there.

"A list," he repeated, shaking his head.

"Yes." She pulled a small piece of paper from her glove and handed it to him.

He stared down at it, then unfolded it slowly.

"There is one name," he said.

"I did not say it was a long list," she returned.

He drew in a long-suffering breath. "Mama—"

"You will call on her tomorrow afternoon."

"I will not," he replied tersely.

"You will," she said. "Or I shall make

certain that the foundling hospital goes to someone you do not admire."

He locked gazes with her. "You would not do that. You are not that cruel."

"I am that determined," she said, squaring her shoulders. "I will not and cannot allow you to keep on this path."

"Mama, I am not on any sort of mad path as you seem to suggest," he gritted. "I am an excellent duke."

"Yes, my dear, you are. So, you will marry. You'll be content. You'll have children. I will be a grandmother, and all shall be well. I have a duty to your father…"

Her words died off, and he understood. More than he wanted to. His mother was in earnest. Some warped sense of duty was pushing her in this. Reason was not part of it. And so, reason would not work with her.

He drew in a long breath. He did not wish to believe that she would do what she threatened, but there was a certain look in her eye that he had never seen before.

"You mean it," he breathed.

"Oh, indeed I do, my dear." She nodded. "Indeed I do."

"You would destroy your own father's legacy, created in the memory of—"

"Yes," she bit out. "I would. For my son, and for the memory of my husband, I absolutely would."

He ground his teeth, resigned to her terri-fying determination to do her duty no matter the cost.

"Travers!" she called to the awaiting foot-man. "Champagne. His Grace will be getting married." His mother gave him a small salute then, as if she understood that she had chosen war over love. "Do not test me, my dear, for I have made up my mind."

And with that, she turned, her ruby skirts flashing over the grass as she whipped away and headed toward the tent—and the await-ing champagne that she had no doubt arranged.

Rafe drew in a fortifying breath. After all, if she was choosing battle, he was not absent arms. He was a man who had negotiated trea-ties, who had led a cabinet, and who had the ear of the most important men in govern-ment. He made policy, he owned half of England, and he was not about to be manipu-lated.

If his mother wanted battle, he would meet her on the field.

CHAPTER TWO

"It does not fit."

Charlotte Browne pulled at the sleeves of her borrowed silk gown and fidgeted in front of the long mirror, a mirror at which she'd never allowed herself to linger before.

Except to clean it, of course.

The robin's egg blue gown was beautiful, trimmed with a darker sapphire ribbon. It should have looked stunning. And it did…on Francesca.

Charlotte swung her gaze back to her stepsister, her heart squeezing as she willed herself to meet her upcoming task.

"No one is going to believe that it belongs to me," Charlotte stated, arching a brow.

Francesca shook her dark-haired head and said optimistically, "I disagree, Charlie. No one will dare question you. You know exactly how to play the part." A look of distress creased her brow as she added, "Besides, you must wear it. You are convincing them you are a lady, after all."

Charlotte nodded, squaring her shoulders. She could not fail. She would not.

And the only thing she feared was returning home without her dear friend and fellow servant, the elderly Stevenson. Just a few days ago, she had attended the Marshalsea Debtors' Prison and had gained admittance. She'd kept her frock on, determined to appear more than a servant. She'd succeeded.

But now that she knew the amount of coin necessary to pay the fees to the Knight of the Marshalsea to release her friend? She had to go in the armor of respectability, lest the man attempt to negotiate with her. Or worse, simply take the money and not let Stevenson go. The jailers were notoriously corrupt.

"Are you not afraid in Southwark?" Francesca asked, her hazel eyes widening with amazement at Charlotte's boldness.

"No," she replied quite honestly.

She had spent a good many years walking the roads of London. After all, when one was treated as little more than a housemaid, one was given a great deal more freedom than, say, Francesca was.

Francesca went to balls, routes, soirees, and musicales. But she was never allowed to leave the sprawling townhouse alone. And she was certainly never permitted to go anywhere outside the wealthiest enclaves of the city.

Their father would never condone it.

Charlotte bit the inside of her cheek as she coiled her blond hair atop her head and jabbed in pins with a good deal of vigor. Her hair was unruly and required a steady hand to tame it.

The truth was, Lord Palmerton was not her father. Once, she had hoped he would fill the painful emptiness her own beloved father had left when he had been taken from her and her mother. Charlotte was but a small girl then.

Her hands stilled on her hair as she recalled that forlorn hope. The way she'd imagined having someone to take her riding again. To lift her up on his shoulders...

Palmerton had seemed as if he might. And then, once the ring had been slipped upon her mother's finger, the vows spoken, and the book signed...things had taken a dark turn.

She swallowed and let her hands fall to her sides.

He had been her father by marriage, but he'd made it clear that he was not interested in fulfilling that role in any way, except for, well, legally. And his idea of being a father to Francesca was to insist she marry a great man who had power and vast wealth.

A spring breeze wafted through the window, bringing in the scent of lilacs and hyacinth from the garden, and those bright, cheerful notes shook the dark thoughts from Charlotte's mind.

She drank in the fragrance. How could one not adore spring? The colors, the sounds of birds, the bright future of flowers and verdant leaves bursting forth from the darkness.

She was like those flowers. She had to be. Pushing her way through the darkness. Determined to see the sun.

Charlotte turned from the mirror and crossed to the window, taking in the beautiful garden created by her own father who had brought back trees and statues from his tour of Europe. She could almost feel him in those trees.

When the breeze whispered through the budding leaves, causing the limbs to dance? She would have sworn it was her mother's voice assuring her all would be well if she kept her shoulders back, if she looked for the chances that this life would bring her, if she but kept her chin up and eyes wide.

The truth was, it was difficult some days to maintain the love of life her parents had both had.

The sound of porcelain clinking cut through her reverie, and she whipped away from the window.

"Are you ready, Charlie?" Francesca asked as she carefully placed the tea things on the tray. "You must go soon. Papa will be back, and if he catches you, you will never get out of the house."

She gave a tight nod. This was a small window of opportunity to go and get Stevenson out of the Marshalsea. It was imperative she bring him food as well. She'd learned prisoners starved to death in that place. So many couldn't afford to buy their own food, and they were not supplied meals. And then, of course, there were those desperate enough to steal food from prisoners who did have it.

Starving. All because Palmerton had wanted her to suffer, no doubt. To remind her of the power he had to harm those she cared about.

She could not believe that a man could be so despicable, but he was.

Palmerton had vast sums of money, but he had accrued a small debt of no more than two pounds in Stevenson's name. He'd refused to pay and arranged for his servant to be collected by bailiffs.

No one would dare question a lord to protect a servant. No one.

She swallowed the acrid bile rising in her throat.

Charlotte eyed herself once again in the mirror, trying to ignore the fact that the hem of the gown was too long, that the sleeves skimmed her knuckles, and that the bosom sagged a bit.

Francesca's figure was the sort that every young lady of the *ton* longed for.

And soon she would marry. Perhaps a duke. Charlotte smiled to herself. She liked the idea of her dear sister a powerful duchess, away from her repressive father.

"I have never been more ready," she declared to Francesca.

And with that, she picked up the tea tray, headed toward the door, and stepped out into the hall.

Francesca followed her, and they made their way quickly down the back stairs into the bustling kitchen, where Francesca was not supposed to go into.

As Charlotte plunked the tray down on the long table, the silver-haired cook eyed them both as if they had lost their wits. She *tsk*ed, shaking a finger gnarled from years of hard work. "You are in for it today—both of you. You are taking quite a few risks by being here together. And you know it."

Francesca smiled, giving Cook an affectionate look. "I shall simply tell Father that I have come down for one of your excellent buns."

Cook blushed before clucking her tongue. "If you do, your father will castigate you and say you won't fit in your gowns."

Francesca winced.

Her father controlled almost everything in her life, including what she was allowed to eat.

The man was a complete tyrant.

It was mystifying how a man could be so two-faced like Janus, the Roman god that Charlotte had read about in books.

"I wish I could go with you," Francesca said firmly, taking her hand in hers.

"I wish you could, too," Charlotte replied. "But you cannot. I shall go for both of us, and that will be enough. I will free Stevenson."

Cook jabbed the tip of her knife into the wood table. "That place is not fit for rats." She huffed, her eyes filling with tears, which she quickly brushed away. "I would not wish my worst enemy, even Palmerton, in that place. He knows nothing of what he's done. He can't. He can't know how that sort of place can break a person."

Charlotte crossed to her dear friend and wrapped her arms around Cook's stout waist.

She knew that the older woman was naive, but even she couldn't make sense of what had befallen what had been such a happy house years ago.

There was nothing to say, and she wouldn't utter falsehoods to the woman who had done her best to care for her, even whilst working from before dawn to late into the evenings.

"Do you have the basket?" Charlotte asked.

Cook nodded, clearing her throat. She gave Charlotte a brusque squeeze, then wiped her hands on her immaculately pressed apron.

Cook blew out a shaky breath. "We must be particularly careful. If his lordship finds out we've taken food, we could all be jailed. The man knows his larder better than most people know the back of their hand."

Charlotte took the wicker basket Cook held out to her.

She looked inside, her heart beating wildly at their audacity.

There were bread, cheese, and apples.

This would hopefully get Stevenson through if, somehow, the Knight would not release him today. Without sustenance, he would weaken. And the sights she had seen earlier this week? They would haunt her dreams for years to come.

It seemed horrifying, indeed, that a man could be condemned essentially to death by starvation for the debt of forty shillings. But there it was.

She'd managed to pay off the two-pound debt and had gone to free him—and learned of the prison fees that had to be paid first. She'd agonized over it. For she had little money and certainly not several pounds' worth.

There had been only one thing to do.

She had sold the last thing in her possession that had belonged to her mother that Palmerton had allowed her to keep. A small gold locket with a fine likeness inside.

It had nearly broken her to sell it, but it had been worth it because, now, Stevenson was still very much alive.

Her mother was also very much alive in Charlotte's memory and always would be. She did not need a locket to remind her of her mother's love.

She cradled the basket against her hip and collected her simple bag, which held the coins to free Stevenson. "Wish me well," she said with more confidence than she felt.

She turned toward the doors, ready to depart, but then Cook called out, "Wait—you must take this with you this time. I couldn't rest for worry when you went a few days ago, my dear. I would send one of the footmen with you if we could manage the ruse. But I cannot see how we would hide it."

Cook picked up one of the bricks used for heating the beds, usually wrapped in a piece of flannel after being heated in the oven, and tucked it into her bag. "Anyone gives you a funny look, and you bash them with that."

Though her insides shook with nerves, Charlotte laughed. "Indeed, I will."

Over the years, she'd learned from several of the female servants how to defend herself. One could not be a maid in this world without knowing how to bash a fellow's head in should the bloke warrant it.

And with that final thought, she headed out of her mother's home, ready to face some of the most dangerous streets of London.

CHAPTER THREE

Rafe strode through the crowded streets of Southwark, drinking in the wildness of daily London life.

As opposed to many of his class, he sought it out.

The vast majority of the *ton* never left the hallowed halls of Mayfair or the west of London unless it was to retreat to their palatial country estates. Whereas he found going into the city and across the river to the South Bank was the most vital part of his existence.

After all, it reminded him that London was the lifeblood of the world. An essential heartbeat, keeping everything in order, not always for good and sometimes great ill. It was the center of a teeming empire of varied people that came and went, ruled by the tides of the Thames.

At this particular moment, despite the city that invigorated him so, he found himself incredibly frustrated.

A night of carousing had not ended it.

He was going to have to pay a visit to his solicitors to see if there was any way he could get around the difficulties. He had plans to expand the hospital, to improve it and make it more amenable, kind, and capable of taking care of more children without them being treated in a cruel way.

He knew the brutality of other such places where children were often tied to beds or never picked up or consoled...

He couldn't save them all. But he would save those he could.

Rafe turned, picking from the warren of roads that headed north. His presence caused people to part for him—something that simply occurred wherever he went.

Just as he was about to head toward the Thames and cross over the river that led to the walk up Fleet Street to Hyde Park, he caught an odd sight.

A footpad in sweat- and dirt-stained clothes yanked at a young lady's wicker basket. Her knuckles were white on the handle, her body taut as she arced in the opposite direction.

The two were engaged in a serious bout of tug-of-war, and the young woman did not look as if she would give in, despite the risks of tangling with a London tough.

Little shocked him. But this woman's defiance of the towering, rough man did.

Her blond hair tumbled about her face in wild curls as she struggled. Her bonnet had been dislodged and now bounced at her back from the plain ribbon tied at her throat.

Pink-cheeked with outrage, eyes flashing,

she yelled, "Get your bleeding hands off!"

The man refused to release his prize as he roared back at her, "Eh, love! I bet you've got coin as well! You'll give it to me now."

No one intervened.

No one would on this street.

The woman, much to his amazement, still did not yield or tremble with terror.

Instead, she hauled one arm back abruptly and looked as if she was about to strike, though such an action seemed a terrible misjudgment. Her opponent was the sort of fellow that only the darkest slums produced, where a grown man might beat a girl into the ground for a few possessions to sell at the secondhand shops.

The tough's eyes narrowed, as if daring the woman to be so foolish.

Rafe's stomach tightened. She clearly did not belong in this part of town. Her frock was too tidy, her face too clean. And she was about to get herself killed over a basket.

Something had to be done. And he would have to be the one to do it.

And so, he strode forward, ready to come to her rescue.

But just as he was about to grab the tough, the woman wound her hand back—a hand he realized clutched the strings to her oddly shaped bag.

She then swung it forward in a forceful arc.

The bag shot out and hit the fellow on his ham-like shoulder.

The man yelled so wildly that people stared as he danced back. He howled again with alarm as he released the basket he'd been trying to steal.

She let out a cry of triumph. "You see, I defend what is mine. I hate to resort to such violence, but it is vitally important that I deliver the contents of this basket. Now, sir, if you are hungry, I shall give you a bun, but that is all I can spare."

The man scowled, his free hand flexing as if he was considering grabbing her by the throat and shaking her like a rat.

Rafe took a step forward and caught the footpad's gaze, arching a brow. He flexed his gloved hands, knowing the man wouldn't dare to attack a peer in broad daylight.

As soon as the tough spotted Rafe, he let out a curse and whipped around, then darted down a narrow alley, his feet kicking up scum-covered puddle water as he went.

Rafe reached out to steady the woman, who had not yet seen him. But she appeared to be off foot.

The moment his hand touched her shoulder, he realized his miscalculation, but it was too late to withdraw. And he braced himself.

As predicted, the reticule came swinging again and landed straight in his ribs. He winced, and a grunt tore out of him. "I do beg your pardon, but I think you may have cracked a rib."

"Oh dear!" she gasped, her bag dropping to her side. "I am so sorry. I did not mean to hurt you."

"Your blow would indicate otherwise," he wheezed. "What the devil is in that thing?"

"It's a brick," she replied bluntly. Her sapphire eyes darted over him, taking in his clothes and his doubled-over state.

"A brick?" he echoed as he forced himself to straighten.

It was no easy task. There was a good possibility she had indeed cracked one of his ribs in her admirable and vigorous self-defense.

It served him bloody right for touching her shoulder without fair warning when he'd known she was *armed*. He was loath to admit it, but her fierce nature, wild curls, and piercing blue eyes had stolen his usually very practical wits.

She was entirely capable, he realized, and he liked her for it. He found himself eyeing her as she righted her cloak. The gown underneath the plain cloak was quite simple. Her earlier speech had indicated she was familiar with a rougher tone, but her accent was rounded and indicated access to the more important families of his own set.

She did not offer him another word, but

clutched her basket and turned away, clearly eager to be off.

"There will be no thanks, then?" he called after her.

She stopped, hesitated, her slightly worn cloak dancing over her simple boots before she turned toward him. Those cheeks of hers were still a glorious pink, and she arched a blond brow. "For getting in the way of my reticule?"

He barked out a laugh. "A fair point."

She inclined her head in acknowledgment.

"Where are you going?" he blurted, then winced inwardly at his ridiculous question.

"It is not of your business where I am going, sir." She traced her eyes up and down his frame, and they widened a little. Her lips parted ever so slightly, and she took a moment before continuing, "I would say, sir, that you are in more danger here than I. Your cravat alone could feed a family for a year."

Her summation of his cravat was correct, but not his endangerment. "Thank you for your concern, miss," he replied. "But I am quite capable of taking care of myself. It is not the first time I have ventured into these parts. Can you say the same?"

Her pink cheeks flushed a deep red. And he was certain now that it *was* her first foray into this part of town.

She cleared her throat and nodded. "Of

course you are familiar with these parts. No doubt you are a rake and a scoundrel, sir, and enjoy slumming with the poor as so many of your class do. And given that, I should not linger in your company lest I should be ruined by it."

He snorted, amazed at her turn of phrase. But to his shock, he found himself *enjoying* it. She was an utter surprise. No one spoke to him thus. High or low. Yet here she was, all but castigating him on the street. All after sorting out a footpad.

She was a bloody marvel.

"How could you possibly be ruined by my company when you are out by yourself?" he queried, cocking his head to the side.

"I am not in need of a chaperone or companion, sir," she rushed firmly, as if she was eager to be on her way. "Now, I have an appointment."

A deep, protective need within him demanded he not let her go alone. "Please allow me to walk you there."

Her lips parted, and her eyes narrowed.

Before she could deny him, he rushed on: "It will ease my conscience. After you were so very nearly attacked, at least, if I keep you company…"

Her gaze dropped to her bag, and her entire body went rigid. A cry of alarm escaped her lips.

The sound of it shook him. "What is it?"

"My bag," she bit out. "It is torn."

He looked, and there was indeed a rip in the green fabric. It was a bag of no account, and he was surprised by her genuine distress, but perhaps she did not have the resources to acquire a new one. He could certainly assist her with that, but first and foremost, he wished to ease her sudden tumult.

He offered a smile. "No doubt it was ripped by the brick inside, which you wielded with such excellent vigor."

She ignored his compliment and began looking about wildly, her eyes frantic.

Dread coiled in his gut. "What is amiss?"

"My coin," she lamented, her breath ragged now. "It is gone!"

The panic in those words could not be ignored. And he was no fool—money mattered. He had vast sums, but for most people, to lose their money would be a calamity indeed.

"Perhaps we can find it," he offered. "Do you think that you lost it here?"

She shook her head, a sheen of tears in her eyes—a completely different emotion from the splendid cockiness she had displayed just moments before.

"I do not know," she confessed. She bit her lower lip and rifled through her bag. "But I must find those coins. It is imperative that I do so."

Her hands began to shake, and the basket trembled as well, threatening to spill the contents.

Gently, he took her by the shoulders, risking being bludgeoned again. "We shall find whatever it is you require," he said firmly.

She gazed up at him, and the pain in her eyes nearly undid him. The fear, the suffering, the loss of hope... They all nearly crushed him.

"You don't understand," she rasped. "I am on my way to secure someone's freedom from the Marshalsea."

"The Marshalsea?" he echoed. This was indeed quite serious.

She sucked in a breath and pulled herself free of his grasp, dashing her hands under her eyes, then placed the basket down.

Desperately, she yanked at the bag, as if somehow another search might reveal her lost treasure.

The crowd about them seemed to flow like water around a rock in a stream, ignoring them.

But he felt his ill ease growing.

The young woman grew more desperate with every passing moment, and the agony of her pain weighed on him in a way he had never felt before. All his life, he had helped others and defended many, but now, his heart felt ripped open by her sorrow.

"There must be something to be done," he said, trying to break through her fear. "Perhaps we can find a way."

"No." She shook her head. "If the money is gone, I cannot secure his freedom. And if he must stay there longer, the suffering he shall endure…"

"Is it your father, then?" he queried, trying to steady her. "A husband?"

Her gaze shot to his, and the stern look in her eyes turned the sapphire into a shocking steel. "Must it be a husband or a father to lament their position in such a terrible place?" she snapped.

"Of course not," he replied, feeling her criticism as if he had been lacerated by a very well-placed whip. "Forgive me. But you must share information with me if I am to be of assistance to you."

Those words seemed to find their way through the fortress of her defense. "He is *like* my father."

"Please allow me to escort you to the prison," he said calmly. "You can take the food to him, and we shall find a solution."

She stared at the muddy ground, no sign of coin anywhere. If there had been coins, they were almost certainly already picked up in the fray by quick hands used to scavenging.

She swallowed. "I don't understand. You would do such a thing?"

"Of course, I would do such a thing."

A muscle in her cheek tightened. "I will not owe you anything, my lord."

The implication of her words did not offend him. Young women were frequently manipulated by men who promised to help them, he knew. "I do not wish anything from you but to see you safely there and to do a good deed."

"Why?" She gave him a bewildered look.

And his heart grew heavier with the knowledge that she had known so little care in this life. "Because it was how my father raised me, and I cannot escape that. If I do not help you, I shall hear him berating me in my dreams for years to come."

"Oh." She blinked. "Well… We cannot have that, my lord. I wouldn't wish that many nightmares on you."

Finally, she was softening. He gave her a smile. "Your Grace, actually."

She frowned. "I beg your pardon?"

"The Duke of Rockford," he said simply, with a slight bow and a flourish of his gloved hand.

She stared at him for a long moment, then laughed. "A duke?"

He nodded.

There was something about her steely resolve that he longed to know more of. He declared in the voice that brooked no argument, "I shall go with you. We shall sort this out. And if necessary, I shall pay the fee. Unless, of course, it is thousands upon thousands of pounds. Is it thousands and thousands of pounds?" he queried, attempting to make her smile.

She did not.

She scowled instead. "It is not thousands of pounds. It is three pounds, ten shillings."

"My God, that is nothing."

"Nothing?" Her eyes narrowed. "It is not nothing to him. It is not nothing to most."

His mouth dried as he realized the horrible faux pas he had just pronounced. "Of course you are correct. Perhaps I shall sell my cravat."

"No," she stated, "I cannot take money from you, sir. I do not know if you are honorable. Nor can I induce a debt. I should not like to be placed there myself. As terrible as it is for a man, it can be far worse for a woman."

"Of course," he said, an acrid taste filling his mouth at the idea of her being locked up in such a hell. "But I will not require any sort of return of the debt. As I shall likely not see you again after this day."

And he found those words did not sit well—the idea that he wouldn't see her again. But he did not wish her to be afraid to take his help, and the best way was to assure that she would owe him nothing. Not even a future meeting.

"It is close," he said, offering his arm. "Shall we go?"

She eyed that arm as if it might bite her, but then she eyed her ripped bag again, and her shoulders sagged. "I cannot let him remain in that place even one more day."

"Then let us not linger here, good lady," he coaxed. "Together, we can ensure his quick release."

"Thank you." She gave a tight nod, turned, and, without taking his arm, marched ahead.

CHAPTER FOUR

One did not expect to be all but rescued by dukes and have them insist on providing one aid. Yet, here Charlotte was, and she frankly had no idea what to make of him or his intentions. Was he trustworthy? All her instincts told her yes, and yet, she knew the world was not a benign place. Her stepfather had taught her that.

Though she was uncertain as to his true character, the stakes were far too high to deny his assistance. She'd have to chance it. Letting Stevenson languish in the prison was not an option she could contemplate.

When Charlotte approached the guard with the disheveled beard standing at the door in his long, dark coat and slightly scruffy hat, the man looked at her as if he had spotted a cantankerous goat.

"Not you again!" he barked.

She quirked a brow, determined not to back down. Bolstered by the towering, ducal specimen of manhood behind her, she declared, "It is I, sir. I have come to liberate Mr. Stevenson."

The guard blew out a derisive snort before his lip curled. "Indeed, you have not, unless you've brought the funds."

"*Indeed*, I have," she said, keeping her chin up. Though she had bandied with costermongers, fish sellers, and chimney sweeps, debtors' prisons were an altogether different sort of negotiation.

What went on within this place was harrowing. It galled her.

"I don't believe it," snapped the guard. "You've got no money, just like most of the other posh, accented young ladies come to rescue their errant papas. You were empty-handed last time, and I'll not budge till I see coin."

The sudden wave of intense indignation crackling off the duke startled her, and his low growl of a warning cut through the air. "You should not speak thus to a lady."

The guard's gaze shifted to the duke, and his brow furrowed. "She has been an unaccompanied person. How much of a lady could she be?" Seeming to draw upon his usual arrogance and power, the guard added, "And that's, of course, if she's a lady at all."

The words stung. She was no lady. Certainly not by the duke's standards. "And yet, I am a person deserving of respect, regardless of any status I might hold—"

"Ha," the guard returned. "Coin gets respect."

Rockford took a step forward. A muscle tightened in his jaw, and he looked as if he might do murder, though his visage remained cool.

The duke arched a brow. "If you do not cease now and do as the lady *bids*, I shall have to take umbrage at your words. And if I, the Duke of Rockford, take umbrage at your words, I shall have to take certain steps. I daresay, the Knight of the Marshalsea will happily listen to my complaints, even if you do not deign to listen to hers. And I do not think that is necessary today. Do you?"

The guard's face paled considerably as he realized her ally was not merely a toffy-nosed blueblood but a duke. From the way he stepped back and cursed beneath his breath, he knew how little power he had compared to the man who was her companion.

He gave a tight nod. "Go in; pay the Knight of Marshalsea. And perhaps Mr. Stevenson can be freed. Be careful with the food, though. Duke or no duke, you might be swarmed."

"I shall make certain the lady is not swarmed," Rockford replied firmly.

And with that, they entered the prison proper.

The agony of those incarcerated, unable to pay their debts, rolled around them like a thick coat of oil.

She hated it. And she hated even more that Stevenson had been there for weeks.

The aging, creaking structure seemed to sigh with the misery of its occupants as Charlotte and the duke entered the courtyard, headed to the office that was the gateway to this hell.

Much to her surprise, the duke let her lead the way, and she cut through the people milling about the rather small common area. She could not understand why he was assisting her. She had little acquaintance with good men, save servants, and she did not know what to make of him.

As they walked inside the prison, the people were dressed from the finest of silks to worn wools.

Every walk of life intermixed here. Some had families that paid for a decent room and food. Others had literally nothing. Not a bed to sleep on or a crust of bread.

Hungry eyes swung to the basket tucked under her arms. Bony fingers fidgeted, as if they could imagine clutching the provisions within.

"Bloody hell," the duke whispered. "Hell is empty…"

Charlotte nodded and finished quickly, "And all the devils are here."

The line from *The Tempest* seemed apropos, not of the tenants of this prison, but of the devils in society who locked men away who could not pay their debts—and who were still expected to pay those debts whilst imprisoned and unable to work.

When she came to the office door, she squared her shoulders and rapped on the wood.

"Come," a voice drawled with little patience.

She drew in a slow breath, seized the handle, and entered. The duke was close behind, a firm presence, and when she opened her mouth to speak, he swung a bag of coins onto the table.

"This is for Mr. Stevenson," Rockford announced. "Release him."

The man sitting at the table, ink-stained fingers scribbling away in his ledgers, looked up.

He blinked several times as he took in the duke. Then, his eyes widened. "Your Grace, it is an honor to receive you. I have seen you speak—"

"Then you should know that I find the situation of the prisons appalling."

"As do I, Your Grace," the man protested. "But someone must enact the law? If not I, then—"

"Can you hear your justification, sir?" Charlotte burst out. "How do you sleep?"

"On a feather pillow, just like His Grace," the knight said.

"Oh, yes, I sleep on a feather pillow," the

duke agreed, a dark wave of righteous anger crackling from him. "But I toil all the hours of the day to try to improve the lives of the people of England. I do not think you can say the same. Or can you?"

The knight, unperturbed, cocked his head to the side. "You are a duke, and born to it, no doubt graced by God. But I? I must cherish my position and be grateful that I am in this office and not in the prison. Or worse, the gutters outside."

The knight's argument rang with surprising truth, and her own rage at the man dissipated, but not at the situation. The knight was a cog in the vast machine, like the machines in the northern factories.

The knight scooted his chair back. "I shall ensure Stevenson is freed this very moment... for a small fee that will expedite the necessary paperwork, which might otherwise take several days."

The duke narrowed his gaze. "Of course. An expedition fee seems perfectly reasonable."

Charlotte swallowed, her chest tightening. She had not brought extra coin. It had not occurred to her that she might have to bribe the knight.

The man slipped out into the hall.

"Your Grace," she breathed. "Thank you."

He shook his head. "It is how these men

make their livings. I knew of the corruption in places such as Bridewell, but I have had the good fortune to not know anyone in a debtors' prison."

"I have educated you, then, again?" she asked.

"Indeed. A fortuitous thing. I cannot fix a problem that I do not know exists."

Was this man real? He seemed so genuinely intent on his view of the world and his role in it as someone to heal it rather than harm it.

"I did not know dukes like you existed," she admitted.

He gave a slow inclination of his head. "A rare breed, I confess. But I shall endeavor to increase those of my ilk."

She stared at his handsome visage and tried to envision what he was like in private. How he might be without the trappings of his dukedom.

For the life of her, she could not.

He wore it like a well-cut coat, his power. And it suited him.

She couldn't even imagine it. All that he could do. All those he could save.

Her life was so little in comparison. All she wanted was to preserve her family's home. To keep that connection to her parents alive.

Whereas he? He longed to change the *world*. Still, he had so little idea of the life of someone like the knight, Stevenson, or herself.

No doubt, he read about them in reports as statistics. The life of a maid, a footman, city clerk—

"Have I grown a second head?" he asked abruptly.

She laughed. "Indeed not. I am merely marveling at your power. If you say jump, people do. If they demand more money, you can give it, no matter the cost."

"I am fortunate."

"Yes," she breathed.

"You say that as if it is a curse."

"Not a curse. But…"

"But?" he prompted, his brow furrowing.

"Will you think about the people here when you leave? Or just the mechanism of the prison itself?"

"I don't understand," he said.

"Well, you said you will try to fix the problem, for which I admire you deeply. But what of the people here now?"

"Ah. The great question," he said.

"I beg your pardon?"

"It is the gap. Between action and plan. You see, I can work all day and night and never sleep, but I still cannot save everyone."

She gaped at him as it suddenly struck her. "But you try, don't you?"

"As many as I can, yes, but there are limitations to even my power."

"Oh"—she smiled slowly—"I doubt that."

"You'd be surprised," he muttered.

Was that so?

"How far *would* you go, then? To save someone?" she asked. "As far as inconvenience? Or true sacrifice?"

He stiffened. "When I offered you help, I had no idea I would have such an opportunity to discover the faults in my character."

Her tongue grew thick with remorse. "Of course; forgive me. I have misspoken."

What a fool she was. No man was Sir Galahad. How could they be? This duke, like all other men, was a mortal with feet on the earth.

And he was far better than any man she had yet to meet.

She gave a quick curtsy. "I do not have the capacity to do good as you do, and here I am—"

"Cease." He groaned. "I did not mean to make you feel as if you cannot offer criticism of me. I promise you I am accustomed to it and can weather any storm. Even one from such a unique source as yourself."

Just as she was about to reply, the door opened and the Knight of the Marshalsea gestured for them to follow.

The whole affair was done in but a few

moments. Charlotte could barely believe it — or the exchange she'd had with Rockford in the office. What had compelled her to ask him such a thing?

Stevenson was brought to the front, and they were ejected from the prison as if the staff could not bear such a group of impossible do-gooders.

The duke stood stunned as they lingered on the pavement. "I have never experienced anything like that in my life," he said.

Stevenson shuddered. "It is a shock, Your Grace."

Your Grace, she thought to herself, truly allowing that to sink in now.

How was it possible that she had been in the company of a duke and not known it? Her stomach tightened. Of course he was a duke — the way he was dressed, the way he spoke, his entire bearing. The power he wielded so easily.

It made perfect sense.

But she did not wish to linger in his presence, lest he make inquiry into her identity. The last thing she or Stevenson needed was for her stepfather to know a duke had come to their aid...and possibly learned of his nefarious action.

The punishments she would receive did not bear consideration.

"We must go," she said to Stevenson,

taking his hand quickly and squeezing it to assure him this was all real. "You are much missed at home."

Stevenson gave a quick nod and looked to the basket, his eyes finally filling with light, losing a touch of the haunted look.

Without hesitating, she passed the wicker basket to Stevenson, who grabbed it with eager hands. He took out a piece of crusty bread made by Cook this morning and lovingly packed by his wife, Mary. Turning away from them, he tore into it and began to eat it swiftly.

Heart aching at his pain, Charlotte forced herself to calm, for he was safe now. She and Mary and Cook no longer needed to stay up through the night, envisioning his suffering, unable to do anything about it.

Her heart full, she turned to the man who had freed him. "Thank you, Your Grace. I truly appreciate everything you have done. I know that it was not necessary for you to do it."

"It was necessary," he said firmly. "I needed to see inside that place. Thank you."

Her eyes widened. "I beg your pardon?"

"Thank you," he repeated. A muscle tightened in his jaw as if he was disappointed in himself. "I knew the ills of this part of town… or so I thought I did. And your friend here? If he is here through no action of his own, the corruption of this place is vast. I shall be the one who ends it."

She noted that he did not bear false arrogance. He made no bold claim that he alone could make the transformation happen. But he was determined that the suffering should not stand. She could see that in the way his shoulders squared and the shadow of determination in his amber eyes.

She drew in a breath as she tried to make sense of the man before her. Was there really a lord—a duke!—who cared about people like Stevenson and herself?

The people at whom the great ones did not look except when tossing them a coat, a muddy pair of boots, or dirty dishes?

"Though it may not matter to you," she said, "I will think very highly of you if you make the attempt."

His gaze locked with hers, and something deep and full of longing lit those amber depths, turning it from stone to the hue of hot whisky. "It does matter, and your approval shall be reward enough."

"You speak of rewards," she exclaimed, stunned that he should think so about her. "But it is I who am in debt to you."

He shook his head, and his dark hair skimmed his hard cheekbone. "There is no debt. Truly, it is I who am indebted to you."

She arched a brow, confused. "I do not see

how that is possible."

"Can you not?" he said softly, his voice a delicious, gravelly query.

Her breath caught in her throat.

The Duke of Rockford and she stared at each other, without title, without rank, and it was the most glorious moment. For in that instant, she was no longer a maid who dusted out the hearths, cleaned the chamber pots, and somehow managed to make sense of household accounts that were wrung of every last penny.

In his eyes...she was glorious.

And she felt it to her very toes.

The sound of a cabby shouting at a coster-monger to get out of the road shook her, and she jolted out of her reverie. She needed to concentrate, for she was expected home.

"I must go immediately," she said, realizing the danger of lingering with him. "I am late."

He blinked, apparently stunned as well. "But could I not at least know your—"

"Thank you for your help," she cut in, her heart shockingly heavy at the realization that she did not dare give him her name.

And with that, she whipped around, took Stevenson's thin arm, and raced away with the older servant.

As they left the duke standing there, Stevenson mumbled around his bread, "That handsome duke fancies you."

"Pffft, Stevenson," she returned. "Dukes don't fancy maids."

"But you're not—"

"I am," she insisted, chin up. Perhaps once she would have had position. But all that had changed when her mother married Palmerton. And when she had died, leaving Charlotte with no protection.

Charlotte refused to look back. To long for what she couldn't have.

No. The only way was forward. She'd care for her family home and estate for as long as she could endure Palmerton. For she could not bear to leave what few memories she had of her mother behind.

A church bell tolled out, and she groaned. They had to get back!

If anyone came to call on Francesca, Charlotte had to be there to serve tea. And if she was not? A worse fate could be awaiting her than a day or two without bread.

CHAPTER FIVE

On shaking legs, Stevenson ran to his wife.

Mary cried out with joy, flinging her arms wide to receive him. Stevenson stumbled into her embrace, lowering his face to the top of her head. He blinked swiftly as his wife wrapped her arms around his too-thin frame.

Tears of joy spilled down Mary's wrinkled cheeks as she clung to her husband.

Charlotte watched, overwhelmed, barely able to process her own feelings at the sight of the reunion. She'd almost failed today. She'd almost failed today and this reunion would have remained a dream rather than a reality, and that? It caused both relief and a note of terror to dance through her. The idea of her dear friend languishing in such a place while his wife waited, miserable and wrought with worry, made her slightly sick.

The duke had made this possible. Her determination alone would not have been enough without his assistance and support.

She'd never felt so much gratitude toward one man in her entire life. She'd never thought she would feel thus toward a man of the nobility, but he had behaved in a remarkable fashion.

Charlotte quickly wiped at her eyes before

daring to embrace the couple. A wave of relief and joy washed over her as her arms encircled their warm, loving forms.

"Come, come, my love," Mary said, then she gave Charlotte a still-worried look before she stole a supporting arm to Stevenson's waist.

Charlotte nodded her approval, and Mary began to guide him back into the house.

Stevenson staggered ever so slightly, as though he had used all his energy to return to this house and its sparkling gardens. "I am very tired, my love," he confessed to his wife, struggling to right himself, and she held him stable.

"I have a bed ready for you," Mary assured.

She glanced back over her shoulder at Charlotte. "I cannot thank you enough for being so daring, my dear. I cannot think of another young lady who would have risked such a thing."

"It was the right thing to do," Charlotte said firmly, then added, "and I did not do it entirely on my own. The credit belongs to another."

Stevenson let out an exclamation of agreement. "I never thought to meet the Duke of Rockford."

"Rockford?" Mary all but yelped. She blinked, gaping for a moment as she studied her husband's face. "I've read about him in the papers, so I have."

Stevenson tutted lovingly. "All of England has read about him in the papers, my love." He then turned a knowing eye to Charlotte. "Very good man, nice fellow—liked our young lady here, he did."

"Nonsense," Charlotte retorted with good humor. "He merely did us a good turn. I think he must be an honorable man."

Stevenson's lips curled in a slight smile despite the fact that his face was haggard. "Oh, he likes you, miss. He likes you quite a lot. I think you should go and see him and—"

"Never you mind," Charlotte cut in before far-too-fanciful thoughts could take root. "I have nothing to do with dukes. I shall never see him again; of that, I am certain. And it's a good thing, too." She laughed. "What would I do with a duke?"

Stevenson pursed his lips before he shook his head ruefully. "I don't know, but stranger things have happened."

Gently, she touched his shoulder and reminded him, "Girls like me do not marry dukes and princes in real life. More like he'd ask me to clean his fire grate."

Stevenson gave her a loving look. "If you insist on thinking so little of yourself, I shall have to take you to task, Charlotte."

"Not now," she said softly, allowing her

hand to slip from his arm. "Though I love you for thinking well enough of me to believe that I could have a duke. Now, you must go and rest. We shall make you soup, and bring it up, and take care of you, and tuck you in, and you shall not move a muscle."

"Good God, what's he doing here?" Lord Palmerton challenged from the entry to the garden. He stood in his beautifully tailored black-and-white, taken from the latest fashions of the day. His silvery hair shone in the sunlight. He was the picture of a gentleman, but there was nothing gentle about his expression as he surveyed them.

Ice slipped through her veins. She had thought he'd already left for Bath and had assumed they would not meet for some time, thus giving Stevenson some peace in his recovery.

Charlotte cleared her throat, then said boldly, "He's been released. Someone's paid his debt."

"Someone," Palmerton echoed, cocking his head to the side.

She lifted her chin and dared, despite the wariness swirling around her belly: "I used my savings."

She wasn't about to tell him about her mother's necklace that she sold, lest he accuse her of theft, something of which she would not doubt him capable.

Palmerton strode across the stone path, his gaze trailing to Stevenson, then back to Charlotte. "I had no idea you had so much money saved."

She made no reply. She had enough experience to know that the more she said, the more weapons she gave him against her.

And then he smiled, lifting his leather-gloved hands and applauding. "Very resourceful, my dear, very resourceful."

"Papa, we're late," Phillip called as he sauntered into the garden. Dressed in bold green, blue, and gold silks, Phillip looked like the ostentatious peacocks that frequented the garden. His curled hair shone like a lion's. "Lord Rutherford and Lord Castlereigh await you at the tables this week."

Palmerton's smile stayed cold and cruel. "I suppose I must go and make our way with the most important lords, since you don't seem to be able to impress them."

Phillip's jaw tightened at his father's mockery and unveiled disappointment.

Phillip was a few years older than Charlotte and was treated as poorly by his father as Francesca was.

It was strange because Charlotte knew that, in a twisted way, Palmerton wanted the best for his children, but he was so unkind to them as he pushed them to be more successful than he had been.

Palmerton wanted his son to have power through friendships, but Phillip did not have a significant title or ancient family name, making such relationships almost impossible to achieve.

Money alone was not enough.

"Come, Phillip," his father instructed. "I shall drop you at your bachelor's lodgings. I expect you to host only the best young lords while I am away."

"Yes, Papa," Phillip replied, his face pale with too much drink and, no doubt, fear of continuing to fail.

"Charlotte," Palmerton snapped.

She jolted, knowing she should have kept alert. It was one of Palmerton's favorite tactics—making one feel as if they were no longer under his notice, then turning back to them with a vicious word. "Make certain that Francesca is always beautifully dressed and her head isn't in her ridiculous poetry. You know the ones."

"Of course," she said with a quick curtsy. But as she bobbed down and she thought of the beautiful books that she and Francesca loved so well from the kingdom that had been destroyed not long after the American Revolution, she blurted, "When have I ever not?"

Palmerton's eyes narrowed. "I beg your pardon?"

She winced. What the blazes was she doing?

The exchange with Rockford must have given her some sort of courage to speak to Palmerton in such a manner. A manner she'd not ventured in years.

Palmerton inclined his head before he started for the front of the house and his waiting coach. "Oh, and Charlotte," he said softly.

She swallowed, knowing that deceptively calm tone. "Yes?"

"Go to the library—select a few of the books from that ridiculous little country next to France. I think it's time we got rid of them. Don't you?"

She swallowed, her heart beginning to pound in her chest. "The books are very valuable," she dared to protest before she could stop herself. "A-and they've been in the family for—"

At those words, his eyes crackled with anger. "Not my family. Get rid of that continental trash."

She swallowed, gave a tight nod, and looked away.

Without another word, he departed with Phillip, knowing he still controlled them all in his grip even without his physical presence.

She refused to let the sound of Palmerton's retreating footsteps quake her soul.

Today had been a good day. Stevenson was free, and that had to be enough.

Even if she was forced to toss out another memory.

It had to be enough. Even if she felt like she was losing a piece of her heart.

CHAPTER SIX

Rafe climbed the lichen-touched steps of the sprawling house located on the very western border of London. The Thames was stone-throwing distance from the porticoed entrance.

It was a surprise to him.

He had been expecting the Palmerton family to live in one of the new affairs close to Green Park. Those gilded monstrosities had been built in the last ten years and spoke of wealth made by an empire—its exports, its imports, and its crimes.

But this house was far older than any of the modern industries that had provided the wealth to his class and those who were rising up from the ranks of the poor, creating a now large and impressive middle class.

No, this house was quite old.

And so, in the massive home by the powerful river?

He felt oddly at home, for the sprawling hodge-podge of added-on bits and pieces and turrets reminded him of his own London abode.

Rafe felt his pocket, and paper crinkled there.

Could the single name on his mother's list

possibly lead to love? Was there any chance the lady might love him for more than his dukedom?

The truth was, he had met many young ladies of the *ton*, and not one had inspired his interest. Not one had cared for his likes or dislikes; they seemed only to want the coronet he could provide. None had seemed to understand that he wasn't looking for the grand show of love, but the small intimacies that sustained a couple for years.

He didn't find the young ladies of the *ton* to be inferior. It was simply that they were raised in such a way that did not allow them to be…well, someone who could be open with him, frank, or give the sort of discourse that would allow him to know them as a true person.

And if he couldn't bloody well know their true person, how the devil could he surmise if he might one day grow to love them?

They were all raised to fawn at him or tell him exactly what they thought he wanted to hear. And so, he'd decided that he would go about this in a very different way than what was the usual state of affairs.

He'd be blunt.

He would tell the young ladies that they could be as frank as they liked with him.

And then he would be able to strike out the name on his mother's list and tell his precious mama that he had met the one lady she'd written down. As she had required. Surely, she would not hold to her claim that he had to announce an engagement at her yearly London ball.

He raised his hand to grab the knocker and let it down. No servant had hurried to the entrance and whipped open the door.

Usually, when a carriage of his import arrived at any such house, he was met immediately. After all, it was impossible to not notice the ducal crest on his coach door.

His arrival was typically met with much bowing and scraping.

He waited, curious now. A good minute went by before he even heard a single stirring within the house.

He raised his hand again and banged the rather large lion-shaped knocker.

At long last, there was a scurrying of feet on the other side of the door. Its heavy oak panel swung open, and he met not a butler at all, but a wrinkle-faced older woman with silver hair coiled atop her head, mostly covered by a limp mob cap.

She wore a simple gown of purple, and her eyes shot wide at the sight of him. Then her gaze swung down to his coach, and she coughed.

He was concerned for several moments that he had stunned her speechless — a circumstance that had not occurred to him in some time.

"How do you do, Your Grace?" she rushed, still gaping up at him.

"I am doing very well, thank you." He smiled, a smile he used on all the grannies on his estates. He was determined to assure her he was no beast with bite. "I have come to see Lady Francesca."

"You've come to call upon Lady Francesca," the older woman echoed, as if mystified by the prospect.

"Indeed. Is this a bad time?"

It was such a shocking thing to say, he barely could believe that he was saying it. There were no bad times for dukes. Usually, people would be fumbling backward to permit him through the door. Instead, the mob-capped woman just kept gaping up at him as if she could not believe the sight before her eyes.

Had he come to the wrong house? She seemed so shocked by his presence, he was tempted to step back and check his paper with the name of the house, which was carved into the stone on the left.

Phoenix House.

Yes. This was it. He looked back over his shoulder, then to her again. "Is something amiss?" he asked. "Have you seen a ghost?"

"No, Your Grace," she said quickly,

smoothing her hands over her apron. "Only, we have not seen…"

"Yes?" he prompted gently, hoping she did not expire on the spot.

"Forgive me for my rudeness, Your Grace." The older woman cleared her throat and began scuttling backward, even as she swept her slightly faded blue gaze over him. "I confess to being overborne. You are quite the specimen."

He coughed on a laugh. He was not usually spoken of thus—not directly to his face, at least. And he found it strangely endearing.

"I do have that effect on people," he said reassuringly. "Silly rank and all that."

The older woman gestured with her gnarled hand for him to enter, but before he could, he heard a voice.

Not just any voice.

That voice.

A voice that danced over him and sent hunger and admiration humming through his veins. Yes, that voice traced through him like warmed honey. Rich but promising delight.

"Stevenson is finally asleep?" *that voice* exclaimed from the foyer. "I did not think that he would."

Rafe called out before he could stop himself: "You!"

The young lady stopped dead in her tracks in the back of the hall—something that he seemed to be doing to the women in this house.

Her eyes widened, and she looked like she was about to whip around and retreat from where she'd come.

"Wait!" he exclaimed, which came out with a good deal more gruffness than he had intended. But fate was shoving him in her direction, and he was not about to lose her again.

Her eyes flared at the sight of him, and she twisted toward the door, her simple linen gown caressing her body.

And not only that, there were several buttons undone at her neck, as if she had been preparing herself to disrobe.

The coat she'd worn this morning was gone, and her blond hair, which had been coiled under a bonnet, now tumbled down her back as if she had allowed the coiffure to come undone on purpose.

As if she preferred it to be free and wild.

It was quite unruly, really, as if she'd driven her hands through it, and he found himself absolutely captivated by her presence. Wishing that he, too, could slide his hands into her curling locks and feel their strands caressing his skin.

It was the most shocking and erotic thought he'd had in some time. For it was completely unexpected. He'd slide his hands into her hair, cup the nape of her neck, tilt her head back, and take her soft lips—

"Your Grace? Are you unwell?"

Unwell? Bloody hell. He felt more alive than he had in years.

Could this be...? Could she be...?

She still looked as if she was seeking the opportunity to dart backward. She tucked a lock of hair behind her ear and asked, "What exactly are you doing here? How did you find me?"

He blinked. "Forgive me, I did not follow you. I've come to call upon a Lady Francesca." He drew in a breath and rushed. "I did not wish to cause you distress—"

"Oh, you have not," the young lady denied. "We are simply not accustomed to such visitors. We keep ourselves rather private in this house."

"Do you?" he asked. She didn't seem the quiet sort. "If you must know, my mother arranged with Lord Palmerton that I should call upon his daughter, Lady Francesca." He stilled. "Are you Lady Francesca?"

Her brows lifted. "I am not."

A strange emotion danced through him. Disappointment. Yes. Good God. He was *disappointed*. And he had no idea what to make of that.

The woman's lips twitched then. "Do you often do exactly as your mother prescribes?"

"She's incredibly wise," he said with a shrug, "and I find it sensible on my part to do as she asks and have done with it."

She laughed, her wariness seeming to dissipate. "I like that reply very much, and if I had a formidable and wise mother, I would do the same."

"Do you not have a mother?" he asked, mesmerized by the sound of her laugh bouncing off the painted mural on the ceiling.

Her smile dimmed a little. "No, not any longer."

"I'm so very sorry for it," he said.

"Thank you." And as if to emphasize what he had surmised, she added, "I have grown accustomed to the state. Over the years, Lady Francesca has been a dear companion to me and given me much comfort."

"Ah, I see," he said, his spirits sinking despite her marvelous presence. "You are related to Lady Francesca."

"Indeed, I am," she said quickly. "She is my…"

"Cousin," the older woman piped up. "And Lady Charlotte has lived with this family most of her life."

"Ah, a cousin," he breathed. Hell's bells, but this was a tricky state of affairs. Lord Palmerton and Rafe's mother knew he was here to visit Lady Francesca. His pointed interest in her cousin and companion would not be politic. "And Palmerton is your guardian?"

Her eyes widened. "Oh, no. My father is away, you see. At our estates in the north. So, while I am here, I stay with my cousin. In fact, I've had the good fortune to keep her company most of our lives. My father prefers me to have female company."

He nodded, slightly unclear as to their family relationships, but such was the *ton*. Cousins were everywhere.

And this was slightly better. He'd hate to have to tell Palmerton he preferred his daughter's cousin. Still, both young ladies under the same roof would prove challenging.

"Are you sure you are not unwell?" she asked, her lips tilting in the most delightful of quirks. "Mary here makes splendid tea to calm the nerves."

Nerves?

"I am perfectly well, thank you." He did not get nerves. Or, at least, he never had before. She was doing things to him no lady had ever done. It was a most unusual feeling.

He cleared his throat and proclaimed, "Nothing like a cousin for a bit of company. I wish I'd had them, but alas, I do not. My mother and my father were both only children. Quite unusual, but there you have it."

It was another reason his mother was determined to see him wedded and with an heir post haste.

"Would you care to come in, Your Grace?" the charming woman asked, her lips twitching as she realized he was still firmly lodged on the threshold.

"Indeed, I would," he replied, and he found himself venturing across the marble.

This was the oddest meeting he'd had since...well, this morning.

"Are you always given to such odd conversation?"

"Are you usually given to such banal conversation?" she asked in return.

He choked on a laugh. "Indeed, I am," he said. "Clearly you do not spend a great deal of time in the House of Lords or at *ton* parties."

"No," she confessed, her smile tightening. "My time is spent in different pursuits."

Different pursuits.

What the devil did she mean by that?

Well, he wasn't about to find out by standing in the foyer. It would be the height of rudeness. And yet... He found himself profoundly curious about her. More curious than he had even been this morning.

"Will you please tell me what I should call you?" he asked. "I do not think I can call you the cousin of Lady Francesca for the rest of my visit."

She swallowed, and her eyes darted to the servant, Mary. Then the odd young lady cleared her throat and said, "You may call me Lady Charlotte."

"Is that all? Lady Charlotte?" he teased.

She placed a hand to her middle and rushed, "Faraday. My father is Lord Faraday."

As soon as the words were out of her mouth, her lips clamped shut, and he wondered again what the devil was happening.

He suddenly felt as if he was in one of Sheridan's farces. Was someone hiding behind a painting? Was this some vast trick?

He did not think so. She was simply a mystery. And he found himself drawn to that.

"Lady Charlotte Faraday," he replied with an elaborate bow. "Though I'm not acquainted with your family, it is a pleasure to meet you formally. Would you keep company for my call with Lady Francesca? Or is she not in?"

"She is in the library," Lady Charlotte managed.

"Marvelous," he said. "I do love a library. Shall we go there?"

"If you would like, Your Grace."

He wanted to go very badly indeed, but not with Lady Francesca.

No, he wanted to go with Lady Charlotte instead.

The maid in the mob cap glanced back and forth as if she was witnessing a badminton match. "Shall I bring tea, then, Ch— Lady

Charlotte?"

Lady Charlotte folded her hands in front of her. Her fingers twisted and fidgeted as if she was hiding them.

They were a bit red. Did she sew a great deal? Or ride without gloves?

Of course not. He had to be imagining things.

"Yes, indeed, Mary," Lady Charlotte proclaimed. "Please do. Ask the cook to send up some buns if any are available. I'm sure His Grace is most hungry. He's had quite a long day." Lady Charlotte smiled gently, and her eyes filled with gratitude as she added, "And this is the duke we owe so much to."

Mary's eyes filled with tears, and before Rafe realized what was happening, she crossed to him, grabbed his hand, and kissed the back of it.

"Thank you, Your Grace," she declared through her tears. "Thank you for freeing my dear Stevenson. I did not know what we would do. You see, this whole situation is quite untenable, and I..."

"Mary," Charlotte cut in softly.

Mary's words died, replaced by a thankful smile.

In that strange moment, he wondered what Mary might have said, but whatever it was, it would not be revealed now.

Mary gave a creaking curtsy. "Thank you

again, Your Grace, for being so kind to some-one so far below your station."

He stilled.

He wasn't entirely certain if Mary meant Charlotte or Stevenson. Clearly, Charlotte was a lady and thus of a suitable station. But perhaps she was impoverished...which would explain why she lived with her cousin, be-haved so strangely, and cared so much about the loss of a few pounds.

What had brought her to such a state? And was she looked after in this house? Or did her uncle merely tolerate her?

"It was my pleasure to help," he said. "If I can do more, I will."

"Oh no. Nothing more is needed," Mary said. "He is quite happy to be back with us, and I am so happy to have him in my arms again. I shall go to the kitchen, then I will go and check on my Stevenson."

"We shall take very good care of him, Mary," Charlotte assured.

Rafe was struck by the clear love and kindness Charlotte felt toward the servant.

In all his years, he had never seen the like. And he found his admiration for Lady Charlotte growing exponentially.

How many other young ladies would take such an active role in caring for the servants in the house? For *loving* them? It was not a done thing.

But in that moment, he realized it should be.

Mary gave another creaky curtsy, then headed into the shadowy hall that no doubt led down to the kitchens.

Charlotte headed toward the hall in the opposite direction, and he happily followed her, completely uncertain as to what awaited him.

CHAPTER SEVEN

If Charlotte could have given herself a good, solid kick, she would have.

But alas, she was not able. Instead, a running commentary of her absolute madness kept racing through her head. What was she thinking?

Lord Faraday!

The duke had been so insistent, and she'd searched for any name. Faraday had popped into her head. After all, they were not a known family, and Francesca had mentioned that the lot of them had chosen to delay their arrival to the Season, lingering in Northern Scotland, since the weather was so fine.

As she led the duke down the hallway toward the library, she winced, grateful he could not see the play of emotions over her face.

Why the devil had she agreed to *Lady* Charlotte? And why had she offered any title at all?

What in God's name had possessed her?

And to allow him to believe she was Francesca's cousin?

Heavens! Her own father had died when she was still in leading strings! She did not know what had come over her when she had denied Palmerton's guardianship, but the words acknowledging his power over her had stuck in her mouth.

What a disaster this all was proving to be! She had not lied so much in her entire life as she had within thirty seconds of being in the duke's company this afternoon.

But she had been dressed as a lady this morning when he had come to her assistance. And she did not know how to explain to the duke that she was little better than a servant. She had not yet changed; she had not had time to, with the reunion of Stevenson to the house. She had been just about to when she'd encountered Rockford in the foyer. Which, of course, was why he so easily assumed she was a lady. After all, even ladies were a bit mussed from time to time when caught unawares.

But the reality was that she did indeed take her meals with the servants, that she slept with the servants, and that she'd not had a new gown of her own in five years.

She did not want him to think…

Well, she did not want him to think that she was acting with nefarious intent and have him report to Lord Palmerton that she had been out and about deceiving all and sundry. Risking Lord Palmerton's wrath was a dangerous thing indeed.

So, she'd thought it best to what?

She ground her teeth.

To lie to him outright—to create an identity that did not exist?

She could only find herself deeply grateful that Palmerton had departed for Bath, visiting a gambling house that he particularly liked to frequent at this time of the year. Strange and ghoulish as it was, his set made bets on who would recover and who would not at the watering pumps.

She did not understand how anyone could be so entirely bored with life, or cruel, that they would make such wagers, but so they did.

"Is the library tucked in some distant part of this rambling house?" the duke inquired, breaking the silence as they traversed the rabbit warren of corridors.

She laughed. "It is a rambling house," she agreed, "and the library is on the other side of it. I suppose I could have called Francesca to one of the front rooms," she mused.

"Oh no," he said happily. "I love such houses. There's so much history in them. I think of all the time and all the lives that have passed since the bricks were laid down and work begun."

She stopped, nearly stumbling at his words, which matched her own thoughts about all such houses but particularly her own home.

Much to her surprise, he was close enough that he collided into her.

His hard body crashed against hers, and she gasped at the feel of him through her thin gown. Warm. Hard. Strong.

He grabbed hold of her, his strong, broad hands circling about her waist. His fingers and palms splayed over her stomach and ribs, steadying her.

Glancing down at her over her shoulder as she whipped her gaze up to his, he studied her.

Her breathing came in slow takes as their gazes met and held.

Her lips parted with amazement at how perfectly she fit against his towering frame.

The duke held her still for one moment longer than he must have intended to, for she felt his soft breath on the nape of her neck, causing the curls at her cheeks to dance. His body... The sinew and bone reminded her of the vital energy she'd witnessed in the Apollonian statues in the long gallery of the house.

Whipcord strong, powerful, barely contained.

She delighted in the feel of him through his perfectly tailored clothes. Yes, she loved every moment that muscled length of his body pressed to hers.

It was the closest she had been to a man in her entire life, and she found herself not only shocked but intrigued.

After all, she read far more than many young ladies were permitted or had time for. Alone in her corner in the servants' quarters, she pored over her favorites, which were the penny novelettes in which romance bloomed between mighty lords and servant girls like herself.

She knew that such a fate would never befall her in real life, but the fantasy of it, the dreaming of it, had sustained her through many difficult periods. No prince was coming to save her, but she liked to imagine being loved. Just as her mother had been by her father.

Now, here she was in a duke's arms. Perhaps it was for a moment and perhaps it was only because she'd tripped on a bit of carpet, but it was quite a surprise.

And this man was not for her.

She'd likely never marry. Allowing herself to pretend he might be like one of the heroes of her stories would be foolish indeed.

"Your Grace, I am quite well," she said, though a dangerously tempted part of herself longed to stay in his arms and see where such intimacy might take her. "Thank you for catching me, but I am very sturdy and can stand on my own."

"Better than most," he murmured, admiration warming his gaze.

Slowly, she stepped out of his arms. His

fingertips lightly skimmed her body, and he let his hands drop to his side.

He let out a small breath of air, then, as if he was astonished by his own behavior and the loss of her in his arms. A strange look on his strong face, he, too, stepped back.

As they lingered in the dark-paneled hall, he stared down at her, his eyes half hooded and his dark lashes thick.

His jetty hair caressed his cheeks as he tilted his head down ever so slightly, and she wondered what he was thinking.

For his gaze roamed slowly over her face, as if he could capture every curve and every angle of it so that he might recall it for the rest of his life.

His sensual lips parted as his gaze lingered on her mouth before his brow furrowed, and then he blinked, the moment gone.

Rockford then blurted, "The history of this place must be fascinating. When I find myself in such an establishment, I cannot help wondering if there are any priest holes about. After all, this place was built in the time of Henry VIII, was it not?"

"Yes," she exclaimed, realizing that they were to pretend the exchange between them had not just occurred. Though her heart kept beating with a far too energetic beat.

She nodded. "It is a very old family house. And you've the right of it. They were Catholic then." She leaned in toward him and whispered dramatically, "And there *is* a priest hole, if you must know."

She paused, thinking about her mother's family. She knew so little, for her guardian had removed all references to family history from the house, including the family bible. But it was impossible not to know some of the history just from the actual building of the place.

She glanced about her and marveled, "It is rather shocking that it survived so many monarchs and so many revolutions and civil wars."

"As did the family," he said softly, his gaze once again full of admiration.

In that moment, she felt as if there was more to his statement than met the eye. Was he suggesting that she was as resilient as the house? As the family that had dwelt within these walls? She rather thought that was his meaning.

"Indeed," she agreed, lifting her chin.

The past held so many secrets, so many tantalizing things. The present, she found, was just one long drudgery after another, in which she had to complete tasks given to her sometimes out of spite.

"Lady Charlotte," he said, his voice a low rumble.

"Yes," she breathed, then nearly kicked

herself again. Why the blazes did her voice sound like that?

"My mother did not indicate that there was another young lady living in this house."

She squared her shoulders, her chest tightening as she realized she had no idea how to explain her situation.

Honesty seemed the best route, even if she had not been entirely honest with him so far.

"Well, it is because I'm a lady of little note or fortune. I do not have anything to recommend me."

"I cannot agree," he stated firmly. "You have a great deal to recommend you."

"But not as much as Francesca," she corrected. Somehow, she had stepped on dangerous ground. She wanted him to *like* her. To *admire* her.

But this was not a novel. A duke would never marry a servant. Or a woman with no title or fortune. She could not forget.

Charlotte whipped around and strode down the hall with purpose. Now that she was turned away from him, she worried her lower lip. She could not have him digging about her past or making inquiries with his mother about a Lady Charlotte living with Lady Francesca.

The duke would find out that she was barely a gentleman's daughter.

Her mother had apparently been related to a noble and inherited their fortune and house. Which Palmerton had put to good use.

And most of that money was gone now. She'd certainly never see a penny, for the law had given it to her guardian.

She drew in a steadying breath that did not quite quell the anxiety rolling about her stomach.

Much to her relief, they arrived at the entrance to the library. She stepped inside the large room, and it was impossible not to find comfort in the books that filled the copious shelves.

The rows and rows and rows of beautifully bound books filled the air with the magnificent scent of ink and paper and leather. She knew that her stepsister was in here somewhere.

"It is a perfect room," Rockford stated, easy in his compliments.

"I agree," she said brightly.

"Some libraries seem bought only to show that the owner of the collection has the fortune to have so many books," he mused. "This looks…"

"Lived in," she offered, all but bouncing on her toes, feeling a personal pleasure. After all, it was her mother's family that had grown this collection over the generations.

He nodded, duly delighted by the sight before him. "You love this place? I can see it plainly on your face."

Tears stung her eyes. "It was my mother's

favorite room, my grandfather's favorite room, and, I do believe, his father's favorite room," she said, blinking rapidly. "As a matter of fact, it was likely the favorite room of every single member of this family for the last several hundred years."

He cocked his head to the side, causing shadows to play over his hard visage. "This was your *mother's* house?"

She swallowed, realizing she'd put her foot in it! If she was a cousin, this shouldn't be her house. It should be Francesca's house. Her mind all but froze then. "Yes…" She hesitated. "You see, my mother was sister to Lord Palmerton."

"Ah," he said, accepting the lie without a commentary.

Charlotte fought a grimace and wished that she could kick herself anew. It was a good thing she could not or she would be head to toe bruises. Still, she was only making a more elaborate set of lies—lies that would catch her up and get her into such trouble. "I have always loved this place."

He studied her, his face warm with admiration. "And yet, one day you shall have to go away from it."

She flinched inwardly. She would not. She'd likely never marry, and this place? It was the last connection she had to her parents. Each room. Each painting. Each tapestry. And she wasn't ever going to leave it. She'd have to be kicked out—something she would not put past Palmerton if she did not keep up his standards.

She tore her gaze away from the duke who elicited such strange feelings deep in her soul. How was it that he could see her so clearly and yet not know her at all? She was lying to him, here in this house that he saw she loved so well. But the lies were necessary.

She loved it, his understanding of her. And she hated it, too, for nothing could come of it.

Perhaps she'd be in luck and Francesca and the duke would have nothing in common and they'd never see the fellow again.

A thought that did not cause her the relief for which she had hoped.

Oh no… It was a very different feeling that raced through her at the thought of never seeing the man again.

"Charlie," Francesca called from the massive fireplace at the end of the library. "Is that you?"

Charlotte could not see her, for she was behind a rather thick stack of books.

"Indeed it is," she returned as they neared the fireplace and she spotted her stepsister ensconced in one of the high-back leather chairs. "You have a caller. The Duke of Rockford."

"What?" Francesca bolted upright from the chair, and the pile of books tilted over, rather like a drunken leaning Tower of Pisa that refused to stay aright.

The books plummeted to the ground.

Francesca let out a gasp of horror, and Charlotte darted forward as she always did to tidy the mess.

Francesca bent down to help, which was nothing unusual, but the duke raced forward along with them, as if a treasure had been spilled upon the ground.

Without a word, he assisted, reverently collecting the books one by one in his capable hands.

After they were placed evenly on the gilded mahogany table beside the chair, he asked, "Have any of the spines been damaged?"

Charlotte gaped.

He cared about the spines of books.

Who was this strange duke with a Herculean physique who went about adventuring in the south of London in the morning only to be caring about the state of books in the afternoon?

He was odd. And impossibly handsome. And interesting. Much like the books she so adored.

And oh, heaven help her.

As she caught his gaze in the soft afternoon sunlight, which floated through the tall glass panes and danced over his features, she knew that she liked him—and that wasn't allowed.

Not at all.

CHAPTER EIGHT

Taking Lady Charlotte into his arms had been chivalrous when she'd tripped in the hall. But the feel of her waist beneath his fingertips?

There had been nothing chivalrous in his thoughts as he'd traced her body when she'd slipped away. Oh no. His thoughts had vaulted into sin.

He'd wanted to take her mischievous mouth in a searing kiss, slide his hands to the curve of her bottom, and pull her up against his hard body.

But he wasn't the sort who took advantage of young women in hallways. He never had been, and he never would be.

But now? With his fingertips merely brushing hers, collecting books from an ancient woven carpet? He knew he was in trouble.

It was not just the fingertips.

It was every damned thing about her. The way she spoke to him without reservation. The way their bodies seemed to dance together without music. Her astute mind and love of history.

Was it possible that he had found someone like himself—someone who was a part of society but preferred the tales tucked in history and books?

And he found that he could not tear his gaze away from Lady Charlotte.

Lady Francesca, the lady his mother had sent him to meet, was but a few feet off, hands folded before her demure pale-green gown. She was a person of great attractiveness, he supposed, and he had made view of her dark hair and her blue eyes and her pale skin.

She had a lovely voice. The young lady likely had all the points required of a young lady on the marriage mart.

But he could not keep from looking at Lady Charlotte. He felt like a magnet pulled to her through the city today.

She captivated him in a way that no other young lady ever had. She challenged him, too.

He was thinking perilously ridiculous thoughts. In fact, his line of thinking was something out of a play, a novel, or a poem.

His work and time spent in the hedonistic upper crust of the *ton* had taught him well that life was not a play or a novel or a poem, but he could not shake the feeling coursing through him that he had found...his other half.

Surely, he had gone mad.

His friend the Earl of Trent, who did not believe in emotional nonsense, would insist he go home and call for the doctor at once.

Was he coming down with a fever? He did not feel feverish, except for the fact his blood was coursing with heat. For her.

It was no fever dream. It was the damned feel of her skin against his. Her curved figure pressed to his…

Lady Charlotte looked toward him, her own sapphire eyes wide, but then she yanked her gaze away, stood, tucked her hands in the folds of her skirt as if shaking off his touch, and crossed to the fire.

"Lady Francesca," Lady Charlotte said in her bell-like tones. Her lips curved in a delicious grin. "Please meet the Duke of Rockford. He has come to call upon you. No doubt he has heard what a delightful person you are from his mother."

"I doubt my mother has ever met her," he said frankly.

"Then how could she know if I'm delightful?" Lady Francesca asked with surprising bluntness and without offense.

He laughed, finding himself more at ease with these two. "Fair point. You must understand my mother knows hundreds of lords and ladies. It is impossible for her to meet everyone in the *ton*. Likely, she asked who the likeliest ladies were and asked her favorite sorts of questions."

Lady Francesca snorted with amusement. "Oh my. How very practical."

He sighed and confessed, "Well, it's true. My mother instructed me to come here to meet you, and, generally speaking, as I told your cousin, I follow her advice."

He noticed Lady Charlotte's shoulders tense, and she darted a glance between him and Lady Francesca, who looked as bewildered as he felt. Then, just as suddenly, they both softened and smiled.

He shrugged but couldn't quite stop his frown. "And as my mother constantly reminds me, which is her duty, I am a duke and I must marry. She has suggested I should consider you, Lady Francesca. You seem quite sharp and no doubt have surmised that is why you were recommended."

Lady Francesca coughed.

"My, you are very blunt," Lady Charlotte observed.

His insides tightened. Was she displeased? She certainly didn't seem bothered that he was here to consider her cousin and not her.

It was a blow.

"Should I be anything but?" he asked calmly, though he felt anything but ease as he swung his gaze back and forth between the young ladies. "You see, I think that there is only one true way to go about this state of affairs. I could prevaricate. Lady Francesca could prevaricate. We could all pretend and talk about the Thames boat races and drink tea. Or..."

"Or," put in Lady Charlotte, her face perfectly astonished but intrigued.

"Or," he continued. "We could be quite honest. What do you prefer, Lady Francesca?"

Lady Francesca blinked up at him, her blue eyes surprisingly kind and bright. There was an element of mischief in those eyes that he found refreshing, but he did not find her appealing in the way that he found Lady Charlotte to be eminently marvelous.

No. Lady Francesca's lips curled in a grin that seemed to suggest that she found the entire state of affairs amusing, but she was not intrigued by him, either.

There was no pulse between them. No crackle. She smiled at him because he was a duke. And that was all. She wasn't a rude person. Of that he was certain.

"Well, Your Grace." Lady Francesca cocked her head to the side, studying first him, then her cousin. "I think that not prevaricating sounds like an excellent idea. Don't you, Charlotte?"

Lady Charlotte looked back to him, her cheeks a slightly ruddy color as if she was contemplating something she couldn't repeat. Which, of course, was absurd.

She squared her shoulders and stated, "I find that lords and ladies never say what they mean, and that causes a great deal of confusion."

"Agreed," Rafe said. "I do not know why society must dance about the truth."

"Don't you?" Lady Charlotte challenged, almost laughing at him.

"You find me *naive*," he breathed.

"I could never accuse you of such a thing, Your Grace," Lady Charlotte countered.

"But you think I should understand why."

She nodded, her eyes bright. "I do, indeed."

"And I suppose you're going to explain it to me?"

Lady Francesca let out a sigh. "Oh, dear. Here we go."

"Is it to be a treatise?" he asked, his lips twitching as he realized he was quite looking forward to Lady Charlotte's pontification on this subject.

For he had no idea what she was about to say. An unusual state of affairs for himself. He usually always knew what people were about to say.

But not with her.

"You have no idea," Lady Francesca all but groaned, but in good humor.

As if indeed about to give a lecture, Lady Charlotte cleared her throat and took a deep breath before she launched into her opinion on the matter. "You see, it is incredibly important for the upper classes to maintain their importance. And the only way that they can do this is by codifying their language to such degree that they say nothing of great import to one another in company."

He frowned, taking in her words, realizing she was correct. He couldn't recall the last time anything of real import was spoken at a ball, a race, or a rout. "Go on," he urged.

Bolstered by his interest, Lady Charlotte continued sensibly, "It is not what they know or how they say it that is important, but *who* and *where* they know in common."

He blinked, this part muddier and not as evident. "I beg your pardon. I'm not entirely certain I follow that."

She grinned, then winked with a good deal of cheek. "I shall speak slower, then."

He laughed again, a bold, surprised sound—something he found himself doing in her presence quite often.

Clearly, Lady Charlotte was an intelligent woman who had given this a great deal of thought. Her observations and skepticism of the *ton* surprised him. She was rather young to have such a jaded view.

But he found himself glad she did not follow the *ton* blindly, as most of the young ladies, desperate for invitations to Almack's, did.

She took a step toward him, her soft skirts

pressing against her legs. "The importance of the nobility, Your Grace, and the way they speak, is in how it *excludes* others. The first thing that I have seen that the nobility does is identify if one knows another noble person well or if they have a great house. For instance, you are only here because your mother knows of my cousin."

"Cousin?" Francesca piped before she nodded brightly. "Oh yes, of course myself." A rather sheepish laugh tumbled past her lips. "How foolish of me."

He paused at Lady Charlotte's skewering commentary. "It is true. We don't let in anyone, do we?"

"No, not unless they have a great deal of money," she said.

"They?" he queried.

She blushed. "We. Of course, I mean *we*. But when one studies something, it is easy to make it a subject outside of oneself."

The edge in her voice surprised him. Her passion was uncommon, as were her whip-smart intellectual observations of class.

There were so many ladies and men of the city who had vast fortunes but were disdained by the *ton*. They were kept out because they knew no one in the *ton*. They did not have ancient houses. No, they lived in new monstrosities and married any lower noble in an attempt to gain entry.

It was not a point of which he was proud.

The *ton* was a very small set.

And he? He belonged to an even smaller subset of it.

More than half of the genteel families that came to London for the Season were simply not deemed important enough to be invited into the rooms he occupied.

After all, his was one of the most powerful families in the land, and to keep that power, he would have to ally himself to a family like Palmerton's. A very old family if not a land-rich one.

He had never met Palmerton and had only heard of him in passing.

There were so many nobles he did not know; his mother, on the other hand, was a master at keeping track of the families in the *ton*.

No doubt, she had a list of pedigrees as long as Hadrian's Wall.

The French clock on the mantel dinged several times, and he found himself disappointed. The time for his visit had ended. He had to leave.

He had to leave *her*.

"Ladies," he said, keeping his voice even. "I find that I must go. Our conversation has been illuminating, but I should like to invite you both elsewhere."

Lady Charlotte *tsk*ed playfully. "I thought you liked libraries."

Damnation, he adored how she loved to set him down. He found it only made him long to growl her name, slide his fingers into her wild hair, and find out if her kisses were as playful as her tongue.

"Oh, I would be happy to sit in this library with you for hours. Unfortunately, I do have appointments this afternoon."

"More ladies?" Lady Charlotte teased, her eyes dancing.

"No, Lady Charlotte," he replied. "Government calls."

"Government?" she queried.

"Several bills in the House of Lords await my vote."

Lady Charlotte's brow furrowed, and he would have given a great deal to know her thoughts just then.

"But I confess, I cannot allow our acquaintance to be at an end."

"I am glad you like Francesca so well," Lady Charlotte piped.

Francesca? Was Lady Charlotte being coy? She seemed incapable of it. But there was a determined strain to her voice. "And you? Do you not think I like you?"

"Oh, I am very forgettable, Your Grace. No doubt, by tomorrow, you won't recall the cut of my clothes, or my name, either, given your vast acquaintance."

Had he made a muck of this meeting?

He'd thought it was going rather well, but now, she seemed to wish him gone.

If she thought that he could forget her, she was utterly mad. "Will you be at a ball this week?" he asked bluntly, determined not to be fobbed off. "There are many, but Lady Asquith's is the most important. I could ascertain invitations for both of you."

"I don't dance," Lady Charlotte declared with surprising ferocity.

"You don't—"

"Dance," Charlotte finished with a tight nod.

He frowned. "How very—"

She sighed. "It is an aversion that I have to skipping about the room. It makes me ill."

"It makes you ill," he repeated. Was she having him on? Or did she dislike him entirely and was trying to be polite about it?

Lady Francesca laughed, a slightly forced sound, before she rushed, "Indeed it does. She comes out in hives."

Lady Charlotte stared at her cousin as if she was going to die on the spot. Or as if she wished she could murder her.

Lady Charlotte did not die. Nor did she attempt to murder the cousin she so clearly loved.

"How terrible," he said, feeling an awkwardness he'd never felt in company. As a duke, he was always feted. But suddenly, he felt as if he was yesterday's tea things ready to be taken to the bins. "Excuse me, ladies, is my company or person so appalling that you would come up with such a story?"

"It is not a story," Lady Charlotte insisted. "I cannot dance at all."

He arched a brow.

She bit her lower lip, then allowed, "The hives perhaps are a bit of an exaggeration. But there is nothing wrong with you, Your Grace. You're quite kind. And personable... for a duke."

"This is the strangest conversation I have ever had." He stared at Lady Charlotte, trying to make sense of her. Of his reaction to her. He could not. "And yet I find that I don't wish it to end."

"Then you are very foolish, Your Grace," Lady Charlotte declared. "For I am clearly impossible and should be avoided at all costs."

Did she wish to be avoided at all costs? It would certainly explain some of her rather odd statements. But why?

"You are not impossible. You are marvelous," he said. And before he could reconsider, he urged, "Alas, my current commitments do not allow me to enjoy your company this night. But please come to Vauxhall in a week's time. Both of you. Let us go and see the fireworks, if you will not dance. My mother could be the chaperone if you do not have any lady in town to look after you. It seems as if your father is away, Lady Francesca?"

Lady Francesca's smile dimmed, but then she crossed to Lady Charlotte, took her cousin's arm, and pulled her to stand behind the mahogany table. "He is away, in Bath. And we accept. Don't we, Charlotte?"

Lady Charlotte's eyes went wide as a slightly muted sound filled the room.

He frowned. Had her cousin just kicked Lady Charlotte behind the table? No. Surely, he was imagining things.

Just as Lady Charlotte appeared to begin to refuse, she let out a small exclamation, then nodded.

"Well, then, ladies," he said, uncertain if he was triumphant or a fool. "In seven days' time, then."

"Until then, Your Grace," Lady Francesca said, curtsying.

"My mother will be delighted," he assured with a bow. "I have finally found two ladies whom I wish to take somewhere."

"She will only be delighted if you wish to marry one of us," Lady Charlotte warned.

"Oh, I think she shall be happy," he said.

And with that, he turned on his booted heel, wondering what the blazes had happened to him.

And if…just perhaps…he needn't resign himself to misery, after all.

CHAPTER NINE

Charlotte paced the length of Francesca's bedchamber, wondering how the devil she had gotten herself into such a horrific predicament. In a gown that barely fit. Again.

A week had passed, and she wished she could be sensible enough to simply say she was ill. But she did not think the duke would accept such a thing without coming to visit her. For he was a thoughtful man. And that was the last thing she wanted.

"Lies," Charlotte lamented. "Lies. I am so deep in them, I am drowning."

"And me," Francesca piped merrily from her dressing table as she stuck a butterfly pin into her hair. She paused, angled herself in the chair, and winked conspiratorially. "I, too, am swimming at quite a pace, hoping to outpace the waves of your nefarious ways. I had no idea you were so duplicitous, Charlie."

"Look, Chess." Charlotte threw her gloved hands up into the lilac-scented evening air drifting in through the open windows. The garden was full to bursting, and the night was heavy with the beauty of it. She wished she could revel in it. She could not! Her stomach was in knots.

"I found myself in a particularly difficult

situation with the duke. I didn't wish the duke coming back to our house last week at the prison, so I did not tell him my name. Truly, I never thought I'd see him again. I was grateful for his help, but now…"

Francesca's merry eyes danced a veritable reel as she pulled on her long gloves one at a time. "Now, you are going to Vauxhall to meet with him, and he is far more interested in you than he is in me. I can tell you that much."

"Do not say such a thing," Charlotte groaned. "He cannot marry a mere maid like me. And I have no wish to marry a duke."

Francesca arched a skeptical brow at that. She shook her head. "He is not for me."

Her sister frowned. "You do not like him?"

"He is a duke. Powerful. And…kind. I barely know him. How can I know if I like him? Do you like him?"

"Does it matter?"

She gasped. "You don't mean it."

Francesca sighed, her shoulders slumping as she faced herself in her polished mirror. She studied her features. "I long for freedom. Don't you? A match would guarantee that for us. Tell him the truth, Charlie. He likes you. He likes you *well*. He might see my father for the villain he is and give you—"

"What?"

"Independence," Francesca said firmly, almost with an edge of the mercenary.

Charlotte swallowed. How she adored her sister. She was everything that Charlotte was not, and she didn't envy her for a second. For her stepsister was but a piece in her father's game.

At least Charlotte didn't have to worry about being forced into a profitable marriage. No, she could stay in her turret, with her penny novels and her chores.

"Whatever he decides, tonight, we shall go and have a splendid time," Francesca said. "And perhaps... You never know. One of us shall be a duchess."

"You don't have to sacrifice yourself," Charlotte said softly. "Perhaps—"

"Perhaps my father won't throttle me if I don't do everything I can to catch the duke. Perhaps I can escape my father with the duke. Or you could steal me away, too, if you marry him."

Tears had filled Francesca's eyes.

And suddenly, Charlotte felt the weight of their situation. It was easy to make light, but the truth was Francesca had to make a good marriage. Her father was counting on it.

Slowly, she placed her own gloved hands on the thin pale silk skimming Francesca's shoulders. "His mother wants him to marry you, not me," she pointed out gently.

And with that, Francesca gave a firm nod, stood, and smoothed down her ice blue, lace-covered skirts. "I don't look too terrible, do I?"

"You look splendid," Charlotte replied with easy honesty before she frowned. "It is I who looks a bit odd."

"No, you don't, Charlie," Francesca countered. "The dress suits you."

Charlotte stared at herself in the full-length mirror.

In all her life, she'd never worn anything like the borrowed soft silk gown that traced her body like a caress. She'd never had cause.

The frock was simple. It was a beautiful ivory affair. Its capped sleeves skimmed her arms. It had a scooping neckline, baring a shocking but fashionable amount of bosom. She felt quite exposed. After all, servants didn't go about in such a state of near undress! It felt like her sleeves might give way at any moment, though Chess had assured her they would not. The gown was made to be flirtatious but not scandalous.

Without jewels, Charlotte had chosen a simple robin's egg-colored ribbon and tied it about her throat. Her blond hair was curled atop her head, with country roses secured into the coils.

She supposed she looked well enough, but she felt like a complete fraud.

She swallowed, panic welling up in her throat. "Whatever shall I do? I am not accustomed to being in company. I do not know how to converse or behave."

"Well, I would say just be yourself, but Charlie, you are a bit of a shock. Perhaps it is best if you don't say much at all, if you don't wish to be noticed."

Charlotte nodded, knowing Francesca was right.

"You are incognito," Francesca said, taking her hand. "Be whoever you wish. Or simply be yourself. For Lady Charlotte isn't real. She's whoever you want her to be."

Whoever she wanted to be? She could scarce fathom it. What if she entered Vauxhall like a grand lady and acted as if she was from a great French family? She could—

She closed her eyes, not daring to be so wild. "I shall sit on the sidelines and be quiet and unobserved and make no notice."

Francesca pressed her lips together before she teased, "Of course you shall, Charlie. Of course you shall."

"What the blazes do you mean by that?"

"Oh, nothing. Except I do not think you could be unobserved if you were wearing a flour sack."

And with a half laugh, half sigh, Charlotte linked arms with her stepsister. "Into battle, then?"

Francesca nodded. "But what is the prize?"

"Why, a duke for you, of course!"

And that was the only outcome there could ever be.

CHAPTER TEN

"I can't believe that you've managed to drag me out. You know I should be home, polishing my swords."

The comment was nearly swallowed up by the crush at Vauxhall and the applause as a tightrope walker performed antics overhead.

The Duke of Rockford looked at George Leighton, Earl of Darrow, and then to the earl's twin brother, Matthew. The lights of thousands of glass lamps illuminated their faces, making their expressions impossible to miss.

Matthew's lips twitched, and he began to say something, but George swung a gaze to his brother that suggested he might murder him in his sleep if he proceeded. "Don't say it. Don't say it!"

Matthew looked away quickly, studiously admiring the young lady in red tights and shockingly short green skirts now taking to the suspended wire overhead. Still, his lips pursed as if it was all he could do not to harass his straightlaced twin.

George rolled his eyes. "Both of you, minds in the gutter."

Rockford laughed, a free sound, at his friend's grumbling. His mind had not been in the gutter since he was a small boy, and perhaps, not even then. But Matthew's mind…

Matthew's mind loved all things sinful, and it was impossible for the man to not come up with the most scandalous of quips or droll replies when given the opportunity.

Rafe gestured to one of the young boys in elaborate costume to bring them more wine. And he tipped the lad well with a silver coin as he took up three goblets of deep red burgundy.

It was a sign of shocking self-control that Matthew refrained from saying whatever limerick he had in mind regarding his brother's wish to be at home, taking care of his extensive armory.

Before George could protest, Rafe handed his friends the globules and offered a salute. "To Wellington and Nelson."

It was a toast that couldn't be naysaid. The twins joined quickly, and they took a drink of the rather rich but surprisingly good wine.

Matthew had fought for Wellington in Spain and was in London now, trying to make his way as the second son…by less than five minutes.

George, like his brother, had served, but he had been a naval man, sailing for Nelson years ago, before he'd taken up his title.

Now, he was ensconced in the halls of power and all that it entailed.

George was also looking for a wife at long last, which was the only reason Rafe had been able to pull the man away from his whetstones and blades. Frankly, Rafe was surprised George didn't just ask his mother, the duchess, to find him a wife.

She was certainly eager to pair up the world.

In any event, Rafe's mother had been incredibly pleased that he had decided to invite two young ladies to Vauxhall.

But much as Charlotte had suggested, she was only going to be pleased if he wished to marry one of them. And, almost certainly, Lady Francesca was the preferred choice.

His mother would have to live with a degree of disappointment and take her win with as much grace as possible.

After all, at least he'd be marching down the aisle.

While he admired Lady Francesca, she was not for him. No, no, if anyone was for him, he was certain it was Lady Charlotte. If asked explicitly, he doubted he could give a succinct reason why.

It wasn't that she was different from other ladies. That was an insult to other ladies. No, she was simply…different. From anyone he'd ever met. Odd. Passionate. Determined.

And he found he liked odd, passionate, and determined.

If all went well tonight, he'd ask for her hand immediately. To some, it might seem a bit mad, picking a wife after a week, but dukes had made such decisions on far less interaction in the *ton*, relying strictly on letters and pedigree.

A loud cheer went up from the crowd as both tightrope walkers headed out onto the line, faces taut with focus as the fellow lifted the lady into the air in a daring pas de deux.

"What the devil are we doing here?" George drawled, folding his hands behind his back as if he still stood aboard, ready to meet the enemy with a full cannon blast broadside. He, apparently, was the only one unmoved by the performers' death-defying stunts.

"We are waiting for two ladies," he said honestly.

Matthew swung him a startled gaze. "I beg your pardon?"

He nodded, determined not to let Matthew get the better of him. "I have invited two ladies here tonight. My mother has insisted that I find a wife, and…"

"And you wish us to help you pick," Matthew said, nodding. "Very sensible. We shall point out their fine qualities and be most discreet about their poor ones—"

"No! That is not what I'm doing," he roared, pulling at his waistcoat. "I've no wish for running commentary on their persons or help in deciding who will—"

"Grace your sheets?"

"I'm going to pop you one."

"Not if George does first," Matt said with a merry grin.

So much for not rising to Matt's bait.

"The boxing exhibition doesn't begin for an hour," George said drily.

Rafe narrowed his eyes. "There's always time for a preview."

"But then your hair would be mussed," Matt mused.

He ground his teeth, wondering why the blazes he'd brought Matt. The truth was, he quite liked the sardonic lord who made merry when the world was so often sad. But one had to be willing to enjoy his cracks.

Tonight, he was surprisingly on edge. And as the tightrope performers bowed, Rafe and his friends turned and wove their way back toward the glittering pavilion lined with an orchestra playing sugary notes.

Matt's eyes danced as he flicked an imaginary bit of lint from his shoulder. "Ah. Amour. It is so hard to decide when there are so many ladies about. I pity you both. Indeed I do."

"No you don't," George said easily.

Matt was a handsome rake. War had lined his face, but he still had a jaunty, devil-may-care attitude that made him the darling of married ladies everywhere—and the center of the set that did not usually see their beds before dawn.

"Why did you invite two?" George asked, clearly perplexed as they found an empty table. He was not nearly as roguish as his brother, and he did not know how to charm the ladies, though his heart was the purer of the two.

"Efficiency, no doubt," Matt offered, apparently determined to find an irritating explanation of Rafe's motives. He flung himself down casually, stretching one leg out, his gaze turning to the dancers on the floor.

"I could not invite one without the other," Rafe explained. "They are cousins. It was difficult."

Matt dramatically fluttered his thick lashes, clearly not buying this explanation for a moment.

"And the lady I do not want is the one my mother expects me to pick," he bit out.

"There we have it," Matt crowed, putting his wine down and clapping his large hands together.

George began to laugh. "My God, my friend, you are engaged in a full Sheridan comedy. How is it possible that you have managed to land yourself so deep in farce? Is someone going to tumble into one of the water displays tonight?"

"I do not know, but I bloody well hope not," he said drily, folding his arms across his chest, not quite ready to sit. "I should have left you both at home."

"Too late. Too late," Matt said, grinning. "Besides, you'd pine for our winning chat. And you need cavalry to manage this mess with your lady."

His lady…

As if on cue, both Lady Charlotte and Lady Francesca approached the pavilion, both looking an absolute picture of English maidenhood.

They certainly shone like jewels.

Another reason why Vauxhall was so popular: the young ladies of the *ton* were veritable entertainment to look upon. He, of course, was used to seeing young ladies trotted out everywhere, but seeing them amass, bejeweled and beautiful in the pleasure gardens? Many found it was quite a sight to be seen, and watching them dance on the open-air dance floor was also something that those in attendance preferred. Sometimes above the many other entertainments.

He hoped—he hoped *beyond* hope—that Lady Charlotte might allow him to ask her to dance.

Surely, she would not indeed break out in hives. Surely, she had simply been exaggerating.

After all, duchesses were meant to dance.

Lady Francesca and Lady Charlotte cut through the crowd as they spotted him.

Lady Francesca's eyes lit with amusement when she spotted the men with him, and Lady Charlotte looked wary, which was quite surprising, because he had not seen her look wary in the entire time that he had known her.

Certainly not on the pavement outside the Marshalsea.

She had seemed indefatigable there. Here, she looked as if she had been tossed into the lion's den and expected to be eaten.

He highly doubted she would be passive.

And for a single moment, another meaning to his words swept through. How he should love to devour her.

But he did not like to consume his partners.

No, he liked it to be a joint venture of passion taken and passion given. There would not be seizing on his part, unless she would seize in turn.

And then...by God, then the fire that might spark between them? He had a feeling it could consume the world in flame.

Her passion would surely be the flint to his steel.

Lady Charlotte and Lady Francesca, at last, stood before him.

Lady Charlotte swung her gaze over the three gentlemen, and, without any segue, challenged, "Where is your mother? You three do not a chaperone make."

Matt all but coughed on a laugh. "The One," he whispered behind a hand.

"The one what?" Charlotte asked.

Before Matt could reply, Rafe stomped on his friend's boot.

Matt yelped.

"Forgive me; I did not see you there," Rafe lied happily.

Matt shot him a wink, despite the way he shook his booted foot. "Very bad of me to put my foot there."

"My mother will be along in just a moment," he assured Charlotte.

"No doubt she is making merry with a musician," George said frankly.

A strangled note trumped out of Rafe's throat. The last thing he needed Charlotte thinking was his mother was a bit of a scandal now. Even if it was true. But he knew his friend meant no malice.

Lady Francesca laughed, and Charlotte's eyebrows popped up as she clearly tried to make sense of their antics.

"I beg your pardon?" she asked.

"I say," George said apologetically. "Have I put my foot in it? You do not know the reputation of the Duchess of Rockford?"

Matthew *tsk*ed, maneuvering his booted feet away from Rafe. "This does not bode well, Rockford, if they do not know your mother's reputation. However will either of them behave as a daughter-in-law?"

"They know?" Lady Charlotte exclaimed.

"Of course they know we are on trial," Lady Francesca said with a delightful shrug. "He is a duke. No doubt everyone knows."

George eyed Francesca with curiosity. "You do have a most skeptical mindset for a young lady," he said without accusation.

"I have a practical mindset for a young lady," Lady Francesca corrected. "There is a difference. You see, I will not be plucked willy-nilly, like some flower in a garden. No, no. I should look out for who shall make my petals grow the best."

Matt's brow quirked, but he remained silent as he studied his twin.

"Do you generally speak in metaphor?" George asked simply, intrigued.

Lady Francesca smiled. "Sometimes I think it best. I do love a good metaphor."

"Do you like reading?" George blurted awkwardly.

"Of course I like reading," Lady Francesca said passionately. "Who doesn't like reading?"

George let out a sigh, but there was a spark of hope in his eyes. "Many, many people."

"Alas, we must grieve for their poor, lost

souls," Lady Francesca replied.

A look crossed George's face as if he had seen heaven and was about to gain admittance.

Matt swung his gaze back and forth between them before he said with some delight, "I dare say, you two must form a club regarding books."

"That sounds like an excellent idea," Lady Francesca said.

"I am full of them," Matt preened.

"What did you read last?" she asked the earl, largely ignoring his twin—a thing that didn't usually occur.

And George took note, angling his body toward her and inclining his head.

Before anyone could say another word, Lady Francesca and his friend were standing side by side, beginning to discuss the latest novels that had come hot off the press.

Lady Charlotte looked positively flummoxed that she'd been left with Rockford.

Matthew let out a laugh. "I shall not be malaprop," he said. "I am going to go in search of a drink. I'll bring you two back something, if you should like." Matt gave him a mischievous smile. "I can tell," he said, locking gazes with Rafe, "what you were saying before, about the difficulty. I see what you mean."

But before Rafe could make a proper

riposte, Matt escaped into the crowd, as Matthew always did, before he could be punished for making ill commentary.

"What the blazes was he talking about?" Lady Charlotte asked with surprising force.

"Nothing. Nothing," he assured quickly, lest she think she and her cousin were the subject of gossip. "Lord Matthew is a devil, and that's the simple truth of it."

"But he is your friend?" she queried.

"Yes. One can be friends with a devil," he said. "Sometimes, he is even most merry and endearing."

She laughed. "Better a devil who is devilish than a pious fool who infringes upon the freedom of everyone and does not allow a merry quip from time to time."

"Lady Charlotte," he said, feeling more and more akin to her sensible sentiments. "How very astute of you."

"Thank you," she said. "I have read a great deal about the Puritan years and their control. I do not think that I could have ever faced it. Do you?"

"I would've faced it," he said with a shudder. "But it would've been bloody terrible. Can you imagine? No music, except liturgical."

"No Christmas," she gasped.

"Exactly! No theater," he added.

"I cannot imagine a world without plays,"

she lamented. Her eyes widened with faux horror. "Or novels. Can you imagine a world without novels or penny novelettes?"

"Indeed, I cannot," he agreed. "The very idea of it sends a shudder down my spine."

"And mine!"

"Can you imagine no dancing?" he queried without thinking.

"Well," she said, "I suppose, since I don't dance, I can imagine such a thing, but I know how deeply it would affect Francesca and people such as yourself. You all do seem to like it a great deal."

He stared down at her as she turned her gaze to the dancing couples on the floor not too far from them. "You truly don't dance," he breathed, stunned. "You weren't trying to fob me off."

"No, I truly don't," she said plainly. "I really have had neither the opportunity nor the occasion to do it."

"You don't go to balls?" he queried, even more surprised. He couldn't imagine her as a wallflower. She was too bold. Too interesting. Too ready to seize the conversation.

She stilled. "No, not usually. This would be my first Season, you see," she said slowly.

He studied her, trying to make sense of the young lady before him. "You're certain you're not trying to assuage my feelings?"

"Have I ever spared you in anything but

this?" she asked.

He snorted with surprise. "I confess you have not. A point to you. You've never been rude, but I know more about your opinions of the world than I do the vast majority of the *ton*."

"Exactly," she said with a pleased nod. "I do not care about massaging your vanity. Life is far too short to waste such time. But I would not hurt you out of unkindness."

Unkindness... He couldn't imagine her being cruel. Fierce? Oh yes. But unkind? No.

"I agree with you wholeheartedly, but I think you are missing a great deal not being able to dance. Perhaps I could send a dancing tutor to you."

"No," she rushed, her body snapping to attention. "No, no, no. Thank you. Lord Palmerton would not be fond of tutors being secured that he does not know himself."

"I see," he said.

The statement—and her sudden change in stance—did strike him as a bit strange.

Usually, anytime a duke paid attention to a young lady, it was a great boon for any family. But there was no getting around his feared difficulty.

Palmerton would no doubt believe that Rafe was going to ask Lady Francesca to wed, not his niece.

Would he take it ill?

Was he the kind of man to take it badly?

From the look on Lady Charlotte's face, he began to think that yes, Palmerton might take it badly indeed.

Oh, he anticipated a bit of disgruntlement but nothing more. He'd find a way to make his future duchess's host pleased.

Lady Charlotte and Lady Francesca seemed to be great friends, but Lady Charlotte appeared to live in a shadow. Had her own family in Scotland sent her to live with Palmerton? And if so, did Palmerton keep her hidden away? Such things happened. Was that why she did not know how to dance? Had she not had a tutor?

The thought infuriated him, and he felt the need to right it.

He extended his hand toward her in a bold move. "Then you must let me teach you to dance."

She lowered her gaze slowly to his extended palm, staring for a very long time. The night breeze danced in her hair, causing her curls to tangle and tease over her face, and her cheeks darkened with a deep rose hue in the lantern light. "I do not wish to make a fool of myself upon the dance floor," she whispered honestly. "I prefer not to draw attention."

"I see." And he felt ever more that he did. Lady Charlotte was a jewel far more precious than any diamond, and yet she had not been displayed. She'd not been to balls.

And now?

Why did she not wish attention to be drawn to herself?

Why was she so concerned about a tutor coming to her house? Perhaps her uncle wished to keep her hidden until the perfect moment to reveal her to society. He hoped that was the case.

And yet he couldn't deny this moment between them.

Vauxhall was the perfect place to take her down a path and to teach her to dance. Young ladies of every walk of life managed to get away from their mothers in this elaborate maze of shrubbery and trees.

It was one of the points of Vauxhall. If a lady wished to go down one of the lit paths with a gentleman? There was no scandal. In fact, it was one of the drawing points of the garden.

No, there was no risk...until a lady wandered off into the dark paths. And then, she might do whatever she pleased, as long as she was not caught.

"I could teach you the waltz," he said softly before he turned his gaze to one of the winding ways that glowed from the golden hue of the lamps swaying overhead. "That way."

She looked in the direction that he suggested, then scowled. "Do I look a complete fool?"

He jolted, stunned by the force of her question. "No, I would never say that."

She pursed her lips and folded her hands beneath her breasts, which plumped them in the most distracting of ways; however, being a gentleman, he yanked his attention back up to her face, then cleared his throat, determined to keep to the right side of virtue. "I will counter, Lady Charlotte, with a point of my own. Do I look like a cad?"

She paused, her mouth opening ever so slightly as she made good view of him.

Oh so slowly, she studied him up and down. And the assessing glance did the most astonishing things to his physique and his psyche.

What did she think of his person?

For it appeared she was judging every inch of him, from the polished tips of his black leather shoes, up his tightly clad calves and thighs. Her gaze lingered for a moment at the placard at his hips, then moved to his waist, where she then raked it up his broad chest and met his eyes.

It was a scorching, slow consideration, that look.

"Oh, Your Grace," she replied. "You do indeed look like a cad."

He swallowed, rather surprised at her

decision. He'd always thought himself to be rather chivalrous and a gentleman, point of fact.

A smile tilted her lips. "I see your distress."

He began to speak, but she raised a hand and rushed in, "Let me finish, Your Grace. You *look* like a cad, and I'm sure many a lady *wishes* that you were a cad. I can see that just looking about tonight. A dozen eyes have already tried to catch yours."

Had they, by God? He had not noticed.

She licked her soft but pert lips and continued, "I'm certain there are hundreds of ladies here who would die of absolute bliss if you asked them to take the dark walk tonight. But let me tell you this: I know you are not a cad, from what you did with Stevenson and what you did in the library with myself and Francesca. You are a good man with a good heart. I'd bet there is not a single shade of gray in you."

He let out another laugh, but it turned into a groan. "Do you think me a milk sop, then?"

"That is not what I said, Your Grace," she returned firmly. "I do not think you are a milk sop, because you are honorable and kind. I can see the strength in you. I will never forget the look on that jailer's face when you made certain that Stevenson was released. I think that London would quake in its collective boots if ever you wanted it to."

It was his turn to study her. Who was she?

How had this young woman become so self-possessed as to tell a duke her thoughts without hesitation?

He did not know, but it drew him to her. Good God, he felt compelled by her and whatever was growing between them. "I do not wish to cause you offense, Lady Charlotte. I only wish to dance with you."

She bit her lower lip, and then something changed. A look of sheer will blossomed in her eyes, as if any fear she'd possessed had been eradicated by their exchange. "I will go down the path with you if you will teach me how to dance, but I will not go into darkness, Your Grace. We must linger in the light. And that way, anyone who sees us will simply say what a silly couple we are for dancing on the path and not on the floor."

She cocked her head to the side, which caused her curls to skim and kiss her neck… just as he wished to do.

How he longed to reach forward, brush those locks aside, and press an open-mouthed kiss to the curve of her neck.

"But no one will ever be able to say that we have been truly scandalous," she said firmly, squaring her shoulders, which caused the bodice of her gown to press against her breasts. "And they will not see my face well. So, no one will be able to say, *Lady Charlotte is a scandal. Lady Charlotte is a fool. Lady*

Charlotte does not know how to dance."

She took a step closer to him, and the hem of her thin silk gown skimmed his boot. "For in the dim light of the walk, we shall be in neither sin nor complete virtue."

"We shall be in the gray," he murmured, understanding her, marveling at her. And feeling that he was about to have her to himself.

At that thought, something deep inside him roared to life and growled, *mine*.

"Can you accept that?" she asked, her chin tilting up as she gazed into his eyes.

He blinked, taking in the power of her meaning. "I don't think I have been in the gray, Lady Charlotte."

A strange look slipped across her face. "Yes, I can tell. You believe things to be white or to be black, to be true or to be false."

"It is how I've always lived my life," he said simply. "I find it easiest to function thus."

She nodded, though she did not look assured. "Sinners are sinners and saints are saints?"

"I would not call myself a saint," he ventured. "But I do think that there is a line one crosses into dishonor."

"And you would never risk dishonor?"

"Never," he replied.

"Come, then," she said with a nod, "let us dance on the path. And let anyone say what they may."

CHAPTER ELEVEN

Much to Charlotte's surprise, instead of remaining in strict book discourse, Francesca went off with the Earl of Darrow and proceeded straight to the dance floor, where they no doubt continued their comparison of the best novels of the year.

The music filling the air made Charlotte long to sway to it.

How she wished she could dance!

Though she had attempted sometimes to practice reels and jigs and the waltz, she never had enough solid time to be able to do it properly. When she did have discussions with Francesca, she was always sewing or polishing or doing some work that allowed her to speak to her stepsister while she completed her tasks. Yes, Charlotte was always either brushing Francesca's hair, styling it, taking care of her clothes, tidying her chamber, or completing the hundreds of other tasks necessary to maintain the house.

So, when she dared to slip her hand into the Duke of Rockford's upon his request, there was a moment of such intense shock as her fingers slid into his.

It reminded her of the morning when he had caught her in the hallway—only this felt *more*. With her gloved hand in his, he took her down the path.

Every step away from the crowd only intensified her breath, which seemed to match the excited beat of her heart.

Was she mad to be doing this?

She certainly was, but she'd had such a little life. She had lived so small that suddenly she found herself wanting, daring to live at the greatest capacity she possibly could.

Oh yes, she had told Francesca that she would hide away and not be noticed this night, but… Fie on that! Fie on not being noticed!

Here under the night sky, the fragrant breeze wafting across her cheek and the sounds of merriment about her? How could she live but a little life?

She had spent her entire existence not being noticed. And here? Tonight? This was a chance to finally be *herself*, and she was not going to give that up.

So, when the immensely powerful and beautiful Duke of Rockford led her farther down the perfectly groomed pathways lined with various trees and shrubberies, the air filled with the scent of roses, she almost swooned with happiness.

It was as if she had stepped into one of her penny novels. And for at least one night, she was going to pretend just as Francesca had said that she truly was Lady Charlotte, grand debutante with a fortune who could marry the Duke of Rockford if he but asked.

As Lady Charlotte, she would be worthy of him.

She would be able to meet him quip for quip, laugh for laugh, dance for dance. And she would never have to be afraid or look over her shoulder, worried that her guardian was coming to tell her to get back to her turret or back to the kitchen, to the stones that always needed scrubbing with sand.

Sand that turned her hands raw.

She angled to Rockford when he paused beneath a particularly beautiful tree with branches that swept low, like an embrace meant to protect young lovers from watchful eyes.

And in the protective arms of that tree, on the shadowy path kissed with lamplight, he slipped his other hand to her waist.

"Now," he began, his voice a dark rumble of temptation. "We shall keep this very, very simple. I shall teach you how to waltz."

A waltz? She was already dancing on air. Or so it felt.

"I think it is the easiest," he explained. "We won't have to learn any elaborate patterns, and you won't have to worry about any other couples or having to go up and down the floor, et cetera, looking for me amidst a sea of unfamiliar ladies and gentlemen."

She gave a nod, her insides fluttering with anticipation. Anticipation of the dance and of being in his capable arms. "That sounds marvelous. And I must confess, I've always wanted to learn the waltz."

"As you should," he said. "Anyone with any sense should long to waltz. For there is nowhere to hide. It is just you. Just me. And the music."

That sounded positively terrifying and completely irresistible all at once.

If she wasn't careful, he would notice that she was trembling. For all this? It was more than a servant could ever dream.

He angled his head down and instructed, "Now, what you must do is stand close to me, but not too close. We are closer than an arm's length, but our bodies should not be touching. My hand will rest just below your shoulder blade, like this."

Carefully, he placed his palm against her back, his thumb tucked under her shoulder blade.

She swallowed at the feel of his hand pressed to her back. There was so little between them. And for the briefest, most shocking of moments, she wished there was nothing between them at all—that she was in his arms. Their lengths pressed together. She could only imagine what it might feel like…

The strength of his body wrapped about her own.

With his free hand, he clasped the folds of her silk skirt and raised them ever so slightly, passing them to her free hand. "You must take up your skirts with your other hand."

The gesture felt deliciously shocking as the silk skimmed up her leg, baring only her ankle. But the touch of the fabric felt like an extension of him, as if it was *he* caressing her.

Slowly, she did as she was told.

"And then we are simply going to walk," he said.

"Walk," she gasped, staring at his cravat.

He was tall. Very, very tall. And she found that she was quite stunned by the breadth of his shoulders, standing thus.

"Yes," he said, the rumble of his voice in his chest as heady as the wine she had tasted one night with Francesca in the kitchens. "Walk. For in walking, we will be able to learn the rhythm of each other; how the other moves; how we sway, and how to go together."

"Together?" she breathed.

"Indeed," he assured. "Look at me, Charlotte."

Slowly, she tilted her head back and met his gaze. And the fire in them. The strength, the crackling promise of this dance?

It sent her blood humming through her

body with a song that demanded he match.

He licked his sensual lower lip and explained, "One cannot dance unless one's body is in accord with one's partner's. There is no point at all, or the dance is jarring and awful. But if we meet together and we find the timing, it is…"

His voice trailed off as he looked down at her, shadows trailing over his face.

"Yes," she prompted.

"Bliss," he replied honestly.

"Bliss," she repeated. "But is such a thing important in the everyday doings of a life?"

"I beg your pardon?" He blinked, caught off guard.

"Is it so very important? Grand moments? I think I would rather be shown small, everyday joys than know one grand moment of bliss."

He stared at her then, as if she had lit some wonder-filled light in his soul.

"Are you unwell?"

"Not at all. You are right, of course; love is in the small things. The gestures that are consistent. Like bringing your beloved hot chocolate in bed each morning."

"That sounds positively decadent to me. But yes, to show up every day. To experience one grand dance here under the trees of Vauxhall is exceptional. But bliss to me? Would be a dance by the firelight every night.

With the man I love."

"Then that's what you should have," he whispered, his face transforming with emotion.

She tsked, her heart beginning to beat quite fast under his gaze. "Ah. It shall never be."

"Never say never, Lady Charlotte," he replied, his voice a low hum, and his eyes danced as if he had seen heaven. She could not understand why. After all, a daily dance by the fire was surely a silly thing to a duke.

CHAPTER TWELVE

This dance was a terrible idea. Of that, Charlotte was certain. But she refused to regret it.

She couldn't. Whatever could he mean that she should have her dance a day with the man she loved, as if he was interested in the position?

Clearly, the very idea was absurd!

And surely, a dance couldn't induce bliss. But in his arms, as he began to slowly move her along the path, easily guiding her feet, stepping backward, then stepping forward, then somehow, miraculously, stepping to the side, she let out a slow breath.

She was dancing! Somehow, the walking was turning into more. Yes, she felt it as they began to bend and sway, and she let go and simply let herself be in his arms...

She was so flooded with joy, and a smile tilted her lips with such vigor it almost hurt.

How she adored the feel of his hard sinew beneath her gloved hand upon his shoulder. She would follow him on any dance floor. For in this moment, she felt like he could teach her to fly if he decided to put his mind to it.

Then...she stepped immediately on his booted foot so firmly he winced and stopped, clasping her to him.

She let out a gasp of horror, her face all but pressed to his chest as he held his breath. "I am so sorry!"

"Oh, my dear Charlotte." He let out a sigh and relaxed, already recovering, then took her chin between his thumb and forefinger, tilting her face upward. "There is no achieving what you wish without a few missteps along the way."

Her brow furrowed as she looked for signs of his disappointment in her ability. There were none. And she was mystified. "Truly?"

"The leader," he said with a nod, "is always responsible. For I did not lead you well, and thus, you stepped on me."

"So it is *your* fault that I stepped on you?" she teased, completely surprised that he was absolving her of all guilt.

He laughed softly, an intoxicating caress in the shadows. "Who else's fault could it possibly be? I am the one who is supposed to ensure that you make it through the dance unharmed. And that you enjoy yourself."

She nibbled her lower lip, confused. "Is that what it's supposed to be like for ladies? It doesn't seem like that's what it's supposed to be like for ladies."

He listened patiently without attempting to interrupt, but his hand had moved to her waist, resting where her hip met her lower back. "What is it *supposed* to be like?" he asked.

She sighed. "Well, from what I see, ladies are supposed to be dressed for men and behave a certain way for men and bear children and take care of their houses."

"Many men feel that way," he allowed, his hand splaying, covering her lower back as he slowly, almost unnoticeably, swayed them side to side. "I don't really care what the rest are supposed to do." His lips tilted in a smile. "I'm the Duke of Rockford. I damn well do what I please, and I'd like you to do the same."

To damn well do as she pleased?

She could not fathom such a thing.

"Am I dreaming?" she asked, half laughing.

"Does it feel like a dream?" He turned them slowly under the bow of the tree, flickering light playing over them.

"Yes," she whispered. "It does."

"Then do not awaken," he urged.

And suddenly, the lantern lights seemed too dim.

She glanced around.

Had they gone off the path? Was it possible?

No. They had not moved. The lantern must have simply run low on oil.

Rockford sighed, stilling as the fabric of

her skirts belled then swung against his powerful legs.

They stood silent for a moment in the growing shadow.

"We must go back," he pointed out, though he did not seem to be able to move.

She frowned, at a loss. Her heart ached, and the intensity of it surprised her as she lingered in his embrace. In the night, the heat of his body under his perfectly tailored clothing felt so...well, perfect. The way they had begun to move together as one?

She had been on the cusp of some unknown feelings. And the idea of losing that? She hated it.

"I did not think our lesson would be over so quickly," she said honestly. "I was enjoying it quite well."

"It doesn't have to be," he said, glancing back up the path, away from the tree and nearer to the hedgerows. "We could edge closer to the light just over there."

"Yes, please," she said. "Let us. I'm not quite willing to relinquish this."

"I am glad you like it, Charlotte."

"Like is not the word."

"Then you find me to your liking, too?"

"I like you well, Your Grace."

"I was quite uncertain," he admitted, and he drew her away from the tree and up toward the lights, nearer to the sound of laughter.

"I do like you," she confessed. "I'd be a fool not to. You're far better than most of the men I know."

"I'm sorry to hear it," he said, his expression genuinely perplexed. "There are a vast many rogues among my sex."

. . .

Rafe desperately wanted to ask her about the unpleasant men in her life. The ones who had taught her that he was a rarity. But he felt it would be a terrible idea—that somehow it would destroy the moment.

There was a darkness in her there, and she did not wish him to cast light on it.

He was certain of it.

So instead, he took her up again in the dance and began a slightly more elaborate pattern, making a curve and an arc on the path, stepping to the count of the dance, though they had no music.

Their bodies dipped and swung slowly together.

She beamed again, just as he hoped that she might, delighted by the movement.

"It *is* heaven," she said at last, when he paused to give her a moment to take it all in.

"A good dance is," he said.

"Do you feel it, too?"

He did not feel the bliss that she might, because he was concentrating so intensely on ensuring that she enjoyed herself, but it was the most wonderful he had felt in years.

There was no question in his mind.

"Yes," he replied. "This is heaven."

And then both of them were gazing into each other's eyes. Silence stretching between them, filling with something else. A hunger for a different sort of dance.

That moment when she had said she longed for the little things, the simple gestures of love… He was lost. She was the only one who had ever suggested such a thing to him. In that moment, he'd felt hope—hope that at last he'd found a woman he could grow to love. And he wouldn't let her go. Not now.

Her face was tilted up to his in admiration and a need of her own, and he was gazing down at her, hunger filling his blood.

He did not wish to stop, and so he did not.

He bent and took her lips in a kiss.

It was soft and slow.

He hesitated for a moment, giving her the opportunity to shove him away if she wished. She did not.

If anything, she leaned dreamily into him.

His mouth worked over hers, his growing desire for her weaving through him, setting his blood afire.

There was something compelling about her that insisted he keep her in his arms. He did not care if all of London saw. He would marry her tomorrow.

And so he kissed her anew.

His hands slid over her back as he pulled her closer to him. His tongue teased the line of her lip.

She gasped and opened her mouth to him.

Her own hands slid up over his shoulders, and she cupped his face. The intimacy of the gesture startled him, and he gasped, too.

She leaned away, her eyes widening.

"What are we doing?" she asked.

"Charlotte—"

"No," she said. "This is not… I cannot."

And with that, she pulled away from him. She began to rush up the trail, and a loud, booming laugh filled the air.

She crashed right into another gentleman who was coming back from one of the true dark walks.

Charlotte whipped away from the man, but not before the gentleman gave her an odd look.

The fellow was a young buck, clearly deep in his cups and having just had a tryst. His blond hair was disheveled, and his clothes were slightly askew.

But once he took one look at Rockford and Rockford gave him a solid glare, the man raised his hands in supplication and went back into the darkness.

Rafe did not make a move until he was certain that the buck had traversed down the path and that his boot steps had faded off into the night.

"He did not see you," he said, hoping more than knowing for sure.

"He did," she countered, her gloved hands twining together. "He most definitely saw me."

"Charlotte…"

But she was having none of his assurances as she burst out, "It does not matter. He did not see us kiss. I was going away from you. I was in the light."

"Yes," he said softly, the pain of their separation shocking, as well as the fact that they'd both risked discovery.

How had he let go of honor? Kissing her in the dark? While of course he would marry her if they'd been compromised, he did not think of the pain the discovery itself might cause.

"My God, what have I done?" she whispered. "I am no lady at all."

"How can you say such a thing? Of course you are a lady. This moment… Our kiss… It was a genuine reaction between the two of us," he said. "Don't you see? We are clearly meant—"

"No," she ground out, her face a pale oval of fear in the night. "We are not clearly *meant* anything, but thank you for this night. It means the world to me."

"Do not go," he insisted, his heart pounding wildly against his ribs as the wonder of the night vanished.

"I must," she returned, her eyes shining.

And with that, she raced up the path, toward the brighter lights and away from him.

He strode back up the path, following her, anger at himself pulsing through his body.

A part of him wished to run after her and pull her into his arms, demanding she see the power of what had happened between them this day. But that would cause the most horrendous scene.

As soon as he had stepped back to the crush around the dance floor, he noticed that Lady Francesca was being pulled aside by Lady Charlotte.

He spotted a scrap of blue ribbon dancing on the ground. Charlotte's! It had been about her neck, teasing her skin. Somehow it had come off, and he found himself compelled to pick it up. He slipped it between his thumb and forefinger, gazing at it as if, somehow, he was holding her in his arms again, transported.

He lifted his gaze to her, ready to return the item, but just as the two entered a rapid tête-à-tête, Rafe's mother sashayed up beside him, her burgundy skirts swinging.

Quickly, he tied the ribbon about his wrist, keeping it secure. Easily, he tugged his shirt sleeve over it and turned to his mama, who looked like the cat who got the cream.

"My darling boy, you do have quite the effect on the young ladies." Her gaze swung to the two ladies in question, then back to him. "Driven one away, have you?"

"Mama," he ground out. "Not now. I don't know why she keeps doing that."

"Doing what?" his mother asked, blinking.

"Running off," he gritted, longing to throw his hands up in the air. "Just when we're about to…"

"About to what?" she asked before she *tsk*ed. "My dear." Her eyes widened with dramatic feigned innocence.

"Not that!" he all but roared, then cleared his throat as several sets of eyes swung to him.

He forced himself to smile and said to his mama, "I like her."

"What is her name?" she asked, her teasing demeanor fading.

"Lady Charlotte."

"Lady Charlotte *what*?"

"Faraday, I believe. She is cousin to Lady Francesca and is staying with her at present. It seems as if Lady Charlotte has stayed there for quite some time, truth be told."

"You do not like Lady Francesca?" his

mother asked with a sigh.

"She's perfectly pleasant, but she is far more along George's line."

His mother studied Darrow, who was currently in conversation with his twin, looking positively enraptured by the whole night's events.

She drew in a long-suffering breath. "Lady Charlotte is not on my list."

"Very few women were," he drawled, wishing he could go after Charlotte. Knowing that she would not wish it. He would call upon her first thing tomorrow. It was the only way forward. He'd assure her all would be well.

He had that power, if she could but see it.

"So, you wish to marry a Lady Charlotte, and yet we do not know anything about her, save she's Lady Francesca's cousin."

He remained silent.

His mother rolled her eyes. "Fine, my darling. I shall indulge your whim. For the moment."

"It is not a whim," he countered. "I am not whimsical."

"No," she agreed. "You are not. Not generally."

His mother pursed her lips, then gave a nod, as if deciding the whole thing. "You like the gel, and so I shall invite her and her cousin to tea tomorrow."

"And me, Mama," he stated, half certain

his mother intended to send Lady Charlotte running for the hills. "You shall invite me as well."

She gave a playful laugh. "Of course, my darling."

He nodded. Somehow this would sort itself. He'd right the mess that had been made, and he'd take her fears away, whatever they were.

Perhaps she had no wish to marry him. But their kiss? Their dance lesson? It certainly suggested otherwise. What was holding her back?

His mother clapped her hands together, her rings winking in the lamplight. "This is working out far better than I ever could have imagined, really. You've found a wife after a week. How marvelous."

"Congratulations, Mama," he returned. As he strode away, though, he did not feel any triumph.

No, he felt as if he was about to be shoved into battle, and he had no idea whether he would come out on the other side, let alone be the victor.

CHAPTER THIRTEEN

"We need to leave," Charlotte whispered as she took Francesca's hand and pulled with more might than she had intended. "We need to go!"

Francesca staggered, stunned and clearly still smitten from the last dance she'd exchanged with the earl. "But I was having the most marvelous time with Darrow."

She longed to be delighted for her stepsister, but horror was cascading through her at a rapid rate. And she felt sick. "You can have a marvelous time with him another day. If he truly likes you, he will come to call. But we *must* go."

"Why?" Francesca asked as she followed her away from the dance floor.

Charlotte swallowed before confessing, "Because your brother is here."

Francesca's face went ashen, and her hand gripped Charlotte's back. "Phillip is *here*?"

"Indeed." Charlotte rushed back toward the entrance of the gardens as quickly as her skirts would allow. "I saw him on the dark walk."

"*You were on the dark walk?*" her stepsister yelped.

Charlotte stopped, which nearly caused

Francesca to run into her, but she grabbed her arms and explained, "I wasn't on the dark walk. I was adjacent to the dark walk. There is a decided difference between being on the dark walk and adjacent to the dark walk. I most definitely was not on the dark walk. I would not have you think—"

Francesca shook her head. "You were not on the dark walk. I understand, Charlie. You sound near hysteric."

"I am! The one night I decide to live, your brother catches me!"

Her face crumpled at the memory of crashing into Phillip's massive and slightly drunken frame. He had been the bane of her life since they were children. He loved making messes for her to clean up, all whilst smiling and giving suggestions on how to best go about it. He also loved lying about her to his father.

Phillip had taken great glee in seeing her switched by his father when she was a child.

"How is this possible?" Francesca asked.

"I don't know." She licked her lips, dreading confessing all of it but having no choice. "He was on the dark walk, and I was on the adjacent path with the Duke of Rockford in the light. Well, mostly in the light. And suddenly, Phillip came onto the path. He must have been having an assignation himself, rogue that he is." Charlotte swallowed as the sick sensation came back. "And he saw me."

"He saw you?" Francesca leaned in, her eyes narrowing.

"Yes. He saw me."

"He saw your *face*?"

She shook her head, hating that she felt unsure. "I do not know. He certainly has never seen me dressed like this before."

Francesca nodded swiftly and drew back. "So, he might not know it was you," she pointed out hopefully.

"A strange look crossed his face when I pummeled into his chest, but I looked away quite quickly. There is every possibility that he did not know it was me."

Francesca drew in a long breath. "Good. But you are correct. We cannot risk staying another moment if he's wandering about."

Charlotte grimaced. "If he were to come by while we were lingering by the dance floor…"

"No, no. I agree," Francesca soothed. "My father would not mind me being here tonight, being the guest of the Duke of Rockford, but you…" Francesca's eyes rounded to twin saucers of horror. "Dear heaven, Charlotte, what have we done?"

"I don't know," she whispered, but then paused, the memory of the dance lesson and the kiss fortifying her. They had been worth it. Those fleeting moments of pure joy? They were worth all of this.

Because for once, she had felt seen and as if the world would open its arms to her.

"It was marvelous, Chess," she declared. "Thank you for bringing me, and thank you for insisting that I dare to be someone I'm not allowed to be. It was the most wonderful thing I've ever experienced in my whole life."

"What exactly did you experience?" Francesca asked, her look of fear dissipating and curiosity replacing it.

Charlotte gave a sheepish smile. "Quite a great deal. Would you like to hear about it?"

"Every last word," Francesca said, her eyes lighting with happiness for her, despite the consequences that very well might be awaiting them both.

"Not here, though." Charlotte lifted a hand to her throat to touch her mother's simple blue ribbon—and gasped. It was gone.

She swung her gaze about, but it was nowhere in sight! When had it fallen off? She no longer had the beautiful pearl drop that had hung from it. The precious piece had been sold to pay for Stevenson's release.

But she had been unable to part with the ribbon. Now, it seemed it was no longer meant to be hers. For she had no idea when she'd lost it, and she could not go back and retrace her steps through the dark of the pleasure gardens. Her finger ached for the loss of it, but she refused to regret this night.

She refused to regret this wild path she was on. She feared it would end in pain, but she hoped—oh how she hoped—it might lead to more.

And she hoped whoever had found her ribbon would care for it as much as she.

CHAPTER FOURTEEN

The Dowager Duchess of Rockford, Rafe's grandmama, had come to London.

He laughed inwardly. His butler had looked a trifle overborne—a rare state for the fellow, but understandable, given the formidable nature of the excellent lady.

Rafe loved his grandmother beyond all things, there was no question about it, but she did have a tendency to take things over like a storm whenever she came to town.

As he approached his library, he slowly opened the gilded door. Rafe peered into the vast chamber, looking for her silvery hair, which some might feel gave her a halo-like effect. And certainly, the firelight dancing through the silver curls did give a glow, but his grandmother could not be mistaken for an angel. At least not the chubby-cheeked kind.

As he strode into the room, he called out, "Grandmama, whatever are you doing in London?"

"Just a moment, dear boy, just a moment. I need to finish the page," she called in a voice that had grown more reedy over the years but was still full of self-confidence.

His grandmother was an avid reader, just as he and his mother were. Rafe knew that he would not be able to get her to put down the book until she had indeed come to a natural pause, nor would he try. So, he approached quietly, his arms across his chest, and leaned against the long table—older than the current monarchial family—by where she perched on her delicate French chair.

She sat with regal attention as she took in the printed words.

The fire crackled happily before her, and she grinned at the page, chortling to herself.

Still reading away, she reached for her crystal flute of champagne on the marble-topped table to her right and drank the bubbling liquid to the dregs.

When she placed the glass back down on the table, she lifted her silvery blue gaze to his. "Ah, dear boy, get me another glass, will you?"

"Of course, Grandmama," he said easily, feeling great appreciation for her robust love of life, even if she was over eighty.

Rafe took the empty crystal flute and turned to the green bottle of champagne. It was one of the vintages he'd recently had imported from France. No easy thing with all the conflict abroad.

Rafe enjoyed the rather cheerful beverage, but more importantly, he knew that his grandmama loved it. He filled her flute, passed it back to her, gazed at the book, and marveled,

"Grandmama, you have read *Fanny Hill* many times."

"It gets better with every attempt," she crowed before she waggled her brows.

He laughed. "And where are you, then, in her rather fraught adventures?"

She *tsk*ed playfully. "A lady never tells."

He fought a laugh.

Fanny Hill was one of the most scandalous novels ever written. He knew it, his grandmama knew it, London knew it, and yet, they all read it.

It was, without doubt, a nefarious, legendary book.

His grandmother read it at least once every year. He supposed he understood why the adventures of Fanny Hill were fascinating beyond compare. Fanny had not taken the role to which she'd been born. No, she had met life with a saucy grin, and despite the many difficulties and dangers that had befallen her? She had never admitted defeat—and she'd been rewarded for it.

His grandmama had lived no small life, either, having been born in the early days of the previous century. She had seen quite a thing or two and had taken London by storm as the diamond of the Season her first year. As one of the most powerful women in the *ton*, she'd had many near scandalous moments, but as a duchess... Well, she'd been able to do whatever she pleased as long as she did what she was supposed to—and did not get caught.

She'd done her duty and always kept out of the mire. No easy feat.

"What brings you to London, Grandmama?" he asked again, leaning back against the table. He had a rather distinct feeling that he already knew.

She lowered her book, though she did not close it. "My boy, it has gotten to me that your mother has given you a list."

"Indeed," he replied, inclining his head. "If one name on a slip of paper can be called a list."

She made a face. "I've seen the list. It's a terrible list."

He laughed, unable to stop the booming sound. "I don't disagree with you, Grandmama, and I'm glad that you shall take my side on this."

She arched a silvery brow. "Oh, my dear boy, your mother is vastly annoying, but she is not wrong in her sentiments. You must marry. I have given some thought to it, and I have a list of my own. A real one."

He suppressed a sigh. He'd take it. And he'd do his duty, paying call to his grandmama's favorites. But first…

"Grandmama, there is a name not on the list that I am most curious about."

"Indeed?" she queried, picking up her champagne.

"Yes. A cousin of the Palmertons."

His grandmother made a face as if she had sucked upon a lemon before letting out a little sigh. "He's a terrible fellow. I would not associate myself with him."

"Truly?" He'd never met the man. After all, Rafe ran in far superior circles. He might have been in the same room with the fellow and simply never known it, of course.

"Oh truly, my dear," his grandmother replied firmly. "I would run a mile, if I were you, from association with him. I suppose he has cause to be an unpleasant person. After all, he lost his wife and child the same summer. His fortune was gotten from his deceased wife, you know. 'Twas a very sad business— long ago, now. But if this cousin is your match, I suppose we can put up with a difficult in-law."

A diabolical smile tilted her lips before she took a quick sip of champagne. "I'm sure we can arrange to have him sent to some outpost somewhere so that we need never endure his presence."

He coughed on a laugh. His grandmama had a solution for everything, and she could be merciless, but she was also kind, deep in her heart. "Glad to know you've got this all sorted."

"I must, Rafe. For you should marry at once." His grandmother grew more serious, cocking her head to the side, which caused her silver curls to glint in the firelight. "You must produce an heir and a spare."

"But I am not—"

"What?" she demanded impatiently. "Inclined? I do not really care what you want, my dear boy. In this particular case, wanting is not necessary. You just simply get on with it. Wants will be for later."

He groaned. "Grandmama, are you telling me that I should go and have affairs after I'm married?"

She shrugged, the lace at her collar dancing, before she rolled her eyes as if exhausted by the youths of the day. "Do not play a naive fellow with me. You know the way of the *ton*, and you have seen the scandals of the demimondaine. You know that half the children born are on the wrong side of the sheets once the heir and the spare have been produced. I think nothing of it; nor should you, my dear. After all, marriage among the *ton* is merely a fulfillment of contracts. Of consolidating power and more wealth."

She leveled him with an unflinching stare. "You know this, Rafe. It is how it has been done since, well, as long as history has been recorded."

He drove a hand through his hair as he

glanced to the fire. "I agree with you, of course, Grandmama, but the idea of having to spend the rest of my life with someone who's rather—"

"You don't, darling," she cut in with firmness, but kindness, too. "You don't have to spend the rest of your life with them. Look at how many houses you have. You could spend the entire year and only see your duchess once or twice. After the deed is done, of course."

"Grandmama, your sense of practicality is most amazing," he allowed. But he felt unsettled by it all, and he dared to ask, "Is that what you did with Grandpapa?"

Rafe had not met his grandfather. He'd barely known his father. And he felt…lost. Was this truly all there was?

The consolidation of power through the generations? It didn't feel enough.

He contemplated his grandmama carefully as she eyed him for a long moment and seemed as if she was girding her loins before she took a long drink.

"No, dear boy, no," she whispered, her gaze softening. "Your grandfather and I were an altogether different thing. Love is a tricky business," she confessed. "When you give your heart to someone truly, and he gives his heart to you, once you've lost it… When that person dies… It's almost impossible to go on.

But I had to go on, you see, because I had your father to raise. I had to make certain that he would become a good duke, find a good wife, which he did. Your mother is a remarkable woman." His grandmother lifted her chin and winked at him. "She and I are too similar, which is why I'm not staying with her at present and why I always stay with you when I come to London. Despite the fact that you are a bachelor and no doubt up to no good."

He laughed. "Grandmama, I do not—"

"You do not bring your scandals here," she cut in.

"No, Grandmama," he assured.

"How very, very pragmatic of you, dear boy, not to mix pleasure and business."

"But, Grandmama," he protested, feeling a bit foolish in his quest for more. He knew in his core that if he did not risk a touch of foolishness, he was condemning himself to a life of bland propriety. "I hope that my wife will bring me pleasure."

A slightly bittersweet expression crossed her visage. "You may hope it, my darling. I certainly brought your grandfather pleasure, and he brought me a great deal of pleasure in turn, but that is a rarity in the *ton*, not the norm. I will hope for it for you."

She extended her wrinkled hand. "I shall spend every night thinking of a young lady who could bring you happiness and joy."

He wrapped his hand around her small one, grateful to her for her hopes. But should he confess to his grandmama?

He hesitated. He had found her already. He knew it in his blood, deep in his bones.

On that street, outside of the Marshalsea? Charlotte had struck a chord in him that was impossible to deny. Surely, he was being fanciful. Could one fall in love so quickly? But when she had proclaimed she longed to dance by the fire every night with the man she loved? He'd known the answer.

No... The idea had to be absurd; and yet, he looked at his grandmama, whose whole spirit had changed as she spoke of her husband, who had died so long ago.

The love was still written plainly on her face.

"It seems a very long time to go without love," he said.

She blinked rapidly, squeezing his hand. "Without love? Never say so! All my lovers are in books, you know. I love my books. I can have as many adventures as I please. I can be as scandalous as I please. As long as I stay within the confines of these books. And I can always be loyal to your grandfather then."

"Oh, Grandmama," he marveled, his heart aching for her loss and yet full at her strength. "How was I so lucky to have you in my family?"

"My darling boy," she began, gazing up at him, "the spirits at large knew that your soul needed someone like me to take care of you. And I shall do whatever it takes to ensure that you are happy. But you will not be happy if you do not get married soon. You must fulfill your duty, my boy. Duty is important. Your mother is correct, and I will support her on that even if I do not like her list."

He swallowed. He'd never held back with her before. She was no frail flower to be protected. So why was he suddenly afraid? He knew… Because he did not wish to go against her. "Grandmama, I…"

"Yes, my boy?" Her eyes widened as understanding seemed to dawn on her.

"Do you think she could be on my list?" his grandmother teased.

A rumble of rueful laughter slipped past his lips. He was grateful to her for her attempt at levity. "I do not know, if I am honest. She doesn't come from a particularly great family, but she is intelligent, and she is strong, and she is kind, and she makes me feel…"

His grandmother's eyes softened. "I see it, my boy. You are already wandering down a path from which you cannot retreat."

"Do I dare?" he blurted. "Do I dare choose someone who is not perfect for my lineage?"

"Well," she ventured slowly. "If she does

not have scandal in her past, if she is kind and all the things that you say, and not manipulating, using, or lying to you, my darling, as so many of the young ladies of the *ton* have been wont to do in the past…"

His grandmother scowled for a moment as she considered behaviors she clearly thought beneath her sex. "It is appalling, if expected, what they will do in their pursuit of becoming a duchess."

But then she shrugged and declared, "I do not care who she is or where she's from. All that I care about is that you love her, she loves you in turn, and that you shall marry her. And then above all? You'll do your duty with her."

He paused at her rather shocking revelation and commitment to his heart and choice. He felt bowled over by it, for she had always shown him so much love in her dry, sometimes witty way, but her allegiance to duty was profound.

Could his grandmother be in earnest?

After all, there was one thing his grandmama certainly knew as well as he.

Generally, young ladies not born to powerful *ton* families who then became duchesses struggled. It was no easy thing to join the *ton*. It could be painful for them because it was very clear that they had not been raised to it. But his grandmother was giving him the stamp of her approval no matter whom he chose. Perhaps she did not think that he would choose someone who did not fit.

The truth was, Charlotte did not fit. There was something about her that was not quite right. Not quite right in all the right ways.

And he adored it about her.

His grandmother laughed softly. "My darling, I see it. I see how you feel. There is nothing you can say to counter it. And I am happy for you. I expect to hear the banns read soon."

"I'm glad you understand," he replied, stunned with gratitude that she was not going to fight him on this.

His grandmama pursed her lips, then proclaimed, "Write to her father. Ask his permission right away. Do not wait."

"You do not wish to meet her first?"

She contemplated him. "Would my meeting her change the way you felt about her?"

"No," he said softly, shaken by her question and the wisdom of it.

"Then I do not need to meet her, my darling. You write, and you ask for permission to marry her, and then I shall greet her with open arms as your future wife when she says yes."

He drew in a slow breath. "Truly, Grandmama, how am I so lucky?"

"It is not luck, my darling." She gave a firm

nod, then, with his assistance, pulled herself to her feet. She took his hands in hers and stared up into his eyes, as if she could drive her point home with her implacable gaze. "It is work. I work to make certain that my family knows love. That you know love. I shall burn the list I made, for it is not necessary. London will be agog, and it shall be the greatest ceremony that anyone has ever seen!"

If Charlotte said yes, of course. Though it was extremely unlikely that a young lady would decline the opportunity to be a duchess.

His grandmama then lowered her hand and took up her champagne, the crystal shimmering in the light. She lifted the glass in a small salute. "We shall make certain that it is so."

The greatest ceremony that anyone had ever seen?

He thought of Charlotte. Would she like such a thing? He doubted it very much. She struck him as someone who would prefer a small ceremony in a Christopher Wren church.

Perhaps that's what he wished for her, too—for himself—an intimate ceremony where nothing but the two of them and their love filled the room.

Love.

Did he dare use this word?

Did he?

His grandmother seemed to suggest that he should. He certainly had feelings for her he did not understand. But he understood one thing. Out of all the young ladies that he had met, the vast number of them, she was the one for him.

He drew in a long breath, wondering if it was possible. Had he truly found the one? The one with whom he could be himself? The one who did not simply say whatever she thought would garner his proposal?

Yes. He'd found his match. She was the mirror of his heart. And he'd be a bloody fool to deny it.

So, he would do exactly as his grandmother suggested. He would write to Charlotte's father, Lord Faraday, and no doubt he would have permission in no time.

Nothing would stand in the way of him and Charlotte. After all, he was a duke. She would say yes. Except…Charlotte was so unlike all the other members of the *ton*. Would she surprise him and alter his plans?

No, surely not, he assured himself. What woman would deny a duke, after all?

CHAPTER FIFTEEN

Generally speaking, letters and invitations did not make one wish to cast up their accounts, but Charlotte was not in the habit of receiving invitations and certainly not invitations from duchesses.

She'd carried it around this morning, far too busy to open it until she'd dared to take a break whilst cleaning the parlor fire.

The thick parchment trembled in her hands.

"Francesca, what are we to do?"

Francesca looked up from her embroidery. "I beg your pardon?"

"It is an invitation from the Duchess of Rockford. She's asking us to tea."

This was no small thing, a formal invitation by the duke's mother.

"To tea?" Francesca gasped before she poked her needle into her embroidery and flung it down beside her.

Francesca leaped up from the beautifully carved bench older than the House of Hanover and crossed over to Charlotte, who was on the floor by the grate.

"I can't go!" Charlotte exclaimed, looking down to her apron. "I'm covered in soot, and she wishes us to be there in but a few hours' time. It's all but an edict! One might think she was the Pope or the King."

Francesca bit her lower lip, then said, "She almost has as much power as a pope or a king. We must go. We cannot deny her or the ruse is up."

"Perhaps the ruse should be up," Charlotte pointed out.

"No," Francesca rushed. "If you tell her right now that this is all a lie, that you are not who you say you are, Rockford is going to storm over here, and Papa will know what we've done. We must carry this out, at least for a little while longer."

Francesca nodded, taking Charlotte's hands before she reasoned, "We will simply allow the duchess to understand that you are not interested in marrying the duke, and that will be the end of it. You can tell her yourself that you do not wish to marry her son, and all will be well."

Charlotte swallowed. All would be well. Was such a thing even true anymore? She was so deep in the mire, she felt as if she were going to drown in it at any moment.

An invitation to the Duchess of Rockford's home for tea!

There were girls all over London who would've expired with delight on the spot at such a chance. She did not wish the honor, but nor did she see how she could wriggle out of it.

She swallowed, crumpled the letter, and put it in her pocket before she continued cleaning the grate, wishing that the heaven of the previous night could become reality. He had been so...wonderful.

But she hadn't been foolish enough to believe in such dreams since she was small.

And she was not about to start now.

. . .

The Earl of Darrow's swords were indeed highly polished.

Darrow had a vast collection of arms. Most of them were hanging on the walls of the long hall in which he engaged in dueling practice.

It was not just his pastime, but a passion, ever since he had returned home from war and his older brother had died, leaving him the new earl.

Very little was able to distract George's mind from his duties except for a good book or the crossing of blades. And, apparently, the promise of love.

Today, of course, as always, Rafe was happy to duel with his friend. Far more so than usual.

Today, he needed a clear mind.

Since he was going to be meeting Lady Charlotte with his mother—a circumstance that required him to be on his toes, as it were.

A good battle this morning would make certain that he would be ready for the war potentially looming later this afternoon.

And besides, his grandmama was on his side. That was all he needed to win.

George balanced his blade easily, swinging the rapier to make certain of its weight before he pulled at his cuffs. He rolled them up his forearms, then took his stance along the dueling strip.

Rafe mirrored his stance. His own rapier was a good, familiar weight of Spanish steel. He had dueled with it many times.

He eyed his friend, raised the gleaming blade, eased back into his balanced stance, then called out, "En garde."

They each began to counter the other, testing each other's defenses, looking for weaknesses.

Neither of them had any, except in the most rare of moments, and those were the moments that could speak victory or defeat.

That he knew from his past encounters with George.

The earl slowly began to make his way up the dueling strip. Darrow liked to engage first.

Rafe was happy to wait and see what the other did, because oftentimes the person who was ready to engage first was also the person ready to make errors. Sometimes, they were the person who was not thinking, who was not watching.

But George did not swing his blade.

Instead, he rocked back and said, "So, your mother has invited Lady Charlotte to tea today."

Rafe shifted his balance and kept light on his feet as he took in the question. "Indeed, she has."

And he took a step forward, getting ready to clash blades.

"Oolong or green?" George asked simply.

"What the devil are you on about?" Rafe demanded.

George waggled his brows. "Do you think Lady Charlotte drinks green tea or oolong?"

He blew out a breath. "You've never cared what kind of tea people drink."

"No," George said cheerfully. "But your mother will care. Doesn't she say that those who drink green tea must not have taste upon their tongues? The only tea is black. She won't be swayed by fashion."

He ground his teeth. "She doesn't like green tea. It's true."

And he found himself wondering what strange machinations lay ahead.

There was a veritable field of potential explosions for Lady Charlotte to step into.

"She's not going to be that particular," Rafe said boldly as he charged up the strip and began parrying with his friend. "She *wants* me to get married."

George rolled his eyes and easily riposted each strike. "You think she's not going to be careful? You think she's not going to care *who* you marry?" Darrow charged. "Your wife will be the mother of the next duke. Your mother will care a great deal. She is going to have to find out everything she possibly can about that young lady before she allows you to marry her."

"Allows?" Rafe growled. "I am the Duke of Rockford." But then he paused, considering George's sensible if rather gleeful information. "You have a point. She may prove a touch difficult."

And then, before he knew what was happening, George swept in and drove his blade forward.

Rafe just managed to deflect the blade away before he whirled back and counterstruck.

George laughed and danced backward. "Your mother is a master. She will have every last little piece of information that she needs from Lady Charlotte before you have even taken off your hat."

"What makes you think that I will *allow*—we'll use the word that you used—my mother to do such a thing?"

George cocked his head to the side. "What makes you think that your mother has not already invited her to tea?"

"Because she told me what time she was coming—" And he stopped.

"Hell's bells, my friend. You are not thinking clearly, if you believe your mother doesn't want a chance at Lady Charlotte alone. Clearly, you are in love."

"I am not in love," Rafe replied honestly. "But she is certainly the only young lady whom I have ever wished to marry. I think that she would be the best duchess."

"Well, if your mother sees that you feel that way, I guarantee that she has arranged time alone with the young lady." George lowered his blade and warned, "You best get over there as soon as possible."

Rafe lowered his own rapier. "Is that why you asked me over this morning, to tell me that I should go to my mother's and wait there for the whole day to avoid subterfuge?"

"Certainly, though I did hope for a few moments of your time. We both needed a bout." George pulled at his linen shirt, adjusting it over his frame. "But if you wish to protect the young lady from your mother's line of questioning, I think it a very good idea indeed that you do so before calling hours begin. You see, I would not be surprised if she has not changed her plans and invited the young lady over for breakfast so that she might make her queries."

"My mother would not be so..." He paused as the truth of the matter sank in. "Oh dear God, indeed she would. I suppose I'd best go."

George gave him an elaborate bow, then picked up a cloth to polish his rapier. "Get thee gone and make certain that Lady Charlotte is not completely trampled by your mother's charge."

He nodded, to himself more than anything. Everything would go exactly to plan.

CHAPTER SIXTEEN

Charlotte sat across from a woman whom she could only define as a benevolent Venus fly-trap.

The Duchess of Rockford was quite a specimen of womanhood. She sat like one could only imagine the great galleons sat at sea.

Her skirts were perfection and crusted with the most beautiful lace and jewels, an emerald sheen that made the entire room weep with envy.

And the room was nothing to sniff at.

As a matter of fact, if she had ever thought she might be transported to Paris, surely this room was the embodiment of it. Charlotte had read so many stories about rooms like this. Even in her own house, there was not a single room like *this*.

The London townhouse that belonged to the duchess sat off of Green Park, and its opulent settings were in the new style made popular by the resurgence of interest in classical architecture.

Of course, Charlotte had seen engravings in the news sheets and gossip rags. But nothing could prepare one for the watered silk of a most beautiful turquoise variety.

The bright, rich color surrounding her thrilled her to her very toes.

Paintings of the most beautiful women from the previous century decorated every wall, hanging in their elaborate frames from golden chains.

Mirrors in gilded frames were hung with care to make certain that the light bounced about the room. Crystals hung from the chandeliers, and the lady who sat at the center of it?

She sat on the most beautiful chaise longue of ivory silk on delicate legs.

It was a spun sugar confection.

Charlotte and Francesca were also perched on matching but much smaller affairs. She clutched at her extremely delicate teacup and saucer, used to the clay mugs in the kitchen.

She did not feel nearly as powerful as the duchess looked, holding court.

The duke's mother lifted her elaborately painted pink-and-gold teacup, carefully balancing the saucer with ease on the palm of her hand. She drawled in her plummy tones, "My dear, what a privilege it is to meet the young lady who has captured my son's heart."

She choked on her tea.

It splattered everywhere.

She grabbed a napkin from the marble-topped table before her and quickly dabbed her skirt.

Lady Francesca grinned at her.

She grinned back, refusing to be daunted. After all, this was absurd!

What else could they do but laugh? If they did not, surely they'd collapse into a sobbing heap.

They were both young ladies with very little experience compared to the woman sitting across from them. Neither of them had anywhere near the same sort of power. And she wasn't going to allow a bit of spilled tea to ruin her day.

She had larger concerns.

Charlotte cleared her throat and squared her shoulders, adjusting the cup on the saucer. "I would not venture to say that I have captured his heart. Does that not sound a trifle dramatic?"

"First, I adore a bit of drama. Second," the duchess countered, bemused, "it does not. I have been trying to get him married for almost fifteen years. And you met him last week."

What was there to say to that?

The words sank in.

When put that way, it did sound quite dramatic.

The duchess shrugged and sighed as if she had no control in regard to the vagaries of love. "And I do think that he would like to marry you."

The duchess swung her sapphire-hued gaze to Charlotte's stepsister and placed a beringed hand over her heart. "Forgive me, Lady Francesca, but it's simply the way of the world. The heart cannot be gainsaid in this."

Francesca nodded. "I understand."

Charlotte squirmed on her seat. She couldn't allow this to happen. Because what the duke and his mother, the duchess, did not know was that she was up to her veritable neck in lies. And if the duke *did* propose, those lies would drown her. And Francesca.

"Don't you think that he would suit Lady Francesca better?" Charlotte asked bluntly.

"Why?" the duchess asked, her eyes widening as she snapped them toward Charlotte. "Is there something wrong with you?"

She nearly choked on her tea again. *Wrong* with her? Yes. There were many, many things wrong with her, like the very fact that she was sitting on this seat at all.

She was not supposed to be here.

She was supposed to be cleaning the fireplace at this particular moment. And then she was supposed to be helping Cook sand out the pans, for goodness' sake.

No, she was not supposed to be sitting in yet another borrowed gown in a room she did not belong in, sipping tea that she would never get to taste at home.

It was quite delicious. Not green.

She did not care for green. She took a fortifying sip, determined to find a solution to this coil. And if anyone could maneuver the duke back to Francesca, surely it was the gorgeous gorgon before her?

But Francesca sat ramrod straight, eyes wide, observing the exchange as she sipped her tea, clearly determined not to be pulled into the tennis match of questions and answers.

"Well," Charlotte began carefully. "Lady Francesca? Her father, Lord Palmerton? He's an excellent man who comes with a very good family, and well, I…"

"Yes," the duchess said. "You? Who are your parents?"

Charlotte stilled. "My parents? Well…"

"Your mother?" the duchess asked.

"Dead," Charlotte said, trying to soften the word, though that never really worked.

The duchess hesitated, and the merry mischief that usually sharpened her gaze seemed to dim. "Oh, dear. I'm very sorry to hear it. And your father?"

"In Scotland," she managed, though it pained her to lie. Again. She hated the feeling crawling through her, but soon she'd find a way out of this. She had to. And the sympathy on the dowager's face only increased her guilt.

The duchess sat up a little straighter,

leaned forward, and said, "That must have been incredibly difficult for you. How did you bear up, my dear, under such strain? Not many young people have had that happen, and it's just no easy thing."

Tears stung Charlotte's eyes.

She was not accustomed to people being kind to her, except for Francesca and Cook and Stevenson and Mary.

She swallowed back the tightness in her throat and managed, "Yes, it was very difficult. But we have nothing to do in this life but to bear up."

"Well said." Her face softened. "You're correct, hard as it is. We must simply get on with life and do our duty, mustn't we? Although, there is some joy to be had. I think that you will find my son to be a remarkably kind husband, and he will do everything he can in his life to make you joyful, especially since he seems to like you so well."

Charlotte wanted to scream with her exasperation. All this kindness would soon be rescinded when they understood the truth! "Yes, but…"

"But?" the duchess challenged, shaking her head, which caused the jewels in her coiled hair to wink in the morning light.

The duchess put her teacup down and smoothed her hands along the front of her glorious skirts. "Am I to understand that you are resisting the idea of marrying my son?"

The note of personal affront and shock was impossible to miss.

Obviously, the idea of any young lady not wishing the honor of being the Duchess of Rockford was impossible to comprehend.

But she wasn't a *lady*. And therein was the rub.

Searching desperately for a logical explanation—any explanation—Charlotte grasped for words. "I met your son but a week ago, Your Grace, and even for a *ton* marriage, surely, this is rather rapid."

"Is that all, my dear? No," the duchess said, waving a hand, dismissing the problem as if it was a bit of bread she did not want. "It is not. As long as you come from a good family—and I don't even care if you have a great fortune—then there is no dilemma."

The duchess sighed and leaned back, clearly relieved. "Quite honestly, it is no difficulty at all. I'm surprised you do not know how quickly these marriages can occur. Often, the groom and the bride have not even met."

The duchess gave her a smile and a nod before she took her tea up again. "We will arrange the marriage posthaste. But first we must have a ball where we proclaim you my son's intended. I shall discuss that with Lord Palmerton—"

Charlotte nearly choked on her tea as dread crashed through her.

The dowager gasped with delight. "Perhaps we shall get a special license. I do not wish anything to impede my triumph."

Charlotte fought a grimace. "Surely, it is no difficulty to wait…"

The duchess's delight faded, and her brow furrowed. "I'm a bit trepidatious myself, my dear. Are you a fly-by-night sort of girl? A flibbertigibbet? Will you be giving me trouble in a few years' time?"

The question was asked with such personal horror that there was no way to make a reply.

The duchess *tsk*ed. "I don't mind a bit of scandal, but I don't want you to make my son unhappy."

"I don't want him to be unhappy, either," Charlotte said quite honestly, wondering how she kept digging deeper into her personal hole that seemed destined for Hell's gates. "But I do not think that I can provide him the happiness that you seem to hope."

"Don't be ridiculous. We shall ensure you do. But why do you think thus?" the duchess asked bluntly.

Francesca squirmed on the seat next to her.

There was nothing for it.

Charlotte was going to have to tell the duchess the truth. She did not want to tell the duchess the truth.

This was going to be devilishly hard, and the very idea of it was beginning to make her feel ill.

She put her teacup down. "Well, Lord Palmerton—"

"Yes," the duchess cut in, as if annoyed by what she considered to be more trivialities. "I sent him a note, letting him know that I should like to meet him quickly, so that we can come to an arrangement."

"You sent him a note," Charlotte said flatly. A chill traveled down her spine. If she had hoped to avoid punishment due to Phillip not recognizing her? That hope was now gone. Her hands began to shake.

"Indeed," the duchess informed. "I say, my dear. Aren't you pleased? You will be able to have your own establishment soon. As I understand, you are not living with your family? How long have you lived with Lady Francesca?"

No...

She didn't want to leave her mother's house. She *couldn't*.

She had lived in it her whole life, and the idea of leaving it to Palmerton...well, frankly, she was afraid she was about to cast up the very fine tea onto the duchess's very fine carpets.

"My dear, you look quite unwell." The

duchess blinked and scooted to the edge of her seat. "Do you need a bit of fresh air?"

"Possibly?" she whispered as Francesca reached out and took her hand.

"I understand the idea of suddenly becoming a duchess might overbear anyone." The duchess gave her an indulgent smile. "Georgiana, Duchess of Devonshire, had been groomed for it since she was a child, and she was not a happy duchess. Perhaps it will serve you well—not being groomed for it, that is. Perhaps it will be quite good for both you and my son to not be prepared to step into such a dramatic role but to discover it together."

With each word, Charlotte felt as if a nail was being hammered into her coffin.

There was no way out of her mess. Just more mess.

"You will not be afraid of him." The duchess cocked her head to the side. "You do not seem as if you would be afraid of anything except moving away from your house. Do you love him, your uncle, so much?"

"No," she said quickly.

Francesca tensed beside her, her teacup clinking on the saucer.

"Oh?" The duchess's brows rose. "You do not?"

"I'm sorry." She took in slow breaths, determined to make it through this without causing a scene. "That sounded very rude."

"It was very frank," the duchess admitted.

She plunked her teacup down and gripped the edge of her chair. "I am only certain that my guardian would prefer that the duke marry Lady Francesca."

The duchess slowly nodded, her gaze swinging between the girls.

"I see," the duke's mother said carefully, before she made a clearly pointed and overly optimistic clearing of her throat. "Yes, well, what man would not want his daughter to be a duchess? He'd be a fool if he did not, but we cannot force the matter. And I do think that Lady Francesca has already caught the eye of a very noble fellow. Haven't you, Lady Francesca?"

Francesca kept ahold of Charlotte's hand, but her own concern faded away for a moment as she obviously thought of the gentleman in question. "The Earl of Darrow is a most agreeable gentleman. How could anyone disagree with such a sentiment?"

"You see?" the duchess gushed. "We could have a double wedding."

And she'd thought the tangle could grow no worse. How wrong she'd been!

Francesca let go of Charlotte's hand and took an indecorous swig of tea. "A double wedding?"

"Oh yes," the duchess affirmed. "I could

speak with the earl. I've known him and his family for ages, of course. Yes, he could ask you to marry him. All would be done in a trice, and everyone would be happy."

"Would they?" Charlotte asked warily.

If the duchess thought Palmerton would be happy with Francesca marrying an earl when she could have had a duke, the duchess was in for quite a shock.

And worse still?

She, a maid? Marrying a duke? Palmerton barely thought her worthy of keeping in the house that should have been hers. And only the fact that her mother had been a lady of breeding had kept her from the orphans' asylum, she was sure.

Charlotte hedged, "I'm not entirely certain that this is how it should be done."

"This is exactly how it should be done," the duchess said. She snatched up a biscuit and took a decisive bite. "It's how it's been done for generations, my dear. Ladies like me arrange everything. If we did not? Society as we know it would end. The men are far too foolish to keep it going. It's hard enough to keep them from never-ending wars and spending their fortunes in the worst places."

Charlotte did not dispute the importance of a woman's influence on society and certainly not a woman like the duchess, but at present, the woman was organizing

Charlotte's doom.

And she had to be stopped. But how did one stop a tide rushing toward the shore?

Charlotte drew herself up and decided to take a leaf from the duchess's book. She lifted her chin and arched a brow. "We must understand each other, Your Grace. I think you are a remarkable woman who has clearly overcome a great deal of strife, wants the best for her son, and embodies her title brilliantly. But I am not the young lady for him."

The duchess's mouth opened and closed, codfish-like.

It was the first time she had looked completely at a loss. "I beg your pardon?" she sputtered.

"I am not the right fit," she said firmly, despite the longing in her heart that fairy tales could come true for girls like her. But they did not. They became tales of horror. And she couldn't let that happen.

She continued with as much authority as she could muster, mirroring the duchess's earlier determination. "And I would prefer that you do not speak to Palmerton about me. It will cause a great deal of difficulty."

"But... But *why*, my dear? Are you already engaged to be married?"

"No," she said quickly. "I am not. But I will not be marrying the duke."

"I see." The duchess's expression changed

to one of genuine dismay. "This is most confusing," she said. "I—"

"Mama!" the duke all but thundered as he strode into the salon. "You are holding an interrogation, and that, I cry foul upon."

Charlotte groaned.

What could happen next?

Surely the universe had achieved enough amusement at her expense! Yes, she'd been arrogant and above her station, indulging in one dance, one kiss… But surely she would not be punished so severely for such a small amount of hubris?

It seemed she would.

She never should have agreed to come, but she had not seen a way out of it, especially since Francesca had been invited as well.

There was no way for this not to end in scandal.

And consequences.

Palmerton knew that they would be there, and she was going to be thrust into the cellars or worse.

What if he kicked her out of the house?

What if she never was allowed to see her mother's house again? What if all the things that she had loved so well were taken away from her? What if she was never allowed to see Mary or Stevenson again? Or Cook?

Panic began to build up in her, and she did not know what to do.

"Francesca," Charlotte managed as her circumstance became more and more impossible, "I think we should go."

"Certainly not," the duke said. "You've only just arrived." He shot his mother an accusing stare. "Haven't you?"

His mother had the good grace to look apologetic. "Oh, no, my darling. No. We've been having the most marvelous conversation for the last half hour, at least. Now, you must sit, because I do think that you might find some of this interesting. I am convinced Lady Charlotte is secretly engaged to a scoundrel. Or a poor tutor. It is the only explanation for her odd opinions."

"What?" the duke demanded, his expression positively stunned.

"No!" Charlotte exclaimed, very tempted to throttle the duchess. But she had no desire to end up in Fleet Prison. "I swear I am not engaged to be married."

"I think she may love someone else." The duchess *tsk*ed.

"*I do not love someone else.*" Charlotte wondered what the blazes was wrong with the duchess. She was completely balmy!

Hanging her head, the duchess continued with a sigh, "But you made it clear that you are not interested in my son."

Rafe swung his stunned gaze from his mother to Charlotte.

"I did not say that," Charlotte rushed, unable to support that lie. Not with Rockford standing right before her, reminding her with only his presence just how very interested she was.

The duchess hesitated, then smiled slowly. "So, you *are* interested in my son? I thought as much. You can't hide it from me, my dear."

Charlotte groaned at how easily the older woman had maneuvered her into a corner.

But the duke looked positively horrified, as if Charlotte did indeed think him the scum beneath her shoes.

She gave him a quick, distressed look, wishing she could assure him that he was lovely. He was wonderful! It was all her own dilemma that was the difficulty.

The duchess then had the temerity to announce grandly, as if she could never disappoint her son, "Whatever difficulties there are, we shall smooth them away, and all shall be well. Yes, we shall announce your engagement at my ball. It'll be a marvelous state of affairs. I shall get you a coronet. The jewels will be brought out for you. We must get you a new gown, though, because that one clearly doesn't fit you, my dear. Who is your modiste?"

She couldn't say anything.

Somehow, anything she said, the duchess had an answer for.

Forget Wellington. The duchess should be sent to the front. Napoleon would be done in a week.

No, there was no resisting this meeting. And she was not going to dig a deeper hole for herself and Francesca. She could already smell sulfur.

Besides, she didn't want to ruin Francesca's chances. She wanted Francesca to be able to marry the earl if she wished.

And at last, she knew what she needed to do. She'd been on the verge of it before the duke's unexpected entrance.

She needed to simply say that she was a maid.

That she had no fortune.

And that her line had lost all its importance. She was little better than a merchant but without the coin.

And yet the words strangled in her throat. For once they were uttered…he was truly lost to her.

The magic she had felt in his arms? It would be gone. And here, with him in the room? The pain of it seemed too much to bear.

But she *had* to. There was no other choice.

Charlotte drew herself up, knowing she had to be brave. "Your Graces, please. I must speak!"

The duke and his mother turned their

attention on her, their own machinations paused, as they both clearly hoped she was about to agree to *the plan* and they could all celebrate. She could see it in their eyes.

Just as she was about to make her declaration, dashing said plan, the door burst open again...

And Lord Palmerton stormed in.

CHAPTER SEVENTEEN

"Ah! Marvelous!" Rafe's mother exclaimed with delight. "You are here. We must make some plans for my ball."

Rafe swung his astounded gaze to Lady Charlotte, to Lady Francesca, and to the recently arrived Lord Palmerton.

The whole bloody thing was turning into a farce, just as George had said it would.

No. It was *already* a farce.

Was this his life now—one strange, amusing, impossible circumstance after the other? It did seem that, since meeting Charlotte, that was what his life had become.

He had no objections.

His last years had been all predictable and rather staid. This was a new and exciting state of affairs, and he hoped that it would symbolize a new beginning to his life, where he had more than just his duty, his work, and the things that he did to make certain that the dukedom survived.

But Palmerton looked as if he had swallowed a bad egg. His gray eyes bulged, and his face was strained, emphasizing the lines. Despite this, his appearance was otherwise pristine. In fact, the man looked as if he had never seen a crease or crumb, his clothing and hair were so perfect.

"How do you do, Palmerton?" he drawled, clasping his hands behind his back. "We have not had the good fortune to meet. As a matter of fact, I am not entirely certain we have ever been introduced."

"My, yes, yes," Palmerton managed at last. In a moment, the fury that had lined his face disappeared, replaced by a genteel amusement that decried his earlier rampage into the room.

Palmerton placed his hand to his cravat, then smoothed his silvering hair, which was heavily pomaded, with not a single strand out of place.

He looked like one of Beau Brummell's devotees. He was dressed with such detail.

His linen cravat was starched to within an inch of its life and dramatically folded, with a beautiful stick pin keeping it in place.

Palmerton looked like a dandy. The idea of spending two hours in front of one's looking glass in the morning always felt a bit precious to Rafe.

Neither of the ladies had such airs about them.

"How kind of you to invite my daughter and her cousin, Charlotte, to tea," Palmerton said.

Rafe paused.

Was there the slight edge to Palmerton's voice when he said Charlotte's name? Was he mistaken?

Palmerton took a step into the room. "I understand that you came to call on Lady Francesca. She is a most beautiful young girl, and I was not at all surprised to find that she might be in the running for your title. As a matter of fact, several gentlemen think…"

"Several gentlemen think what?" Rafe cut in, finding Palmerton's comments most off-putting.

"That my daughter is a prime catch," he said with a bold smile. "That several offers were incoming this Season."

"Oh, indeed?"

Bloody hell, he thought to himself.

Palmerton was one of those kinds of men who thought that if a young lady was in demand, it drove up her price, so to speak. But Lady Francesca was not a mare at market.

He had no intention of involving himself in some sort of bidding war over a young lady. Ever.

And whilst he thought her fine, he would not be asking for her hand. So, he inclined his head. "I am sure Lady Francesca is going to find a suitable husband, but I had the good fortune of meeting Lady Charlotte the day I came to call at your house. And we share an affinity for many things."

Palmerton tensed. "An affinity with *Lady* Charlotte?"

Lady Charlotte put her teacup down and folded her hands in her lap.

"Yes," Rafe said. "As a matter of fact, I should like—"

"Your Grace," Palmerton had the temerity to cut in. "I think it would be best if we carried this conversation on at another time, and certainly not in front of the young ladies. Don't you agree?"

Rafe ground his teeth together.

He hated the fact that Palmerton had cut him off and was now in control of the conversation. Especially when the man seemed determined to ignore Lady Charlotte's presence in the room.

He knew that he should call on Palmerton officially to court a young lady in his house. Since her father was in the North and she was a guest of this man, it was the right thing to do. But something was strange here, and he couldn't quite put his finger on it.

"We must have a meeting, Lord Palmerton. Would you like to come to my club soon?" Rafe offered, knowing it was an impossible boon to resist.

"I would," Lord Palmerton said, and he looked beyond pleased, which did not surprise Rafe at all.

His club was the most exclusive in London and incredibly difficult to get into. Palmerton was not a member.

The duchess let out a relieved breath and said, "There. You see—all is right with the world. Now, if you would just allow me to squire Lady Francesca and Lady Charlotte about London, we shall make one another's acquaintances and become good friends. The gentlemen shall do what they do. The ladies shall do what we do. And in the end, we shall come together with a merry outcome. Don't you agree, Lord Palmerton?"

His mother waited for the man's assent. It was, of course, what his mother was accustomed to. She always got her way.

It was impossible for anyone to deny his mother. He knew it. Even he couldn't do it. Palmerton smiled slowly. It was tight at first, but then that smile grew, and he placed a hand to his heart. "Of course, Your Grace. It is a privilege to have my daughter in your company. And her *cousin*, of course."

"They are a delight and a credit to you, Lord Palmerton. You have taken such care of them both. How I shall adore having such wonderful company."

"Now, I think we must away. We must reunite and share all our news," Palmerton said brightly.

Then he gave a deep bow. And with that, he said, "Come, ladies. We must go. You have taken up quite enough of the duchess and the duke's time. At least until the duke and I have met at his club."

Lady Charlotte and Lady Francesca got up immediately and, without question, went out into the hall. Rafe did not even truly get to bid them adieu, they escaped so quickly.

"They're such well-behaved young ladies," Palmerton said before he exited with them.

"Well-behaved young ladies," the duchess said, her voice mocking Palmerton once the man was gone. "Does he know the two at all?"

"No," Rafe said lowly. "I do not think he does."

He strode to the window and watched the three as they rushed quietly into Palmerton's awaiting coach.

The door slammed shut, and the vehicle rumbled down the exclusive cobblestone road toward Hyde Park.

It was the oddest circumstance.

The last thing he felt Lady Charlotte to be was a *well-behaved young lady*. Oh, she was exemplary, but *well-behaved*?

That was how Palmerton defined her?

Rafe wasn't entirely certain that was the phrase he would've used for her. But of course, Palmerton wanted a good marriage for his daughter, so he could not have the duke thinking that they were a pair of harridans.

But still, something felt off…

He drew in a deep breath. No doubt it was nothing. Both girls were well-educated, intelligent, bold in speech, and Lady Charlotte was certainly kind to her servants.

Likely, Palmerton was simply a selfish old dandy like most of the *ton* who did not think much beyond the young ladies in his life except for the advantages a good marriage might bring.

Yes, that was it. The man was no doubt obsessed with a good match for his daughter.

He turned to his mother. "Mama, what do you know about Palmerton?"

"Not much, my dear," she said, picking up the novel she had placed under the pillow on her chaise longue. "A friend of mine recommended him as a gentleman of good taste. My friend also suggested his daughter would be a perfect match for you."

She fanned open her book, skimming the lines as she looked for her last place. Pausing, she looked up, clearly trying to recall more details. "He comes from a good family, has a large fortune from the death of his wife, and he is talked of as a gentleman who appreciates fine things. Lady Francesca is spoken well of throughout society. She plays the pianoforte apparently quite well and sings. She also is well-read, my dear," his mother said, saluting him with her book. "I know that matters to you. It seems Lady Charlotte shares similar skills, though her conversation style is certainly more robust. Lord Faraday has given her a very simple but good education. Though her manners are a trifle rustic. But since her family is in Scotland—"

"Thank you, Mama," he cut in. "Did you know Lady Charlotte cannot dance?"

"What?" His mother gasped, disbelieving, as she lowered her book to her lap. "She cannot dance?"

"No," he stated, wondering at it now in the light of day.

"She is odd, my dear," his mother said softly. "And she does seem uncertain about a match between you."

"I have no desire to force her inclination, but in our private conversations... I like her above anyone I have ever met."

His mother was silent for a moment, and then she held out her hand to him.

He took it. He might be a man, independent, and capable of running a good part of the country. But he cared about her. And he knew she missed the love she'd had with his father.

"That is wonderful, my darling. Despite what I say about her unusual character, I like her, too. I took note of the way she drank her tea and the way she was so frank with me. Not many young ladies have the courage to say what she did."

"And what did she say, Mama?"

"Oh, only that you should marry Lady Francesca."

He groaned. "She did not."

"Indeed, she did."

He stared at the door. "Am I making a fool of myself?"

"I don't know, my dear." His mother squeezed his hand, let it go, and returned her attention to her book. "We shall have to wait and see."

"That wasn't what you were supposed to say, Mama," he said drily.

"Was it not?" she asked, turning a page.

"No."

Her lips curved. "Was I supposed to assure you that the young lady would fall madly in love with you and that you two would run off into a passionate sunset together where nothing could stand in the way of your amour?"

He laughed, unable to stop the rumbling sound. "Yes, something like that, Mama."

"You know me too well for that. I am far too honest." She did not lift her gaze, but she lowered her book to her lap as she whispered, "What your father and I had was incredibly rare. Your grandmother and grandfather, too. Just as your grandmama made plain to me the lay of the land this morning, I hope for it for you as well, my darling. Even it didn't last very long for us, you know."

"But that was because he was taken," Rafe said, despite the dust from the chimney settling in his tight throat. "Not because…"

"My darling," she said, turning another page. "Let us not speak of it. You know how much grief it gives me."

"I do know," he said softly, placing his hand gently on her shoulder. "And I'm sorry, Mama. I would not give you sadness for anything."

She placed her cheek on the back of his hand for a moment. "Thank you, my love. She's known sadness, hasn't she?"

"Charlotte?" he asked.

She lifted her gaze to him, shadow touching their usually merry depths. "Yes. I think she has. She is a young lady who has lost a mother quite young. It is a good thing that she has a cousin like Lady Francesca and a house like Palmerton's to which she can retreat. I hope that they have been kind to her."

"So do I, Mama," he said on a sigh. "So do I."

CHAPTER EIGHTEEN

The silence terrified Charlotte far more than any screaming could have done.

Palmerton sat opposite her on the damask-covered coach seat, his hands resting on his knees as he stared straight ahead.

She and Francesca remained in absolute stillness, waiting… Waiting for the explosion that was sure to come.

But perhaps, just perhaps, if she and Francesca were quiet, somehow the worst of it could be avoided.

If they just held still enough, if they did not move, perhaps they could avoid his fury.

If they were careful, if they didn't say the wrong thing, perhaps, just perhaps, somehow they'd escape it.

After all, a duke was now within reach. All the power and influence that Palmerton craved was at his fingertips.

Would that not mollify him?

Of course it would not. Not if the duke wanted Charlotte.

She could scarce breathe, as if a storm was rolling in, ready to crush her.

The waiting nearly undid her.

Francesca was pale, her body rigid.

She knew she must be, too. The blood had

drained from her stepsister's face, and this was significantly due to her own doing. Her lies. The duke was meant for Francesca, not for her.

It was not her fault that her guardian was selfish, manipulative, and able to make the lives of those within his power hell.

But she was in his power. As was Francesca.

When she had gone to rescue Stevenson, she had not meant for any of this to happen. How could she have foreseen it?

In her wildest dreams, she truly could not have believed a duke would be pursuing her. Even if it was because of her lie.

Lady Charlotte had unlocked a set of events that was unavoidable now. Lady Charlotte wasn't afraid. No. She was bold. Fierce. And nothing stood in her way.

And suddenly she found herself blurting, "This is all because you had Stevenson locked away out of malice toward me. I met the duke, and he was kind... Unlike you—"

"Quiet," her stepfather snapped, his eyes crackling with such anger that her breath was sucked out of her lungs. "You are still mine by the law, Charlotte. And you will obey me."

The intensity of Palmerton's voice shook her.

The clatter of the wheels on the cobbles, the loud crowds hawking their wares, and the general din of London vanished as his anger cut through the coach.

Charlotte snapped her mouth shut, her defiance dimming as the reality of her situation came back to her.

Francesca carefully took Charlotte's hand under their skirts and gripped it tightly.

Palmerton had been violent before. But it had been years since they had felt his blows. He was more clever now about his punishments.

No, having raised his ire? His cruelty wouldn't just be directed at her.

It wasn't she that he would strike.

He might strike Francesca or go at Mary or Stevenson or the cook.

Palmerton was wily that way and a master of subtle brutality. It had been remarkably foolish of her to think that she could get away with any of this. To think that she should dare to have one night, one moment that would not have consequence.

Her whole life had been one long set of consequences.

The consequences of her mother picking this man.

And of course she would face recrimination for daring to want just a bit more, even for a few hours—the dream of being more; but she was not allowed dreams. She knew that now. And what a fool she had been.

The coach finally stopped before her ancestral home—a home that should have been hers and hers alone.

But due to marriage laws, it had passed on to Palmerton.

If she left the house? She might never see it again.

He did not shove the door open as she thought he might.

No. He waited as a good lord did for the footman to jump down and open the door.

Palmerton waited for his daughter to get out, and then Charlotte, a good gentleman. She and Francesca walked with trepidatious steps up into the house, knowing that once they were through those doors, all bets were off.

For there would be no prying eyes to see, no one to stop his shouts or threats.

Francesca, of course, went first into the foyer, because she was the lady in the house.

And Charlotte had been merely a servant following closely behind.

As she entered her childhood home and took Francesca's things, her hands started to shake. Not only with fear. But with fury of her own.

How had it all come to this? She was supposed to have had a home.

At least enough to see her in comfort?

But all that had been seized from her.

Palmerton had insisted for years that he kept her out of the goodness in his being. His charity.

But he had gotten her house. Her mother's money.

And she was supposed to be grateful she had not been sent to a poorhouse?

She was not grateful. She was furious.

To Palmerton, she was nothing and never would be anything except a servant—someone to keep in control.

And she hated that she allowed him to tie her to the house, tie her to Francesca, tie her to Stevenson, Mary, and Cook.

If she could somehow manage to let go of all that, she would be free of him for the rest of her life.

But she couldn't go. And she likely never would. For she could not abandon the people she loved and who had loved her in turn when she had been orphaned, though every fiber inside her screamed that she should run.

As she turned and gazed up at the crenelated ceiling, her heart sank. If Palmerton cast her out and exposed her lies, where would she go?

She drew in slow breaths, desperate not to quake in the face of what Palmerton might do as he mounted the steps behind them and came into the foyer.

The fear... It whispered through her. A

voice listing all the terrible things awaiting an unattached woman in the great city that ate people up and spat them out.

She could try to be a shop girl, where she'd live in poverty until death, or she could go and turn the trade, as so many young ladies did along the banks of the Thames and in Covent Garden.

But that way—that way lay a world of danger far more frightening than the one she was in now, despite Palmerton's cruelty.

And she did not have the courage to risk it.

Not yet.

When Palmerton reached out, it was not her arm that he grabbed but Francesca's.

"A maid," he hissed in his daughter's face. "A maid takes the duke's interest. Not you? What are you? Are you some milquetoast fool of a girl who can speak of nothing that might tempt a man like Rockford?"

His lip curled as he looked at his child with utter disappointment. "You are no daughter of mine. All the money that I have spent training you up," he spat out. "You lost him to a servant?"

He shoved Francesca away from him as if he could not bear to touch her any longer.

Charlotte's hands curled into fists, longing to strike, but she knew that would only result in a far worse punishment.

Francesca stumbled and hit the table by the wall. A cry of pain slipped past her lips as she crumpled. She just managed to hold herself up, her gloved hands planted into the tapestry-covered panel.

And then Palmerton whirled around to Charlotte, advancing slowly, his whole body seeming to radiate his disgust.

"My God, what a minx you are. You have your mother's blood in you. Don't you? She knew how to tempt a man. And you are just the same."

"What?" she rasped, astonished by this new line of insult. "My mother was—"

"Your mother was born to mediocre gentility. She had a good house and a bit of money. It's mine now. And you are mine, too, to do with as I please."

He smoothed his hand down his waistcoat as he stared at her with eyes so cold, it was a miracle the room was not covered in ice.

"My God," he spat. "You are naught but a bit of rubbish, and I wish that I had chucked you out the day your mother died. You have caused nothing but trouble since, and you will not ruin this opportunity for Francesca. Do you understand me?"

"Of course I understand." She licked her lips, feeling more danger from this brittle hostility than she ever had before. "I will never see him—"

"Oh no," Palmerton cut in with a bitter smile. "That is not what I said. You *will* see the duke again, and you will make certain that he has no desire to marry you. You *will* make certain that he transfers his interest to Francesca. I have spent a great deal of coin to ensure that Francesca falls into his eye. It was a bad bit of business that he came to call at the moment I was away."

A bribe? She swallowed. Was he so duplicitous? So desperate to see Francesca married to a duke? Yes, she realized, feeling sick at the weight of it.

He shook his head, his brow furrowing at his frustration. "I had it all thought out, all arranged. And who would've thought that this could be the outcome? That he'd meet you on the road and be charmed by your rustic strumpet of a self. But it can be fixed." He bent down and locked gazes with her, his face mere inches away. "Can't it, Charlotte?"

"Yes," she said, swallowing. She'd always known that she had been a thorn in his side. But today... Today, she felt as if he hated her.

Hated every hair on her head, every fiber of her being. Every breath she took.

"Good. I knew you could fix this," he said with forced joviality. "You're so good at fixing things—broken vases, bits of furniture, torn dresses. I think that you will do a very good job of putting the duke off, making it clear that you are never going to marry him, and proving that Francesca is the one for him.

"Isn't that right, my darling?" He whipped around to his daughter.

Francesca gave a quick nod with her back still pressed to the wall, knowing that she had no other choice but to reply thus.

Not if she wished to make it through the night without corporal punishments or other manipulative cruelties.

Charlotte paused. It was as if someone else was taking her over. Lady Charlotte. She kept trying to rise up in her. No matter that she kept shoving her down.

"What if I don't?" she blurted out.

Palmerton stilled, then gave a single nod. "If you don't?"

Her heart began to beat wildly, and she wished to God that whatever rebellious part of her had been awakened a moment ago would go back to sleep and stay that way.

"You've liberated Stevenson from debtors' jail," he said evenly. "Very noble of you, Charlotte; very skilled. And now that I know that you're so entirely skilled, I'm going to have to put your abilities to better use."

Slowly, he raised his hand, let it hover, then tucked one of her wild curls behind her ear.

It was all she could do not to flinch at his touch, but she refused to give him the satisfaction. Instead, she forced herself to meet his gaze and hold it.

"But know this," he said. "If you think the worst I can do is have Stevenson admitted to the Marshalsea, you are indeed a fool who has not been paying attention to my abilities."

He wound his fingers around a handful of curls at the nape of her neck and held it. "I will make your life utter hell by destroying the people you care about. You see, I care about no one but myself and my daughter and my son. It is my job to make certain that we are important in society and finally given what we are due, and you will help with that. If you don't, you will regret it dearly. You understand?"

Her stomach coiled as he slipped his hand out of her hair and stepped back. In this moment, she knew that he was capable of almost anything.

A friend in the Marshalsea was but the beginning of the lengths to which he'd be willing to go to see her under his control.

"Good," he said. "Nod your head so I'm absolutely certain you do understand."

She nodded, even as that rebellious spark in her burned even brighter.

"Now, what are we going to do?" he asked in a sickeningly sweet voice.

She cleared her throat. "I'm going to make certain that the duke chooses Francesca."

"Yes, you are." He smiled now, which hopefully meant the worst of it was over.

"And we all know now what a tremendous actress you are. Perhaps that's what you should do when all this is done. I should drop you off in the West End and find you a job doing exactly what you do so well—lying."

With that, Palmerton tugged his waistcoat down. "You two are to go nowhere without my permission. And Charlotte? Go clean the drawing room chimney. There is not to be a speck of soot when I go out for the night."

Palmerton turned and left them there, no doubt to take a brandy with his son before they got ready for a night of gambling in the houses of sin.

It was then that she began to shake.

Francesca grabbed Charlotte's hand as her eyes shone with unshed tears. She blinked rapidly and gave her stepsister a look of resignation.

At least none of them were going to be harmed at present. And her stepfather was right. She *was* good at fixing things.

Somehow—she did not know how—she was going to find a way out of all of this for herself; for Francesca; for Stevenson, Cook, and Mary.

Palmerton thought he had won. He thought he had put her back in her place.

He was wrong.

She would not be a victim all of her life. And she would not let him win.

CHAPTER NINETEEN

Palmerton was being perfectly amenable in their meeting at his club. Gone was the odd, brittle air that had slipped past his ingratiating smile the day before.

No. Palmerton was all pleasantness.

Rafe poured another brandy into two of the Irish crystal snifters his club preferred.

He handed one to Palmerton, then lowered himself in the high-backed, leather-bound chair opposite the older lord.

As he took a slow sip of the brandy, savoring the heady cherry and oak notes, he studied Palmerton. "So, you do not object to my marriage to Lady Charlotte? I know she is only your niece, but I'm sure you feel responsible for her, and I was to call upon your daughter—"

"No, not at all," Palmerton cut in easily, holding the crystal up to the candlelight so that the amber-hued liquid glowed gold. "Since the girls are such good friends, I only hope that such a connection will ensure that my daughter Francesca will also make a great match. It seems it may already be so?"

Rafe laughed, thinking of his mother's delight at the potential of arranging multiple weddings. She did seem determined to take the two young ladies under her care, since neither had a mother.

"Oh, don't worry. Lady Francesca most certainly shall. She's already garnered, as you say, great interest. And the Earl of Darrow will no doubt offer any day. I've never seen him so besotted."

It was quite a thing to behold the way he and George had fallen into the ranks of marriage-minded men so quickly.

But wasn't that what titled men did? Marry?

Yes, they were doing their duty, with the added benefit of finding simply marvelous women.

"Darrow," Palmerton drawled, the name rolling around his mouth as he considered it.

He swirled his brandy now, making a show of appreciating the fine notes wafting from the glass.

At last, Palmerton smiled and lifted the snifter in salute. "A very good match, Your Grace. You are right. He's incredibly wealthy, owns a great deal of land, and his family is old. She could not do better. Except you."

Rafe tensed. What was he to say? "I take your compliment, my lord."

Palmerton inclined his head. "It is the truth, Your Grace."

"I am sorry that I cannot oblige you in this," he said, choosing his words carefully.

Palmerton clearly wasn't the sort of man to prioritize feelings or inclination in his daughter's choice.

Rafe sighed, deciding honesty was the only thing for it. "I do not generally follow the idea of indulging one's feelings in duty, but in this particular regard, I will. Lady Francesca is of course a perfect choice for a man like me. Everything about her indicates that she would be an ideal duchess. You've raised her very well."

He hesitated. How did one put into words the feelings that had been racing through him since Lady Charlotte had clobbered him with that brick? And those feelings? They kept growing. Intensifying. His admiration? It had only increased with every exchange, as did his desire to take her in his arms and strike up a blaze with her that would consume them both.

Rafe cleared his throat and adjusted his seat, forcing his mind away from thoughts of Charlotte's lush mouth and mischievous eyes. "When I met Lady Charlotte, I simply *knew*. I knew that she was *the one*. She and I are of an accord on the small things that make a marriage successful."

"*The one?*" Palmerton asked and let out a bellow of a laugh.

When his laughter met silence, he coughed and blinked. "Oh my, Your Grace. You are quite sincere."

Rafe drove a hand through his hair and shrugged. "I know it sounds like an incredibly naive, foolish sentiment one might hear in a three-penny novel or a melodrama. But she hit me with a brick, and I've never quite been able to forget the impact it had on me—both on my skin and my mind."

"She hit you with a brick?" Palmerton held his snifter aloft, halfway to his mouth.

"Yes," he mused. "When she was freeing your servant from debtors' jail. I assume you did not do the same because you were away."

"Stevenson is not a good person," Palmerton said tightly, his face growing most serious. "Charlotte is very kind, and she wished to do him a good turn. And she has known him since she was a child. What she did was incredibly dangerous and incredibly foolish, as you know. I cannot believe she went to South London by herself. She could have been killed."

"Yes," Rafe agreed, resisting the temptation to join him in castigating such a risky choice. "But she seemed, I don't know...at home there."

"Did she?" Palmerton asked. "In South-wark?"

Rafe hid a wince. His words could easily be taken wrong. But the truth was, she had been in her element on the pavement in the wild chaos of London. He could not think of another young lady who would have managed herself so well. "Yes."

"And you didn't find that odd?" Palmerton queried.

"Well," Rafe began, taking a sip of brandy. "I did think it a bit strange, but she was so determined that I—"

"Yes, yes, she is determined," Palmerton interjected. He cleared his throat and flashed a quick smile that did not reach his eyes. "She is a remarkable young woman. No one else like her in London. And I shall be happy to attend her wedding at...Westminster? St. Paul's?"

Rafe stifled a groan. "I haven't decided yet. My mother would no doubt prefer Westminster. But St. Paul's is undeniably beautiful."

"Indeed." A strange look passed over Palmerton's face before it vanished behind another smile. "I'm inclined to St. Paul's. Westminster can be dreary with all that darkness. All those memorials and history."

Rafe stared at the other man, stunned. Did he not know Charlotte at all?

Charlotte would adore the tombs, the history, following in the footsteps of kings and queens.

"Has she stayed with you long?" Rafe asked. "Is she generally given to impulse?"

"Yes. She has. She's stayed with us *very* long. And impulsive? It is her nature. It was her mother's nature, too, and she cannot escape it. She was a wild thing, her mother, and not well at the end, sadly."

The words came out in a rush, piling up on one another, and then Palmerton lifted a hand to his lips as if afraid he'd said too much.

"Not well at the end?" he repeated, wondering why the devil Palmerton would reveal such a thing at this moment. As if it was a stain on Charlotte.

Palmerton let out a beleaguered sigh. "Yes, very melancholic, you know. Fits. It was very difficult to watch. But I am glad I can help and look after Charlotte now."

"How hard for you all," Rafe said. "I'm so sorry."

"Thank you. It was such a tragedy." Palmerton's brow furrowed, grief darkening his eyes. "Her mother was beautiful. But her spirit was…I don't want to say weak, but she struggled with the cares of this world. She was so fiery when Charlotte was born—so determined to change everything, to right it. But I think that, over time, the exhaustion of it all simply wore her down."

"It wears many people down," Rafe replied, including himself. And he found himself wishing he had known Charlotte's

mother. "She sounds like she was a remarkable woman."

"Oh, she was. She was," Palmerton declared. "And I am grateful to be able to assist
her daughter and more grateful that she will
make such an advantageous marriage. When
shall the wedding be?"

Excellent. Back to the topic at hand. There
was only one thing holding back the official
proclamation of their engagement—approval
from Charlotte's father. No doubt Rafe would
receive a response to the note he'd sent after
speaking with his grandmama.

"Given all goes well, we shall announce
the wedding at my mother's annual ball at the
end of the Season and then marry soon after.
I think that's best. Don't you?"

"Whatever pleases Your Grace,"
Palmerton said with an inclination of his
head. "Is there any chance that I might become a member of this club?"

"Indeed," Rafe said, amused but not surprised. "It is the least that I can do, since we
are to be so closely connected."

"Yes." Palmerton lifted his snifter, his eyes
gleaming.

The duke lifted his own snifter in reply.

But he did not feel at ease. Palmerton's
presence had awakened a series of misgivings.
The man had a secret. Of that he was certain.

He could not shake it: Something was

amiss. Something about this whole affair was not right.

The dream that he sought? The bliss? The heaven that he had felt that night in Vauxhall was slipping through his fingers...and he did not know how to get it back.

CHAPTER TWENTY

"Surely cotton or linen would do," Charlotte protested.

The duchess looked appalled, as if Charlotte had just committed blasphemy.

Sitting on the small, striped, silk-covered ottoman, sipping champagne from a crystal flute, the dowager instructed, "My dear, do not say such outrageous things. You shall give me apoplexy, and then I shall have to take to my bed for a month. We have far too many things to accomplish for me to do that."

The duchess hesitated and gave a wicked smile. "Though, taking to one's bed can be quite fun."

Charlotte blinked. "I have never done so."

"You will, once you are married," the older woman said lightly. "I promise you shall have every opportunity to take to your bed, and the servants shall bring you every meal that you wish, and we shall all entertain you, especially when you are with child."

Charlotte's eyes widened. "Your Grace, you cannot possibly say such things to me."

"Can I not?" she replied before taking another drink. "Did I not just say them, or should I just refrain from saying the word *child*? A duchess *is* expected to have a child."

"Yes, but what if I don't?" Charlotte rushed, unable to be discreet with her concerns. "Besides, I have not agreed to marry your son."

"No," the duchess agreed, arching a brow of surprise.

Charlotte groaned as she stood in front of the three mirrors that showed her reflection in an unfinished but exquisite gown. "This is most outrageous."

"And don't you just absolutely love it to bits?" the duchess asked, grinning.

"Yes," Charlotte confessed. "I suppose I do. You are unlike anyone I have ever met."

"My darling, the compliment!" she trilled. "You could not give me a better one. Now, have a glass of champagne."

The duchess waved her hand, her emerald-jeweled fingers winking in the morning sunlight, summoning someone to do her will.

"But, Your Grace…"

Her brows rose. "What?"

"It is *morning*."

"Well…" The duchess pursed her lips. "Perhaps I can ask her to put a raspberry in your glass, so it can be breakfast."

Charlotte tried not to gape.

"Now, now, my dear. Everyone knows that drinking champagne is really the best thing for one's skin."

Charlotte began to laugh, then swallowed

it lest she get herself into trouble.

In her experience seeing the nobility, drinking champagne was the worst thing for one's skin, but clearly, the duchess had a good regimen and was quite fit.

"Do you not like silk?" the duchess asked.

A maid dressed in a perfectly cut gray gown passed Charlotte a champagne glass. She nearly grasped the flute but then took it by the stem just in time.

Such a thing would've given her away immediately!

She knew the right things to do, but she never had to *do* them. Charlotte held the champagne glass carefully by its delicate stem, leaned forward, and took a sip.

The bubbles shot right up her nose, and the fizz swept over her tongue in a bright, sharp manner. It had a slightly acidic taste, if she was honest, and she wasn't entirely certain that she liked it, but then she felt a glow wash over her, and she smiled.

"You like it?" the duchess queried.

"Yes."

"And you like the silk?"

"Yes, I do," she confessed. "I've just never had the opportunity to wear something so…"

"I know it's frightfully expensive," the duchess whispered dramatically. "But it's all right, my dear, if you don't bring a fortune to this marriage. You make up for it with your personality."

"I *should* take that as a compliment," Charlotte said warily.

"Indeed, you should. It was intended as such." The duchess winked playfully. "You have a good old family and a good old house, and that is wonderful. My son loves it. He went on about it for an hour at dinner last night."

"He did?" she gasped.

"He did." The duchess sighed, then smiled. "You both love architecture. I can see it now. You shall buy up all the old houses in the countryside that don't have owners and care for their neglected rooms."

"Can we really do such a thing?"

The duchess stared at her for a long moment before assuring, "My dear, you will have almost as much money as our monarch. You can do whatever you please."

Her heart pounded against her ribs. The very idea was beyond her.

But it was what the duke had wished for her at Vauxhall. To damn well do what she pleased...

She could not even truly imagine such circumstances.

She had spent so much time sweeping up dirt, cleaning plates, and taking care of everyone else's laundry that she could not imagine the idea of owning multiple houses, let alone being able to buy old ones in excess. She couldn't even imagine having her own servants and ordering them to do what she was so used to doing herself.

And she never *would* know it, because she would never marry the duke.

She bit the inside of her cheek to keep her distress hidden and looked down at the gown.

It was a soft rose color that accented her blond hair to perfection. It skimmed her body and gave the appearance that she was almost naked.

The gown was not translucent, and yet the fabric was shockingly thin. Given her daily sturdy wear, it was scandalous. The neck scooped low, almost baring her nipples. She couldn't believe that anyone could wear such a thing and be considered a lady, but there it was.

It was the present fashion.

Gold filigree was stitched into the sleeves and hem, where the skirt had been embroidered with rosebuds.

"This is the most beautiful thing that I have ever worn," she said honestly.

"Well, this is just an evening gown," the duchess informed. "Wait until you see what I have in mind for what you're going to wear to my ball."

"Something grander than this?" Charlotte queried.

The duchess nodded. "If you're going to be the next Duchess of Rockford, this is but the beginning, my dear."

"And what if I am not the next duchess?" she ventured.

"Now, my dear," the duchess said, clearly frustrated. "You like my son?"

"Yes, I do," she said without guile.

"Is there something that you need to tell me? Because I will find out, you know. I'm terribly good at finding things out. And your continual intimation that you are not the right young lady for my son does give me occasional pause, despite how much I like you."

Charlotte wanted to tell her the full truth so badly it hurt.

The pain of it was agonizing.

The words were on the tip of her tongue, and they almost poured out of her mouth, but then she thought of Francesca, of Stevenson and the Marshalsea, of the cook, of Mary, and of the horrors that could befall them if Charlotte were not there to shield them from Palmerton.

He could have them put in workhouses. The lot of them. He could marry Francesca to an old, awful man, and he could put Charlotte out on the street without a character.

No, she could not speak, no matter how her heart longed to.

And she prayed that she could find a way

out of this soon. But first, she had to follow Palmerton's demands. And since he insisted on keeping up her ruse? She was in dire straits. It was galling.

She forced a smile. "No, of course not. I do like your son. It's simply that Francesca? She was born to be a duchess. I have not had great entrée into society. I do not know how to be a duchess."

"Oh, my dear," the duchess began kindly. "Don't worry. My son shall teach you, and I shall take you in hand. There's nothing to fear."

How she wished that were true.

But the duchess was mistaken.

There was very much to fear, indeed.

CHAPTER TWENTY-ONE

The excellent cut of the children's clothes told Charlotte a great deal about the care given to them.

She stood in the main hall of the foundling hospital with Francesca by her side, barely able to draw breath. Not out of horror, not out of frustration, but out of astonishment.

The small children all looked, dare she say, happy.

Such a thing seemed quite strange, given that they were all orphaned. In her experience, orphans in London were not happy at all. Sometimes they were in care of people who were trying to make London a better place, but those people still believed that strict discipline and privation was the best way to teach children how to live.

It seemed the Duke of Rockford did not agree, or at least his family did not.

There was a warm fire crackling in the long hall.

It seemed that there were fires crackling in every room.

As opposed to cold austerity and the scent of lye, the whole space felt…well, if she was honest, warm. Children were walking back and forth in pairs, chatting away.

She continued to marvel that their green uniforms were sewn beautifully. She'd yet to see any sort of ill-fitting or poorly dyed clothes.

Some of the children's homes in London were reputed for their blue shade, because blue was the cheapest dye that could be found, but not here. The clothes were simple but beautiful. A bright Lincoln green.

And all of the children seemed in good health.

She was amazed.

Her own childhood, without her parents, could not be compared to children who were adrift, but she had been living in austere conditions since she was small. The cold room at the top of the house, where fires were not permitted; the clothes that were handed down or barely fit. She was lucky she could read, truly.

That ability had allowed her to teach herself so much.

These children went back and forth, books in their hands, and slates, too. She'd never seen such a thing in all her life.

Francesca stood beside her and took her hand. "Are you seeing what I'm seeing?" she breathed.

"These children do not look unwanted," the duke offered, stepping up behind them.

She whirled to face him. "Yes," she said.

"That is exactly what I see. How is such happiness created?"

He paused. "I will not deceive you. There are many struggles. The children have much to overcome, whether it be feelings of rejection or the struggles of an early life in the worst conditions, but the people who have been chosen to work here are kind, patient, and understanding. Many of those who work here now were raised here but choose to stay on to help the other children transition to a life outside these walls."

She marveled at him, his clear dedication, and the way his family had chosen this cause.

As she took in the Duke of Rockford, her heart sank. She wished it would soar like it had at Vauxhall. She admired him. Greatly. How she wished she could be free with him and revel in the fact that he wished to share this with her.

But the truth was she was in dire circumstances.

Palmerton had made it absolutely clear that she was to turn the duke's attention to Francesca.

And yet here in this establishment that his family had made, that he'd supported? It was clear he wished her to see it.

Though she hardly dare admit it, even to herself, a part of her wished... She wished that she had been born to a position which might have made it possible.

Facts were, well, facts. And the sooner she helped Rockford understand that she was not the right woman for him and that Francesca at least could be, the better.

Galling as it was, she ignored the bitter regret growing inside her and drew in a deep breath.

"Yes, well, I'm sure it costs a good deal of money," she said. "But you see, Francesca is the one who really knows about such things. I don't do any charitable work, you see, whereas Francesca is always…"

Francesca brought her foot down on top of Charlotte's. She bit her lip to keep from yelping and tried not to hop.

The duke's brows furrowed. "Is that really true, Lady Charlotte? That doesn't seem to be in keeping with your form. After all, I met you on your way to the Marshalsea, where you gave me a great deal of education about the inequities of it, and you were determined to free a servant from there. I don't see how it's possible that you are not interested in charitable institutions."

Drat! Caught out by her own actions. Words were very difficult things. Actions made it impossible to lie. Actions were much harder to deny than words.

He was quite correct. She had been doing those things, and the truth was Francesca did donate things to charitable institutions. She had sewn many beautiful small garments and shawls that had been sent to many of those in need. But she did not take as much active interest as Charlotte did.

"Well." She laughed—not convincingly. "You make a fair point. I have just been so busy of late that I have not been able to…"

"Well, as my duchess, you will have all the time in the world to do it," he assured confidently. "You can choose whatever charity you like to support."

"I can?" she said blankly.

"Oh yes," he said. "This is mine. I don't expect you to take it up. Well, it's not even mine yet. My mother has promised it to me, but I always took a particular interest. You see, I loved my great-aunt dearly."

The hard planes of his beautiful face softened with memory. "I met her when she was quite old, and she was kind to me. She had a small house on the family estate. You see, things had gone terribly wrong for her when she was young, and she's the reason why the foundling hospital was created."

Charlotte must have looked confused, because he smiled kindly and continued, "My great-grandfather did not take kindly to my great-aunt falling in love with her tutor. She was cast out, with child. And the tutor? Poor man, he died of smallpox. The babe did not survive infancy, and the poverty my great-aunt faced without her family... She lived a miserable existence until my grandfather found her and brought her to his house once the old duke had died."

He shook his head, as if ashamed that someone so cruel had been a member of his family. "It's remarkable how who's in power can shape events, isn't it?" he asked softly.

Was he talking directly to her?

Could he see that she was the victim of such circumstance—that if someone else had the power of her life, things would be different? Surely not. He had no inkling.

"And so a foundling hospital was created?" she breathed.

"Yes." He paused as he let his gaze lift to the children who were now congregating by the fire. "My great-aunt's baby died because they were so poor. She didn't have money to buy fuel, and she couldn't support or feed him. The winters were cruel. It was the most horrific of stories. She shared it with me when I was old enough to understand. She told me how important it was, the work that my mother's family had begun when she'd returned to the estate, how women needed to have a place to go when no one wanted them to have their babies, and that those babies should be cared for and raised with love, not cruelty.

"I've seen the other kinds of places," he

said tightly.

"So have I," she whispered. And she knew what it was like to be unloved.

Charlotte bit down on the inside of her cheek before she could confess such a thing to his sympathetic nature. What the devil was she doing? She couldn't say such things.

As if the duke sensed that she was uncomfortable and did not wish to talk of her own family, her own loss of parents, he guided them down the hall and into another large, comfortable room.

"Your Grace, Your Grace!" several of the children called out in chorus.

He laughed as he headed to the excited group. "Good morning, children," he said.

He bent down to chat with a little girl who was sitting on a long bench. "Why, Elizabeth," he asked, "whatever are you reading?"

"I am reading a most merry tale," she said, her eyes bright with pride. "I am reading about King Arthur."

"Are you indeed?" he said.

"Yes." She scowled. "I don't like what they did to the queen. I think it's terrible."

"To Guinevere?" he asked.

"Indeed," she said. "I don't think that the queen should have gotten into such trouble, and I don't like that part of the story."

"How would you tell it, then?" he prompted, sitting down beside her.

Charlotte's throat tightened as tears stung her eyes. How was it possible that he was so kind and caring?

"I think I should say," Elizabeth began, lifting her chin and tucking a curling lock behind her ear, "that Guinevere did nothing wrong and was a great queen. It wasn't her fault that she couldn't have a little boy and people simply wished to besmirch her because of that and they said terrible things about her and Lancelot."

He nodded gravely, took the small book she was reading, and said, "I think you tell a much more believable tale. You're absolutely right. People say the worst things about a person to villainize."

"Yes," the little girl said firmly, "I agree."

"Now I think it's time for some ginger nuts, don't you?" the duke asked.

"Oh yes," she cheered. "That would be delightful, Your Grace."

"Hooray!" the other children in the room called.

"Have you been reading to them, Elizabeth?" Rockford asked.

"Yes," she said, "but it's always better when you read to us, Your Grace. You do the best voices."

He did the best voices.

Charlotte swallowed, regret and disappointment burning through her.

As if Francesca knew, she took Charlotte's hand and squeezed. "Would you read to us, Your Grace?" Francesca asked.

"Oh, do you think I should?" he asked. "I would like to show you the rest of the house."

"I think this shows us exactly what this house is about," Charlotte said firmly.

"Do you?" he queried softly.

"Yes," she breathed. "It's about love, isn't it?"

"I beg your pardon," he queried.

She took a step toward him, their gazes locking over the heads of the children. "It's about showing people that they're wanted — about the small, everyday things. Like reading stories."

His eyes widened as if someone was truly seeing his intent for the first time.

"You read to them often, don't you?"

"The duke often comes in the evening," Elizabeth piped up.

A little boy with mischievous brown eyes and a pointed chin added, "Yes, His Grace comes sometimes three times a week. He'll read a splendid, ripping tale of adventure." The boy pursed his lips. "I like *Robinson Crusoe*, if you must know. Though I don't think he's very nice to his friend Friday."

"I rather agree with you," Charlotte said, her heart swelling. "Can you imagine what it would be like to be on an island all by yourself?"

The little boy frowned. "Well, when I was small, I was alone," he said. "Quite a lot, actually, whilst me mummy was out working. But then I came here, and things got better, and I have friends all the time. Friends are important," the little boy said sagely. "As is a nice place to stay."

Charlotte leaned down and looked the little boy square in the eyes. "I couldn't agree more," she said.

And though she'd not been born into abject poverty, she felt an affinity with these children that she'd not felt with anyone in quite some time.

She glanced away quickly as a shocking wave of emotion stole over her.

The duke began a book given to him by Elizabeth, and the children listened, rapt, quite happy, as a servant came in and handed out milk and the ginger nuts and brown bread. Nice, thick slices covered in butter.

She couldn't understand what she was seeing. Most places like this were full of gruel and cruelty and crumbs of bread and children who barely survived and unkind prayers from morning till sundown.

This was so different.

He lifted his gaze and met hers, and then, with a start, she understood he didn't care about coronets and gold. Oh, he cared about what the gold could do, and he knew that she understood, too. And for the first time, she realized that was why he wanted her.

It rattled through her, the understanding that he didn't want her because she was a lady of the *ton* who could dance a perfect minuet.

He wanted her because she saw the world the way that he did.

A place where there should be more love—a place where children should be validated and truly cared for.

And Charlotte could not think another word as she felt her world swing, and she understood that her heart, her dratted heart, was being taken by him.

. . .

"Show me the house," Rafe said to Charlotte.

Palmerton perked up and put his gold-painted teacup down on the table beside his spindly but expensive chair. "Francesca would make an excellent guide as well, Your Grace. The two young ladies are wonderful together and know details about the house that not even I know."

The duke fought a sigh. He was not entirely certain why it was so difficult to have Charlotte alone for a few moments, but he did understand that Palmerton was being wise.

A chaperone was necessary even though

they were going to be married. And so he inclined his head and said, "Of course, the two young ladies are marvelous company. I enjoy them wherever we go. Our last outing was a success."

"Oh yes," Francesca said. "It was absolutely wonderful. I truly enjoyed the ginger nuts!"

"You were both marvelous guests," he complimented, hoping to smooth Palmerton's feathers. "The children were talking about you for hours on end afterward and asked if you would be coming back."

"Certainly Lady Francesca would be pleased to come again," Palmerton assured. "She's wonderful with charitable institutions."

The duke blinked. "Yes, so Lady Charlotte told me," he replied.

He wanted out of this room, though it was beautiful.

It was not like the rest of the house. The study, which he assumed was Palmerton's, was a rather fussy affair. It bore the fashion of the present day, with Egyptian antiquities everywhere, white walls, and rather vapid furniture.

He far preferred the rest of the house with its dark wood and ancient furnishings.

The library, of course, was his favorite, and he recalled, "I saw some rather marvelous books the other day when I was here. From the Continent. Do you think I might get to have a look at them?"

Palmerton paled. "I beg your pardon, Your Grace."

"There was one—a set of fairy tales," he explained. "I thought I might be able to translate some of it for the children. Of course, I have my own copy of it, but your edition seemed particularly beautiful."

"Well," Palmerton hedged, "I don't know what's happened to it. Do you think you could show it to him, Charlotte?"

"No," Lady Charlotte said tightly. "It's gone missing."

"Missing?" Rafe said, surprised. "How unfortunate. I already noted how much you love the books in the house. And the house in general."

Lady Charlotte winced.

"Oh, you have?" Palmerton clucked. "What a misfortune. Charlotte is the one who suggested that we get rid of them. Isn't it true, Charlotte?"

"Oh yes," she said quickly. "The collection was growing rather crowded, and we had far too many fairy tales about. I don't care for such silliness."

He stared at Lady Charlotte for a long moment. Surely that was not possible.

"Come along," Lady Charlotte said abruptly, heading for the door. "We mustn't waste any time. Surely, Your Grace, you have places to be?"

He wondered at that comment, too.

Did she wish him to leave? They had always gotten along so well, though their encounters had been few, and he began to think on what his mother had said—how she did not wish to marry him.

It made no sense.

Surely, any young lady would be thrilled to marry a duke, but she did not seem to be. In fact, she kept trying to put Lady Francesca between them wherever they went.

They went out into the hall, and just as before, Lady Charlotte stood on one side of Lady Francesca and attempted to make certain that the duke stood on the other.

But as they headed down the hall, through the long corridors of the house, Lady Charlotte transformed.

He wasn't surprised. In fact, he was relieved.

The tense position of her shoulders slipped away, and he began to wonder about the relationship between herself and Palmerton. They didn't get on.

Of that? He was certain. There was a strange arrangement between them. And he couldn't put his finger on it.

That strange little exchange between the two of them felt proof of it. But she clearly loved Lady Francesca. Families were the oddest things, and though he wished it wasn't true, discord was quite common.

As they headed out toward the great rooms, he marveled at the portraits. Oh, he had a grand house, too, but there was something particularly charming about this one. The coziness of it; the cramped corners, the intricate woodwork, and the towering portraits.

So many families were determined to forget the past and change their great old palaces into modern French designs.

"I think it is remarkable," he mused, hands behind his back, "the way that your family managed to preserve so many details of a bygone era."

Lady Francesca remained quiet as she studied her cousin.

Lady Charlotte beamed at him. "It is, isn't it? I particularly love to examine so many of the little pieces in the woodwork. Wonderful things have been engraved there, don't you think?"

"Oh, indeed," he said, relieved to see the excitement back on her face.

"Do you see there?" she said, pointing upward. "It is Anne Boleyn's symbol, a falcon. Our family was decided Boleynist. Poor Catherine, of course. I do have sympathy for her, but the pomegranates were long ago cut out of the walls."

Lady Charlotte tilted her head to the side as she contemplated a man in seventeenth-century dress. "And of course, my family was never particularly interested in the Stuarts."

He gazed at her. "Your family?" he prompted, confused. She clearly meant her mother's side and not the Faraday clan.

"I don't know a great deal about them," she admitted. "But I've read everything I can about them."

"And you love the history of the house?"

She did not need to reply. Instead, she smiled. A smile so beautiful he could neither think nor reply. Here, without Palmerton or society? She glowed.

Rafe followed Lady Charlotte and Lady Francesca, who continued to say little, through the rooms, not really looking at the beautiful surroundings. No, he could not tear his gaze from Lady Charlotte or the way her face lit as she talked about the people who had once filled the corridors, danced in the rooms, played music, and eaten by the fire.

After several minutes, Lady Francesca swung her gaze to him and then to her cousin. "I beg your pardon, but I must bid you two adieu. I have a letter to write to George."

Lady Charlotte tensed. "Surely not. You are to stay here with me and the duke, are you not?"

Lady Francesca smiled wanly, but she was

clearly determined to go. "I trust that you two shall not get up to anything you shouldn't, but I do not wish to keep George waiting. I've kept him waiting far too long."

Lady Charlotte's face paled. "You cannot, Francesca. Your father would…"

Lady Francesca gave her a hard look. "Yes, my father would prefer a great many things, but at this particular moment, I do not wish to keep the earl waiting."

Lady Charlotte swallowed.

Rafe noted it and said carefully, "George is an excellent fellow, and if you have put your heart on him, I salute you. We shall be great friends, all of us, and often dine together. It'll be wonderful."

Lady Francesca smiled. "I hope that it's true," she said before her smile dimmed and she assessed him with shocking frankness. "You think that I am a kind person?"

"Yes," he offered easily.

"And I would be a good match for George?"

"Yes," he said, wondering what the devil this all signified.

Lady Francesca drew in a long breath as she smoothed her hands down the front of her gown. "Good," she said, and then her gaze narrowed and she asked boldly, "And you're certain that I would not be the right person for you?"

He blinked, astonished at the forwardness of such a question.

"Lady Francesca," he began, more than conscious that the woman he was falling in love with stood beside him. "I can tell you quite honestly that from the moment I met Lady Charlotte, I was intrigued by her, and from the moment I met you, I knew you were excellent. But I also knew that you weren't the lady for me. I can tell that you are educated, interesting, and kind, but Lady Charlotte has a sort of passion about her and a pragmatism that I admire so much I can barely put it into words. After our exchange at Vauxhall, and then again at the foundling hospital..." He paused.

"Well, I knew that she was the one for whom I was best suited, with whom I might be able to..."

"Yes?" Lady Francesca prompted fearlessly.

He cleared his throat, then said, "Be happy."

• • •

Charlotte's heart beat wildly in her chest.

This couldn't be happening. What was Francesca doing? Was she going to willfully provoke her father?

But the truth was, Francesca was simply revealing what they all knew but Palmerton refused to accept.

The duke was never going to ask for Francesca's hand. He was committed to Charlotte because he did not know the truth of things. And even if he was? He did not feel an affinity for Francesca.

And she didn't know what to do about it.

How could she drive him into Francesca's arms, a place he clearly had no desire to go? Should she stomp on his foot? Should she be cruel to him?

"I don't think it is a good idea that you and I wander the halls alone together," she bit out.

He sighed. "Perhaps you're right."

Francesca gave a quick curtsy and turned, giving Charlotte a firm glare. "You two should have a moment."

And with that, Francesca hurried away.

Charlotte let out a blow of frustration.

"Are you afraid to be alone with me?" he asked, his brow furrowing.

"No," she replied, exasperated, longing to be with him but knowing she could not be. "Not at all."

"I'm glad," he said, his shoulders relaxing. "For a moment, I began to fear you thought little of me."

She swallowed, her heart aching. "I think a great deal of you, Your Grace. More than anyone else."

His eyes widened as he took in her words. "Then why this sudden distance?"

"I can't explain it," she said. "I just don't think…"

"What?" he asked softly. "You don't think what?"

She pressed her lips together, struggling to know what to say. "That I'm the right person for you," she rushed.

"And who has told you that?"

She didn't know how to reply.

How did she tell him that Palmerton had slammed her up against the wall? That he had hurt Francesca? That he had threatened Stevenson and Mary?

That's exactly what she should do, of course. Maybe he could rescue them, then. If wishes were horses…

No, if he knew the truth, he would be disgusted. She was a servant and a liar.

"Charlotte," Palmerton called from down the hall. "You should not be alone with His Grace."

The duke drew in a long breath. "It is time I depart, in any event."

He strode into the shadowy hall. Away from her. And her heart wept, for despite Francesca's determination, she knew she could never have the duke. No matter how much she wished.

Too many lives were at stake.

CHAPTER TWENTY-TWO

His mother's ball was in less than a week.

The marriage was destined to be announced to an eager and bejeweled crowd. Or so he had thought.

As it was, he wasn't so certain.

A rare state for a duke.

Over the last week, Rafe and Lady Charlotte had attended many events together, from boating escapades to races to card parties.

They had played bowls, they had taken chaperoned walks along the Serpentine with half the *ton* watching, and yet he had spoken to her less in that week than he had in the entirety of the first day that they had known each other.

He could not quite put his finger on what had happened, but whatever it was, that unique light that he had experienced with Lady Charlotte was fading.

And it was fading fast.

What was it?

Had the affinity between them been his imagination?

Had he made up their passionate exchange of minds and mouths at Vauxhall?

Was she so little interested in him that she

was merely humoring him with every day that they spent together?

Much to Rafe's dismay, he was beginning to believe she was forced to entertain him by her uncle.

He didn't understand. He simply couldn't grasp how he could feel so close to someone and then...distance.

He didn't *want* the distance. Lady Charlotte seemed to be imposing it. Politely.

Was he so arrogant that he had assumed that she would just marry him because he was a duke? It struck him now that he'd assumed she would accept his proposal without question.

It was galling. Apparently, he'd made a vast many assumptions.

And yet he had thought they were more than the simple arrangement that society required. He had thought that Charlotte liked him.

Hadn't she intimated as much? She'd bloody well kissed him as if she liked him.

But every day that passed seemed to suggest that not only did Charlotte not like him, she had little interest in him at all.

It was a bloody appalling state of affairs.

Hell and damnation, he had been the most sought-after bachelor in all of England for the last five years.

No, that wasn't true. The moment he'd

turned eighteen, mamas had been inducing their daughters to drop handkerchiefs in his vicinity.

For years, he'd warded off the hopes and attentions of the horde. A horde that he'd respected and understood yet wished to be no part of.

And now the one woman *he* wanted seemed to have no desire for him at all.

Even after the intimacy they had shared.

It felt like a laceration on his heart. Not just a laceration but an open cut that someone had poured salt upon.

Bloody hell. When had he taken to melancholy?

Outside the Marshalsea, apparently, and then again at Vauxhall. And every encounter since.

Rafe stared at her across the ballroom packed to the brim with gilded lords and ladies drinking punch, flicking fans, snorting snuff, and doing their damnedest to outdo one another in their grandeur.

Lady Charlotte was speaking with George and Matt, having a merry time with Lady Francesca.

A muscle tightened in his jaw. Was he jealous? *He!* Jealous!

The truth was, he wished he was having a merry time, too, and did not know how he'd ended up outside the circle of friends.

George was still pursuing Lady Francesca, though the young lady had grown quite reserved. But the truth was, from what he could see, Lady Francesca and George were perfect for each other.

If George had his way, their engagement would be announced soon. Lady Francesca would go up the aisle with her earl, and then the two would hie off to Europe for a grand tour on their honeymoon to view books and blades.

Palmerton would not be so pleased as he'd be with a duke for a son-in-law, but an earl was quite a triumph.

Rafe would be left in England, wondering what the devil had happened to his plans.

He drew in a long breath and folded his hands, determined not to act a fool.

God, Lady Charlotte was beautiful.

Tonight, she looked like the duchess he wished her to be in truth.

Much credit to his mother and her modiste, Lady Charlotte's gown was perfection. It was an ivory affair, embroidered with silver flowers and bejeweled with crystals. She shimmered in the candlelight.

Her golden hair coiled atop her head, and diamond flowers from his mother's chest of treasures had been placed artfully in the curls.

A single curl had been pulled free and draped over her shoulder, so the end danced over her breasts when she turned and chatted.

And yet, Lady Charlotte did not look as if she was bound up by the rules of society like so many of the other young ladies did.

There was something free about Lady Charlotte—something wild. Rafe did not know how she did it, but even in the room with hundreds of people looking on, she did not appear as if she had been cut from any mold.

Lady Charlotte was an original.

Much to his amazement and agonized delight, Lady Charlotte bounced on her toes, gestured wildly with her hands, threw back her head, and laughed at a joke that Matt told.

It drove him positively mad.

He ground his teeth.

She had not laughed at anything he had said in the last week. In fact, she had barely deigned to raise her brows when he spoke, giving nods and mere murmurs and polite, one-word answers to his questions and comments. It was enough to send a man into fits.

But he was no coward, and he wouldn't be downcast yet.

Taking in a fortifying breath, Rafe crossed the room, hoping that tonight would be different. He carefully wove his way through the ballroom, easily making his way past befeathered ladies and powdered gentlemen.

They parted for him. After all, he was the Duke of Rockford.

Many of them gazed at him with longing, hoping that he might notice their daughters and eschew whatever interest he had in Lady Charlotte. He ignored them.

Though, at this rate, he did not see how anyone might think he would marry Lady Charlotte, she paid him so little attention. When at last he stopped before her, George, Matt, and Lady Francesca making merry, he found himself placing his hands behind his back and waiting to be acknowledged.

To his chagrin, Lady Charlotte did not oblige.

Lady Francesca suddenly grew quiet, whipping out her fan and beating it quickly, which blew her curled hair away from her face.

Matt and George then swung their attention to him, both of them shifting awkwardly on their booted feet. Mirrors of each other in their blacks.

Matt clapped Rafe on the back. "Old boy, good to see you here."

"You conversed with me but an hour ago," he drawled.

George laughed a little too loudly, as if Rafe had said something hilarious.

There was a moment of awkwardness.

Had they been discussing him? Was that it?

George extended his hand to Lady Francesca. "Might I have this dance?"

Lady Francesca hesitated as her gaze swung to Rafe, but then she nodded. "I do adore a reel."

And off they went, bouncing along, joining the crowd on the dance floor, springing from foot to foot.

Rafe turned his gaze to Lady Charlotte. "Would you care to dance?" he asked before realizing his error. Lady Charlotte didn't know this dance.

She gave a slight shake of her head, avoiding eye contact. "I do not dance the reel."

He swallowed.

She was staring out at the sea of dancers, turning her body away from him.

"Of course," he replied. "How foolish of me."

He *knew* that she did not dance reels or jigs. She had made that quite plain a week ago, but he had not been certain if perhaps she might not give it a try, which of course was ridiculous.

Who would wish to make such attempts in front of everyone? But then, much to his shock, Matt stuck his hand out and said, "Would you not care to try? I'm sure that I can lead you around the room in a merry jaunt."

To Rafe's horror, she beamed at Matt. "Of

course, my lord. I will do my best with you, good sir."

And she went with his friend.

Rafe gaped at them. What the hell had just transpired? Were they all in cahoots against him?

Standing awkwardly on his own, he longed to throttle the lot of them. All his life, he'd been confident, assured, capable.

But now? He had no idea what to do.

He dug his nails into his palms, keeping his face unreadable.

He looked about the room, trying to find answers.

It was then that his mother sauntered up beside him and said, "There seems to be trouble in your paradise, my darling boy. Is all well with Lady Charlotte?"

"No," he said flatly. "And I know you well enough to know that *you* know that not all is well. She has been avoiding me. I do not know why."

His mother unfolded her painted fan, which was the same hue as her wine-colored gown. She smiled as if she had not a care in the world, then leaned in toward him and whispered, "Have you given her some offense? She's a girl of good sense. I cannot imagine that she would be blatantly rude for no reason."

He tensed but then sighed. What point was

there in indignation? He needed answers.
And growing defensive would not assist him.
"I do not think that I have."

"Ask her," his mother urged simply. "It is
the only thing that you can do at this point."

Before he could reply, she frowned, a brief
break in her perfect visage. "You may have to
wait, though. In a moment, the performances
will begin. The young ladies will be trotted
out to be made good view of by Lady
Greenbridge's guests. Lady Francesca is first.
She will sing, I hear."

"Oh God," he groaned. "Affronts to the
opera. Why must the *ton* afflict such things
upon their daughters? And the rest of us."

As the reel came to a close, the vast company began to file into the grand salon to take
their seats.

He sighed. There was no escaping it. He
had assumed he would sit by Lady Charlotte,
enjoying her company, feeling free, knowing
she would be his wife.

He did not feel free. He felt trapped, suf-
focated.

It was not his favorite part of an evening,
the musicale, but it was part of being a duke,
listening to young ladies of varying degree of
talent perform for an audience, showing off
their skills in the hopes of finding a husband.

He did not know what would happen now.
For Lady Charlotte, as far as he was aware,

was not in the habit of performing. At least she never had before, as he understood.

Without ado, Lady Francesca was led to the pianoforte by George.

Lord Palmerton stood at the side of the large room, his back to the green silk wall, his eyes narrowed as if he was displeased by his daughter standing up with the earl.

There was a brief moment in which Lady Francesca caught her father's eyes, and she slipped her finger from the earl's gloved hand.

Palmerton's arms were folded lightly over his chest, which emphasized his perfectly tailored black evening coat and snowy cravat. His chin was high, as if he was expecting a grand performance, before he glanced over at Rafe. He beamed, giving the appearance of a doting papa.

The whole moment had been most odd. But any sort of disapproval had vanished from Palmerton as the man smiled at Rafe.

Had he imagined the exchange? Possibly. He felt on edge.

Rafe and his mother crossed into the room and stood where they could make good view of the performances. Lady Charlotte took up a spot with Lord Matthew near the front and watched, her lips tilted in a smile.

And for a single moment, she glanced back over her bare shoulder and met his gaze.

That shared gaze crackled like the air before a thunderstorm.

It went straight from his heart to her heart and back again.

He knew it.

There was no denying the power of it traveling through him and in her.

Her lips parted, and her gloved hands tensed around her fan. Her eyes widened ever so slightly, and he could see her chest rise and fall in a quick breath.

A wave of relief crashed over him then, and it was all he could do not to go to her, take her in his arms, declare her as his and he as hers before the entire salon, and have done with waiting for a grand moment at his mother's ball.

It was there in her eyes, that hot glow and recognition of a like-minded soul.

She did *not* dislike him.

She was *not* completely disinterested.

But then, she whipped her gaze away and returned her view to her cousin.

He felt the loss of her gaze as strongly as one might feel the loss of an embrace.

He squared his jaw, knowing he had to be patient. He would speak with her soon. Any wrong would be righted, and then all would be well again, as it was before.

Quickly, George escorted Lady Francesca to the seat before the pianoforte.

Lady Francesca smiled at the earl, then trailed her fingers over the ivory keys.

With a single, broad gesture of her arms, her fingers hovering, she began to play. And soon her voice joined.

Lady Francesca sang one of Mozart's arias. It was one of the most beautiful, sprightly love songs. It spoke about the difficulties of love but how it would always triumph in the end.

It was a suitable but extremely difficult song for a young lady.

Lady Francesca's voice was not at all what he had expected. It was perfect and pure, a soprano to rival anyone he had heard on an operatic stage. Her father looked pleased beyond all compare, as if he had been preparing for this moment for years. No doubt he had, and Rafe noticed that Palmerton snuck a glance at *him*, as if he was waiting to see whether Rafe approved of Lady Francesca or not.

Unable to avoid it, Rafe inclined his head.

The room took note.

The duke approved. And a hushed whisper went about the salon.

He winced.

It was damned difficult to always be on public view.

As soon as Lady Francesca was done, he applauded, ignoring the pointed conjecture and stares of the guests.

As he did, the entire room applauded with enthusiasm.

Despite his discomfort, he was glad that they did. Clearly, Lady Francesca had worked hard for this moment and would likely be the best performance of the evening.

Lady Francesca stood, gave a quick curtsy, smiled modestly, and then returned to the crowd.

The applause dimmed, followed by an odd silence.

There was a lull and rush of gossips, as if there was a confusion as to who was to perform next.

Then the lady of the house, Lady Greenway, stood before the pianoforte. She gave a girlish, nervous giggle, ill-suited to a woman over forty. But then she coughed and said, "I do believe Lady Francesca's relation, Lady Charlotte, is next."

There was a murmur through the crowd, for Lady Charlotte was a newcomer to the *ton*.

Charlotte's frame went rigid, and she did not appear as if she would be able to move. She let out a peep of resistance. "Oh no," she protested. "Surely not, I—"

But Lord Palmerton took a step forward. A tight smile pulled at his lips as he gave her an intense look, which he likely thought was supportive.

The strained force of it was not encouraging.

And again, Rafe was struck by that sense that something was amiss here.

The entire state of affairs felt strange, and suddenly he was deeply concerned for Charlotte.

Did she sing well?

Was Palmerton setting her up for failure?

After all, many times, people liked to compare cousins or sisters with each other, to show off one and abuse the other. He would not have Charlotte hurt or harmed.

Rafe took a step forward, but his mother gently touched his arm. "No, my dear, no, do not intervene yet. Charlotte is a quite capable young lady. Let her handle this, my dear."

"Palmerton does not act in her best interest in this."

His mother's expression did not change. "You may be right, but let us wait one moment and take Lady Charlotte's lead."

He swallowed, though it took everything in his power to hold himself back. "You are right," he whispered.

And then, Lady Charlotte stepped forward, her chin high and shoulders squared.

She crossed before the audience and stood in front of the pianoforte. "Francesca," she said, her voice shaking slightly. "Will you not play for me? You know I do not play well."

The admission startled the audience.

It was incredibly rare for a young lady to state that she did not do anything well. After all, young ladies of breeding were supposed to excel at everything they attempted, even if they did not.

Lady Francesca nodded and quickly crossed to the pianoforte and sat down. She looked pale, as if she was uncertain what might happen next. And she clearly did not feel as confident for Lady Charlotte as she had for herself.

The two whispered together.

He waited, his insides tense.

What would Lady Charlotte choose? Would it be some German opera, something French, something Italian? It was impossible to know. After all, ladies were versed in the most popular arias of the day. Their instructors knew well to keep them in fashion with the best composers from the Continent.

What would Lady Charlotte sing?

But as soon as the tune began, the entire audience fell hushed.

This was no great aria.

This was no work by a renowned composer. It was the most simple and melancholic and heartbreaking of country ballads being played from the lowest public house to the crossroads of England.

This tune had been played on accordions and fiddles, on tin whistles and sung without music behind it for the last several years on street corners.

Lady Charlotte turned her face to the crowd and opened her lips and sang with the purest heart. In all his life, he had never heard anything like it. It was no bright coloratura, no rich, dripping soprano. It was something so full of emotion that he felt the entire room gasp as she began the words of "Brokenhearted I'll Wander." As she began to sing about Boney, the cannon blasts, and the charge of her bonnie light horseman, tears filled her eyes.

And as he looked to the guests, he could scarce believe what was transpiring.

It was the most shocking thing. Young ladies were not supposed to emote in performance. And yet the passion of her words touched the hearts of the audience, for many of the lords and ladies in this room had sent sons to die in Spain.

Oh, they had been officers, but they had not been free of Napoleon's brutal columns or his booming guns. Many had been young cavalry men cut down in war, cut down before their youth could truly bloom.

The room fell completely silent as she sang the story.

And as he listened to her song and the

brokenhearted notes of the young woman who mourned for the loss of her love, how she longed to fly over the salt sea to her light horseman's grave, where she could be with him again, his own memory filled with the remembrance of faces.

The hundreds of faces of the young men with whom he had served who would never come home filled his mind. And suddenly he could not breathe.

Her passion, her sense of honor, and her grief filled him to his very core. Suddenly, he found himself stepping back against the wall.

His mother discreetly touched his hand. "My darling, are you all right?"

"Yes, Mama," he whispered hoarsely. "I'm as all right as anyone else in the room at this moment. She has captured us all."

"Indeed," his mother agreed. "Lady Charlotte has won this night. I think, perhaps, she has won their hearts for all nights to come."

CHAPTER TWENTY-THREE

When the last notes of the song resonated throughout the crowded salon, Charlotte realized that the room was now consumed with silence.

Swallowing, she gazed out at the rapt members of the *ton* who stared back at her, their eyes full of emotion.

She did not know what she had expected, but the amazement and now passionate applause was not it.

The clapping began slowly at first but soon became a crescendo that was nothing like the delicate, if enthusiastic, approval of Francesca.

This applause washed over her and was accompanied by the intense emotion of those in the room.

She pressed her lips together, wishing she could shout at them all to cease.

She swung her gaze to Palmerton, dreading what she would see there.

He looked enraged. His face was a mask of mottled fury.

Charlotte had been so sure that if she chose a simple country ballad, everyone would find her to be...embarrassing. Gauche, even. The *ton* would think her to be without culture, without importance, without intelligence.

Her voice was not trained. She did not have the skills to do the intricate play of scales that Francesca did, yet here she was with the entire company of Lady Greenway's guests in awe of her selection.

Much to her growing horror, many of them looked as if they had been touched deep within their souls and hearts by her song.

Tears gleamed in the eyes of many of the mamas and young ladies who had no doubt lost loved ones on the field of honor. Gentlemen stood, their faces strained with grief as they no doubt recalled sons, brothers, and fathers who would not return.

And suddenly she knew she had made a profound mistake.

She swung her gaze then to the duchess and to the duke.

They too were staring at her as if she was a revelation.

Something had just happened.

She did not know what it was, but the duke looked as if he might lie down at her feet in that moment and offer his heart up to her.

She wanted to take it—dear God, she wanted to take it—but she could not. She had to give that heart to Francesca.

Somehow, she had to find a way not to fail in this. And yet she *was* failing. Every day she tried to make him abandon her, and yet he would not. His heart was loyal and true. He could not be distracted by her distance. And she admired him deeply for his true nature.

Now? Now he looked as if he would follow her to the ends of the earth and back again.

And his passion for her, his admiration? It was more than she ever could have dreamed of in her little turret room.

But this dream was not for her. She'd never be allowed to have it.

Her own heart broke in that moment. It spasmed in protest against her ribs, and she couldn't draw breath.

She glanced back at Francesca, who was beaming with pride at her. And yet, there was a melancholy in her eyes, as if she knew that none of this would end well. Of course she knew.

After all, a happy ending for either her or Francesca seemed impossible with Palmerton in control of their fates.

Tears stung Charlotte's eyes, and she strode out of the room as quickly as she could.

Heavy steps followed behind her. She tried to outpace them, desperate for cool air and a moment alone to collect herself.

A hand grabbed her wrist in a viselike grip.

Palmerton whipped her about. "You are making a muck of this, girl."

"I know," she countered, unwilling to whimper as he no doubt wished. "I'm trying."

"Try harder," he growled quietly as he tugged her into the shadows of the hall.

"I will, but I need a moment."

And with that, she yanked her hand free from his bony grasp and left him open-mouthed and shocked by her defiance.

Charlotte strode down the hall as if the devil were on her heels, for it felt he was.

She stormed through the corridors, searching for a way out, when at last she spotted tall, open doors leading into the garden.

She dashed through them, then down past the stone balustrade, out into the moonlit night.

She crashed through the shrubberies, looking for isolation, for solitude. She did not care if she was risking scandal.

More the better if she found it! For if she was caught in scandal, she would not be able to marry the duke. She would be free of this whole situation. She would be free of lying to him and of having to drive him away.

She stopped abruptly as the thought crashed in on her. Once she succeeded at the task given to her, she would be free of Rockford, and her life would be so empty. Hollow. Bereft.

It was going to be so cold without him to warm her days. But she did not know what to do.

The sound of water trickling over stone filled her ears, and she realized she had entered the mouth of a hidden grotto.

The elaborate hiding spot was tucked away from view of the house. She'd wandered quite far through the elaborate gardens.

A single lantern flickered its ruby hue, welcoming those seeking solace. Charlotte drew in a deep breath, taking in the scent of damp stone and moss as she entered deeper into the beautiful embellishment that was as welcoming as a cocoon.

It was beautiful, this small space.

She had little doubt, given its discretion and distance from the house, it was a place meant for a lovers' tryst. She wrapped her arms about her, taking in the beautiful bench, which was laden with cushions and covered in a woven linen shawl.

It was a warm night, but she did not feel warm. She shivered with dread at what was to come.

What was she going to do? Why did poor people have such little power? And she was a girl to boot. Her options were few.

Palmerton could not be stopped.

Every tack she took seemed to backfire, too, as if the fates were determined that she not deviate from the path she'd been put on the day she'd met—

"Charlotte," a voice called softly behind her.

Rockford.

That deep rumble of a voice, like rushing water over river rock, skimmed her skin, and she closed her eyes.

For it filled her with agony and delight.

She wanted to drink in the sound of it. She wanted to never forget. She longed to embed it in her soul so that on cold nights when she was alone, she could take it out and remember that once she had been adored and wanted.

"Charlotte," he said again, "turn and face me, please."

Slowly, oh so slowly, against her own better judgment, she did as he bid. She did not meet his eyes. She could not. For if she did, she would be lost forever in a storm of emotion... Of love.

Yes, *love*; she dared name it. For that was what she had begun to feel, even on that first day, though she had resisted it.

She was falling in love with this man.

She had already lost her heart to him. She was no fool—she could not deny it. Nor would she try to deny it now. The look in his eyes when she had finished her song?

Yes, it was love she felt—a love she could not keep.

"Charlotte," he began, taking a step toward her. "Why have you forsaken me this week? Have I done something to hurt you?

Please allow me to apologize if I have. I promise that I will. I will make amends."

"No," she rushed, hating that he sought to blame himself. "You have not. It is not you. You are…"

"What?" he prompted gently, closing the distance between them so that his scent of citrus and leather mixed with the night. That heady aroma was intoxicating, and she longed to lean into him.

"You are more than I could have ever hoped for, Your Grace."

"More than you could have hoped for?" he asked softly, his brow furrowing as he clearly sought to understand. "You sound as if you are saying goodbye. Are you?"

She opened her mouth to say goodbye indeed. As she should. But found she could not. "I… Forgive me. I am out of sorts. The song."

"Yes," he breathed, "the song. You sang it so powerfully. Did you lose someone in the war?"

She shook her head. "No, I did not. But you see, I have missed my parents so terribly over the years that whenever I think of such a loss as in the song, I can imbue it with my grief."

"I am so very sorry, Lady Charlotte," he said sincerely. "I can see your pain."

She licked her lips, then dared to admit, "When I am alone in my room and the wind howls outside my window, my soul cries for the loss of love."

"I will give it back to you," he promised. "Let me, Lady Charlotte. Let me give you the love that you have lost."

"You cannot," she protested, her throat tightening. "It does not work that way, Your Grace."

He winced. "Please don't call me 'Your Grace,'" he cut in. "Rafe. You must call me Rafe."

"Oh, Rafe…" she whispered. Sorrow squeezed her heart in its painful grip. For all this was but a fleeting dream. A dream she could never have. "I cannot do this. You ask me to do something that I cannot do."

"What?" he asked, cocking his head to the side, which caused his dark hair to tease over his hard cheeks. "Love me? If you cannot learn to love me… *Charlotte*, I will let you go. But at least help me to understand why. I thought you felt as I did."

"I do. I can!" she rushed before she pressed her hands to her face, hating how conflicted she felt. She sucked in a sharp breath, lowered her hands, and said, "I do feel as you do. I have never met anyone like you, Rafe. You transcend your title. You are kind and you are good and you make me feel completely alive."

He was silent for a long moment, and then,

oh so gently, he took her gloved hand in his and wove their fingers together. "Then why have you avoided me this last week?"

The touch of his hand stole her resolve. It shoved her fears away. And suddenly she could not think of the consequences. "I cannot explain it. I thought... I think..."

"Yes?" he prompted, tracing her knuckles with his thumb.

The words slipped past her lips before she could stop herself: "I am not worthy of you."

"Charlotte," he rasped. "Don't you dare say it."

"Even if it is true?" she demanded.

He gazed down at her, seeming horrified by her admission. But then, his expression changed to one of determination, as if he would show her how well he thought of her. Of how much he desired her. And with that, he pulled her into his arms.

"I will not let you criticize yourself," he growled. "No one will speak ill of you, Charlotte. Not even you. Can you not see how glorious you are? Can you not see that you are better than any duchess? Any queen?"

Would he think such a thing when he knew the truth? The agony of it was almost too much.

He studied her face, his gaze darkening with his passion. "Yes, you walk upon the ground, Charlotte, but you make it glorious simply by being you."

"Rafe," she whispered as tears threatened to fill her eyes, "please don't."

"Please don't what?" he demanded softly. "Tell the truth? Tell you I adore you? Tell you that all I want to do is to know you, to give you what you desire, to make the dreams that you have a reality, and to be with you? I think you want to be with me, too."

He arched her into his body, holding her tight to him. "Tell me I am wrong."

She shook her head. Words were not necessary as she allowed herself to press into him and feel his hard muscles against her curves.

This was where she belonged. This was where she had always been meant to be.

With him.

She could not have it. Not always. But now? She could not tell him lies.

At her surrender to his hold, Rafe's lips took hers, soft, tantalizing. He worked magic over her, a spell of desire and seduction. He trailed kisses over her cheeks, gently pressing her eyelids, her forehead, the place where her hair met her brow.

And then his mouth was back upon hers, stealing her breath, giving her his. Her mouth opened, and the soft caress of his tongue touched hers. She could not have imagined the hypnotic temptation that he could offer her.

No story or penny novel could have prepared her for his kiss.

It was beyond imagining.

When his arms stole about her body, his hands splaying over her ribs, she knew that she wanted all of him.

She wanted all of him tonight, because if she did not have him, here, in this grotto, she might never know him. She wrapped her arms about his shoulders and kissed him as passionately as she could, given how little she knew about kissing.

At the tantalizing dance of their kisses, she moaned into his mouth and allowed her body to be bowed as he bent her over.

His hand slid to her buttocks, cupping her through her silk gown, and he rocked her hips to the hard evidence of his desire.

And suddenly, Rafe began to pull back. "We must go to the house."

"No," she said, holding tightly to him. "Please don't leave me."

"But Charlotte," he whispered against her ear.

"No, I don't wish to stop," she declared vehemently. "Please show me. Show me what can be between us. I need to know."

Though he appeared mystified, she knew exactly what she was saying, and his eyes widened.

"You wish me to…"

"Yes," she urged, "I wish you to take me. Here and now. Don't hold back." She lifted her hand to his cheek and looked deeply into his eyes, determined to make him understand how much she needed this. "Promise me you won't hold back."

"I promise, Charlotte," he said simply. "I will hold nothing back if that is what you want. But—"

"No," she cut in, placing her gloved forefinger against his mouth. "There will be no buts this night. There will only be yes."

CHAPTER TWENTY-FOUR

In all his life, Rafe had never agreed to do something that could lead him into dishonor. And he was determined that this interlude between himself and Charlotte would not, either.

Tonight, in the silver moonlight with the stars shining high above London city, tucked in the grotto, he knew she was giving him her innocence.

He was in awe of the gift.

But it was something that he had sworn he would never do to a young lady outside of matrimony. It was not the kind of man he was. Oh, there was no question that he'd been a rake.

His years at Oxford, on the Continent, and after seeing the wars in Spain? He'd indulged in the carnal sports, just as other young lords did.

But he had never stepped off the honorable path into the darkness like this. Gentlemen did not risk the reputation of unmarried ladies.

But she was going to be his.

And it was what she was demanding of him, what she wanted, and who was he to deny her what she so claimed to wish?

And he wished it, too. There was no questioning it. In his mind, he was certain that if he did this for her, if he gave her what she wanted, she would be his.

It was clear to him now.

Much to his relief and happiness, she *did* want him. She'd freely admitted she could love him. And this? Here, their bodies twining with passion, was the moment of declaration for both of them.

Reason had been abandoned when he had stolen her lips with his kiss.

He let his fingertips trail over her face, lingering along the line of her chin. Rafe splayed his hand along her jaw, pressed his thumb to her chin, and tilted her head back.

"I will want you," he confessed, "for all my years, and I cannot tell you how glad I am that you bashed me with that brick. You woke me up, Charlotte. I was sleeping, and I don't ever want to go to sleep again."

Her eyes shone with emotion in the moonlight that spilled into the grotto, mixing with the lantern.

"Kiss me," she urged simply. "Please."

He ignored the fact that she did not reply to him in kind.

He ignored the fact that she made no bold pledge like he had to her, but she had begun this foray into their intimacy.

She had told him what her heart felt and

how she thought of him. And that had to be enough. Surely, it could be enough. For now.

This was just the beginning for them. This was the moment when love began. He lowered his mouth to hers, taking it in a searing kiss, determined to devour her, to awaken her as he had been awakened. To make her body light with hunger. And with the slow kiss, her mouth opened, and she arched her breasts into his chest.

Her hands slid up his shoulders and into the hair at the nape of his neck, and he loved the feel of it.

Charlotte pulled him down toward her as if she could brand herself with his mouth. He took that passion of hers and fanned the flames with slow caresses and open-mouthed kisses.

Slowly, he walked back toward the wide cushion-covered stone bench in the darkest shadows of the grotto. A place designed for lovers.

He lowered himself to the bench and pulled her between his legs. He trailed his hands over her hips and gazed up into her eyes.

Her face had transformed to one awakened with hunger. Hunger for him.

In one quick move, Rafe pulled her onto his lap. A gasp escaped her lips, and he placed a kiss on the curve where her neck met her shoulder.

She groaned and tilted her head back, offering the sensitive spot to him.

"This is what you want?" he murmured against her skin.

She blew out a shaking breath. "Could I be any plainer?"

"No," he said, teasing her, slipping her capped sleeve from her nearly bare shoulder, biting her ever so slightly. He paused, then lifted his gaze to hers. "You could not. But Charlotte," he said softly, "I have never done anything like this."

Her eyes lit with amusement for a moment. "I do not believe that to be true," she countered.

"No," he said with a groan. "That is not what I mean. I will not have either of us regretting this. I cannot go back from this, nor can you."

Her face grew serious, and she cupped his jaw and stroked her thumb over the hard lines of his cheekbones. "I don't wish to. You are all I want."

His eyelids grew heavy, and desire pulsed through the length of his body, her words the most erotic thing he could hear at this moment. "That is all that I needed to hear."

And then he kissed her again, winding his arms about her body, and he knew in that moment that he had found the love he had sought his whole life.

That he would never feel alone again. That he had found his mate, and that the future that now awaited him was bright and hopeful. She would no longer avoid him. She would no longer be distant, and all that he had feared would disappear. Replaced by the possibility of love.

He kissed her again and again, letting their breaths intermingle as he slid his hands down her back, stroking it lightly.

She tilted her head, giving him better access to kiss more deeply. And then he swung her around, bracing her so that she could lie back on the covered bench.

She gasped with surprise.

"Is that all right?" he asked. "Is it uncomfortable?"

She laughed softly. "No, it is not uncomfortable. I have slept on far worse."

He frowned.

The admission seemed strange to him. She had slept on anything worse than a feather bed? Surely not.

But before he could allow this distraction, her hand went to his cravat and tugged at it. "How the devil do you get this thing off?" she asked.

He smiled slowly. "Let me show you."

CHAPTER TWENTY-FIVE

Rafe eased her back onto the soft cushions draped over the bench. He gazed down at her, hunger in his dark eyes.

She could scarce draw breath at the sight of the desire upon his face and the promise of what was to come.

He circled his hand around her silk-stockinged ankle. Taking his time, he dragged that hand up over her calf. His fingertips slid under her skirts, skimming over her knee.

And then his hand was tracing over her thigh, slipping upward to the soft center between her legs.

When he gently met her most intimate place, her lips parted with amazement.

Her eyes widened as she studied him, stunned by his actions.

"What are you doing?" she breathed.

"Giving you pleasure," he replied easily.

"Pleasure?" she queried. She'd felt nearly undone by his kisses, pulled by some unknown force to share this intimacy with him. But pleasure? The feelings coursing through her body now seemed almost impossible. Could she feel more pleasure than this?

He nodded, hair wild from her earlier forays with her hands. "I promise if I pay attention to you, if I listen to your body, this will give you pleasure indeed."

"I want you," she whispered.

"And I you," he returned, his voice a low rumble of passion. "But I will think little of myself if I do not bring you bliss, Charlotte."

She sucked in a sharp breath at his proclamation that felt more like a vow than anything else.

She nodded, and then his fingers slipped to her folds.

As he realized her body was slick, he let out a low growl of appreciation before using that slick, wet heat to tease her.

The sensation that came over her then was powerful and drove her nearly wild with hunger.

Her whole body seemed alive at his ministrations. It was as if he knew exactly how to touch her, the spot to find, and the pressure to apply to take her thoughts away and leave her nothing but sensation.

Rafe leaned down and took her mouth in an open-mouthed kiss as he kept circling his strong fingers over her, relentlessly teasing her beyond all possible imagining.

She gripped his shoulders instinctually, holding tight as though if she let him go this would all disappear and she would find herself waking up alone and cold in her turret room.

But she wasn't alone. Or cold. She was here, hot with hunger for him. And he was gazing down at her as if she were the center of the world.

Was this the secret, then? What could happen between a man and a woman? Or was it something that could only happen between her and Rafe? Whatever it was, she wanted it. Beyond all things.

Beyond reason.

Charlotte felt as if she was completely possessed by the need to let him touch her however he pleased. For it seemed what pleased him…was what pleased her.

And it was so perfect.

His tongue teased the inside of her mouth, dancing with her own tongue, matching the rhythm of his fingers below.

And then he was kissing her down the line of her throat, working his way down to the swells of her breasts. She drove her hands into his thick hair, arching up, reaching toward something she couldn't quite understand.

A growl of pleasure slipped past his lips, his breath hot against her skin. And then his fingers pressed and circled with a different pace and ever so slightly more pressure over her slick heat.

An intense cry escaped her lips, which he muffled with a wild kiss.

As her muscles tightened and wave after wave of bliss pulsed from her core, she held tightly onto his shoulders, needing his power to truly give in to this moment.

Rafe's breath was ragged and wild as her release took her.

At her surrender to his touch, he seemed to have lost all sense of reason and logic.

His hands worked swiftly at the buttons of his breeches.

She drew in slow breaths, but she did not feel complete. She needed something more. And as he eased his body over hers, she felt the hard tip of his sex slide against her slick entrance.

This was what she wanted more than anything in the whole world—to experience this with him.

This was her only chance, she knew deep in her bones, to have him, to have this here in a hidden garden, London's silver moon spilling in, the scent of flowers in the air.

With all the magic that one might hope between a lady and a duke, she was amazed by her own boldness at seizing this moment.

Rafe eased her thighs apart and rested his hips between them.

He rubbed that hard shaft up and down her slick, hot core. She couldn't believe how incredible it felt, that friction.

Charlotte bit her lower lip and let out a

low moan, her body straining toward him, urging him on.

The pleasure that had just come to her seemed nothing now with the promise of their union.

She widened her thighs, desiring him to take her.

She'd read about risks that many lords and ladies were willing to take to play bed games. And she understood the technical parts of what was to take place.

After all, she had read many novels that had discussed the subject, but this did not seem real or possible.

At this moment, nothing seemed real or possible.

With the duke, everything felt as if it was a dream. And she refused to wake. Yes, she was savoring this dream, giving into it and indulging it.

When he thrust against her, she let out a stifled and surprised exclamation of pain. He was large; the pressure was immense.

Rafe let out a rough exhale but hesitated.

He dipped his head and kissed her softly. The kiss distracted her from the intensity, the fullness his body created in her.

And then he began to rock back and forth. Oh, so slowly, his hands skimmed over her body, teasing her, tossing her into temptation again.

His mouth kissed again and again, softly, then wildly. Each kiss meant to make her drunk with need. His hips rolled, causing his pelvis to tease against her sensitive spot.

And the pressure that had built so intensely began to dissipate.

"This may hurt," he whispered against her lips.

"I don't care," she whispered back.

She was familiar with suffering and pain, and he had given her so much pleasure that a moment of pain seemed nothing.

Rafe nodded, his face tense with his own concentration and promise of wild satisfaction.

He rocked his hips back, then thrust deep in one smooth move. Her fingers dug into his shoulders, and her entire body tensed around him.

It did hurt. One sharp pierce of it…then it was gone. She stared up at him, amazed that the pain was already gone.

Rafe held still for a moment, gazing down upon her face, studying her to see if he had gone too far.

But he had not. She knew he had not gone even close to far enough. She wanted what came next, and so she parted her lips and urged, "Do not cease."

. . .

Rafe did as she desired, nearly overcome with the power of their bodies moving together.

Though he was the one with experience, she was in command. For it was she who had made it clear that this was what she wanted, to be taken in the garden, before their declaration of union.

And he was more than happy to give in to his pleasure, in to the passion that brewed between them. And soon, he'd have her always.

Her slick, wet heat circled him, and he could barely hold himself together as he caressed the inside of her body.

Knowing that she desired him so much, feeling her body so ready and tight?

It was both heaven and hell. Heaven because of the promise of coming, and hell because it was agonizing to be as careful as he needed with her untried body.

Her muscles squeezed around him, bringing him delicious intensity as he rocked against her.

Her breathing changed, and her hips began to arch to meet his thrusts, proof of her growing desire.

Rafe embraced her and increased his pace to a seductive rhythm. He wanted her to never forget this, and not just because it was her first time.

He wanted her to remember the pleasure

that he could give her, the way he could make her feel.

And so, he began to increase the tempo, undulating, hitting that spot he knew would bring her the most bliss. He slid his fingers between them, stroking that sweet spot that he had found only moments before.

Just as he intended, her core began to ripple and tighten around him.

Her eyes widened with shock. And then she let out a cry, his name upon her lips and her legs circled about his hips.

That very movement, that claiming of him as she circled her legs about his body, drove him over the edge.

Rafe pulled back and thrust home in one solid glide. He held her tight, shuddering against her, barely able to think, barely able to breathe.

Her name was a whisper of adoration on his lips.

This was what he had been looking for his whole life.

This moment and all the moments he knew were there in the future.

Rafe kept her in his arms as waves of bliss brought delicious shocks through his body.

This was just the beginning for them. And he felt a happiness that he had never known. He'd found love. Just as he'd always hoped.

CHAPTER TWENTY-SIX

Only the sound of water slipping down the sides of the stone grotto filled the silence as they dressed each other carefully.

Charlotte's heart was breaking open in this moment.

She did not know what to say to him. He looked so hopeful, so happy. She did not feel happy, though. After all, she could not keep him. She had only borrowed her happiness. Now, she had to let it go.

She had misled him in this. She knew that he thought she was giving herself to him, not just this night, but forever. Just as he had promised to love her for the rest of her life. But she could not do the same.

She daren't.

There was too much at risk, too much danger.

Or could she?

What if she dared to throw her lot in with him? What if she married him in defiance of Palmerton? Wouldn't Rafe protect her? Wouldn't he protect them all?

But he did not know the truth.

It shot through her then—like lightning, the pain laced through her body. She had not told him the truth before she had given herself to him. He thought her a lady. He thought her so many things that she was not.

Why hadn't she had the courage to tell him?

But she knew why. She'd deliberately withheld the truth.

She had wanted this too much. She had wanted to see the adoration in his eyes. She had needed to have this one night with him where she had given herself freely and he had given himself without holding back.

If she had told him the truth that she was no lady, that she was barely more than a serving girl, she might never have had this. He might have looked at her with disdain and disgust.

Oh, no, he would not disdain her because she was a servant. But a duke such as he? He would never love someone who had no position in society. He *couldn't*.

This was no fairy tale. Nor a novel churned out by the writers she so adored.

Rafe's whole life had trained him for power.

And now, she had gone too far. The lie had gone too deep.

How she wished the world was different. That her circumstances were different.

Rafe laced her gown at the back and took her hand in his.

"We must go back now," he said.

She nodded. "Of course."

"Are you in any pain?" he asked, smoothing her gown into place.

She smiled tentatively, though her soul was heavy. "No, I am not."

As a matter of fact, her body felt liquid. Almost perfect. The way he had loved and worshiped her had transported her. But now she was coming back to the earth.

And these were her last moments with him.

She gasped for air.

"I am sorry if this has overwhelmed you," he said. "Perhaps it was a—"

"No," she protested. "It was not a mistake, but…"

"But what?" He gazed down at her with concern. "I thought you said no buts."

She forced a smile. "No buts. And no regrets."

Then he lifted her hand and brought it to his lips. "My love, please, tell me that we will announce our marriage tomorrow night at my mother's ball. It will give me a great deal of relief to hear you say yes."

Her mouth dried. More lies. They stuck in her throat. She swallowed and managed, "It has been a most confusing week. None of this has come to be as I thought it might."

"Nor I," he said gently. "I had no idea that morning when I was walking in Southwark that my life would change forever. For the better."

She nodded. She could not reply. And she couldn't lie anymore.

Her life had not changed for the better, but she would not regret knowing him. No doubt, after this night, her life would be one unrelenting hell, but she would never forget him. Oh, how she wished she could find a way to save Francesca and the servants who had been her family. Palmerton would destroy them without hesitation if she failed in her task. She could never marry the duke—not after the lies she'd told. He would hate her. And rightly.

She dreaded the look of loathing on his face that would drive away his tenderness when he learned the truth. She was going to have to let him go to save Francesca and her dear ones, but she would hold this night and all their moments together close to her heart.

She would try to make amends somehow. She did not know how, but somehow, she would find a way to show him that she had not used him—that she was doing what she was doing because she *had* to.

And that she'd simply wished to feel loved by someone like him once in her life.

As he led her back up toward the house and into the light, she paused and said, "We must not go in together. It would cause too great a scandal."

He laughed softly. "I don't want anyone thinking I'm marrying you because I have to," he said. "You make a good point. Shall I go in and then you?"

She nodded firmly. "I think that a very good idea."

He started for the stone stairs but then hesitated. With the glow of the house behind him and the scent of lilacs in the air, he smiled a slow smile. "Charlotte," he said, "I love you."

Those words, which should have filled her with joy, made her ache so intensely she nearly cried out.

Though she knew she shouldn't say it, she could not stop herself. "I love you, too, Rafe," she whispered. "Thank you."

"Thank you?" he queried, his brows rising. "For what?"

She swallowed, hoping he would think of her last words to him and not the way she had misled him. "You have shown me how beautiful this world can be. You have shown me that the promise of love still exists even when those around you would try to take it from you."

"Charlotte, I will show you every day from this one to our last how loved you are," he vowed, his voice deep with his intention.

The wind rustled through the trees and

danced through her hair. She looked away, pretending to push her hair out of her face, unable to meet his gaze.

He was envisioning them growing old together, sitting in front of one of his houses, watching their children and their grandchildren play.

It was a fantasy.

Something that would never occur, but she would not take it from him this night.

"Go," she urged.

"Soon, you will be mine, my love."

She said nothing but watched as he strode back into the Greenway townhouse, his shoulders back, his head high as if he were walking on air.

She wished she felt the same.

She was crashing. Crashing from the heights he'd taken her to. And soon she would be crushed upon the ground.

Agony at their parting filled her, but she would not regret this night for anything.

"Good God, girl. What an actress you are," Palmerton mocked from the darkness.

She jolted and nearly tripped as she spotted him in the shadows of the balustrade. Fear laced through her blood. What had Palmerton seen? What did he intend?

"Come along, Charlotte," he said. "I think it is time to pay the piper."

"You speak in riddles, sir," she bit out.

He stepped out of the shadows, his gaze narrowing. "You have failed. You have only made him love you more this night. Everything that I asked you to do, you have failed. You are a complete and utter failure."

"I am not a failure," she snapped, pouring all her pain onto her guardian. "It is *you* that is the failure. You are cruel and selfish, and you know nothing of love."

"Love," he echoed coldly. "Love means nothing in this life. It gets you nowhere and nothing. All that matters is status, money, and prestige."

She let out a harsh breath as something struck her. "Did you love my mother at all?"

He made no reply. And that was her answer.

The realization that she had been in the care of a man who'd never felt anything for her poor mama seemed particularly cruel.

No wonder he'd never shown Charlotte the smallest kindness. "You did not deserve her," she declared.

With her condemnation, a muscle tensed in his jaw, and he grabbed her hand. "I will never allow you to marry Rockford, Charlotte. I have another plan for you."

"He is not going to marry Francesca," she pointed out harshly.

"Perhaps not," he agreed. "Perhaps it might be too late for that, but that does not mean that all my plans are dashed."

Dread pooled in her stomach. "What possible plan could you have now?"

"Oh, Charlotte," he said as if he despised how foolish he thought her to be. "I have had this plan since you were a child, but I did not think that I would have to act upon it so soon. You have pushed me into a corner, and now," he said, "the plan is in action. You will not be going to the ball tomorrow night, and you certainly will not be announcing any sort of marriage."

"No," she replied. "I did not think that I would."

"You know," he said with a hint of a smile. "I had no idea that you had such talents for duplicity. The poor duke is absolutely besotted. In another life, you might rival me for it. And it is a good thing, because you are going to convince your darling duke that you are desperately in love with someone else, and that is why you cannot marry him."

She shook her head, not understanding.

"Deeply, my dear. You've been in love with him for years. Admiring him and longing for him since you were a child," he all but crooned. "You will tell the duke and the duchess that, though you could not resist the duke's charms and handsome face, it is my son whom you have always loved. And of course, once Phillip learned that you might be taken? He proposed, and now all your dreams have come true."

"I am not in love with your son," she growled, taking a step back.

"Oh, Charlotte, you know that doesn't matter." He took a step toward her, negating the one she took to get farther from him. "You are going to marry Phillip."

"No," she said, panic rising up in her. "I am not. He's a bully, and he is—"

"The only man you will ever marry. I promise you that."

Palmerton's hand darted out and seized her.

She opened her mouth to scream, but he clapped his free hand over her lips, muffling the sound.

Panic raced through her brain, muddling her thoughts as she struggled to breathe. She couldn't let him take her. She couldn't allow him to get away with destroying her life.

She struggled to get away, but he pinched her nose and pressed his palm over her lips. And as he hauled her back into the shadows, she understood that she had been right.

There would be no happy ending for a girl like herself.

CHAPTER TWENTY-SEVEN

The family engagement rings were strewn out over Rafe's desk. He peered at each of them carefully, trying to decide which one would be ideal for Charlotte. He wanted to find the perfect one—the one that matched her; the one that would show the world how beautiful she was, both inside and out.

He picked up an opal, then placed it down on the velvet cloth upon which the jewels were nestled.

Carefully, he contemplated a large emerald that shone and sparkled with green fire inside its depths.

He then turned to a diamond. It glistened and spoke of a cold, stunning beauty.

It did not match Charlotte at all, so he easily glanced over it.

The seriousness of the moment weighed on him, for he was determined to find the jewel that would meet her approval and cause her eyes to light.

And then at last he set his eyes upon the sapphire—the sapphire that had been his grandmother's engagement ring. It was large, with diamonds surrounding it.

At first glance, it appeared too large for Charlotte, but he knew in his heart that her personality, her soul, and her heart were larger than what society might imagine.

And a jewel of this magnitude would match that. She would not be overwhelmed by it. No, she would wield it.

He picked it up, stared into the beautiful, dancing lights within the stone, and held it up to the candlelight. Yes, this was the one.

He could scarce believe it. He was going to ask her.

As soon as he had permission from her father, he was going to ask her to be his duchess.

Each day had proven how much he liked her—more than anyone in London, more than anyone in England, more than anyone he had ever met before. And he wasn't going to risk losing that. He lifted the wine goblet beside him, took a drink, and allowed himself to smile as the possibility of love finally felt within his reach.

All his life, he'd had to be careful. People pursued him, oftentimes hiding their true selves to gain favor with him. Everyone always cared what a duke thought. Everyone always tried to appeal to him, to appear as if they were of the same mind.

Often, they hid what they thought he wouldn't like.

But not Charlotte.

Charlotte was always herself with him,

telling him things he did not always like but needed to hear.

And he loved that about her.

He loved the fact that she did not try to hide her spirit, her inestimable soul. And that...that was the greatest gift anyone could have given him.

The door to his study opened, and his butler coughed. "Your Grace."

"Yes, Wooster," he said, pulling himself out of his musings and hopes.

"There is a note for you."

He winced, hoping it was not from the halls of government. Or worse. Could someone have been hurt? "It is an emergency?"

"Yes, my lord," his butler said firmly. "It came hand-delivered by a footman, and I was told to give it to you immediately."

"Well, then hand it over," he urged, stretching out his palm, his ruby signet ring shining bloodred in the shadows.

Wooster crossed quickly and handed him the small envelope, which had been sealed with red wax.

He took it and stared at the family name. *Faraday.*

Good God.

Charlotte's family.

Had something gone awry?

"Thank you, Wooster," he said flatly, his insides coiling with a strange anticipation.

Perhaps Charlotte's father was eager to approve? "That will be all. I'll call for you in a moment if a reply is necessary."

Wooster nodded. "Yes, Your Grace."

Rafe waited until his butler had retreated into the hall.

He stared at the creamy, folded parchment.

A great wariness washed over him, a sense of dread. Had her father said no? Surely not. But what would warrant such a missive in the middle of the night?

Or perhaps he was simply so excited for his daughter to marry a duke and become a duchess that he had not been able to wait and had sent the reply by footman.

Rafe snapped the wax and quickly unfolded the parchment. His eyes danced over the scrawled black words, and his stomach sank with horror. He could not draw a breath as he read and reread the words.

He grabbed his glass of red wine, lifted it to his lips, and drank it to the dregs. It couldn't be. The words couldn't be true. But he read them again and again, willing the words to change.

Your Grace,
Of course, I should be happy for you to marry my daughter, but since you have never met her, I think that we should begin a line of conversation about your intentions. If you

wish to marry my daughter truly, then of course I will be happy to make the arrangements for you to meet her, court her, and ascertain whether you are a happy couple. But I do not see how you could admire her turn of phrase and her spirit, since I do not think that you have ever been in a room with her, and certainly not in the last month…

The words scoured his soul, leaving him bereft and empty of hope.

It couldn't be true, and yet it had to be; Lord Faraday had no reason to lie. Which meant his Lady Charlotte was…who? Confusion rocked him, leaving him shaken to his core.

Who the bloody hell was the woman he'd met outside the Marshalsea?

A con? Surely not, for she lived with Lady Francesca.

But she was a liar. And an excellent one.

He crumpled the paper in his fist, not certain what to do. The jewels before him now seemed to mock him, and he sucked in a harsh breath as pain hit him.

Love. He'd thought he found love. He'd found lies instead.

Rafe's mouth dried.

Slowly, he turned to the fire as everything he thought he'd known, everything he thought he'd understood slipped away from him.

Fool that he was, he'd been so certain she had finally been the one to be truthful and honest with him, but in fact, she had lied the most.

For he did not even know her real name.

• • •

Shimmying down the side of the house with a rope provided by Stevenson, in the pouring rain, in the dead of night, was far more difficult than Charlotte had anticipated.

Of course, she would have preferred to go through the house, but Palmerton had locked her in. And no one had a spare key. Certainly not Mary or Cook.

Palmerton did not trust them. The lock had been surprisingly elaborate, and no attempt had managed to unlatch it.

Descent via the face of the house had become the only option.

And Stevenson had stepped in, managing to get a rope with a stone tied to the end through her window. It had been quite a feat of aim and skill in throwing.

Charlotte's feet hit the muddy ground, and Stevenson clasped her hand.

"Come, Charlotte," he urged, and despite his age, he ran into the night with her.

He hailed a hackney cab at the road, and she climbed in with the older man, desperate to explain things to the duke as best she could.

She knew that she could not escape her fate, but at least she could make certain that she did not completely abandon him and leave him thinking the worst.

Though Charlotte had wanted to avoid telling him the truth, to spare those close to her, that was no longer possible. If she allowed him to think what Palmerton wished? Surely, he would hate her for the rest of his life. And it felt as if a danger was growing as the lies increased, as Palmerton held her in his control.

And she could no longer bear the idea that he would think her the cruelest of schemers who had no care for him.

That she had used him in the most brutal of ways — she could not leave him thinking that.

The hackney raced through the London streets, and with each mile, her heart hammered against her ribs.

The city was dark with few lights now, and as soon as the hackney halted before the duke's impressive townhouse, she gave Stevenson a hug.

The older man kissed the top of her head. "Be true to yourself, my pet. I know you wish to keep us all safe. But Palmerton is the devil, and deals cannot be made with him."

She nodded against his chest, focusing on his even heartbeat. How she wished she could follow his advice entirely.

Dealing with the devil was dangerous indeed. And she was in quite deep.

Still dripping wet, Charlotte climbed down from the rented conveyance, grateful that it would be waiting for her with Stevenson to comfort her when the duke threw her out.

Drawing upon her reserves of strength, she mounted the steps and banged on the front door.

The butler wrenched the door open and gazed upon her with dignified horror. "May I help you, young woman?" he demanded, clearly appalled that a drowned rat of a girl might try to gain admittance to such an establishment in the middle of the night.

"I am here to see the duke," she explained.

"The duke does not see strange young ladies at night." And with that, the butler slammed the door shut.

She stood underneath the portico, tears slipping down her face. What was she going to do? She needed to see him. She banged on the door again, and a voice yelled, "Go away!"

"Please!" she hollered. "Tell him Lady Charlotte wishes to see him."

There was a long pause on the other side of the door. "Wait a moment," the butler called at last.

And after several moments, the door

swung open on its well-oiled hinges, and Rafe stood in the candle glow.

"Charlotte," he rushed, though his face appeared grim. "What in God's name are you doing? What has happened? Is Lady Francesca all right?"

He was so kind to worry for her. It only made her realize how lucky she had been to meet him and how wrong it had been to hide the truth from him.

"Francesca is perfectly fine," she assured, her insides tightening with an ever-growing anticipation that her world was about to come crashing down around her. "But I must speak to you."

Her voice nearly broke on her last words.

He held out his hand. "Come in."

She took his outstretched palm, knowing it was likely the last chance she'd have to touch him.

Quickly, he led her to his study.

A fire crackled in the hearth, and he brought her before it. He whipped her soaked cloak off and began rubbing her arms.

He did not notice her gown—how simple it was, how it was clearly not the gown of a lady.

No, he merely tried to warm her, pulling her before the fire, staring at her. It broke her heart.

The silence that stretched between them

was filled only by the crackling fire, until at last he said, "Why are you here?"

She licked her lips, shaking now. "I have to tell you the truth."

"The truth?" He tensed for a moment, his voice hollow, completely unlike the rich tones to which she had grown accustomed. "What truth? What could you possibly tell me that would send you out in the middle of the night in the pouring rain?"

"Rafe," she began, "I am not who you think I am."

He stared at her, his hands stilling. "You aren't Lady Charlotte Faraday," he stated flatly.

"No," she rushed, the words trying to tumble out of her. "I am not."

A muscle tightened in his jaw. "Go on."

His response was so…strange. His face— his beautiful, kind face—was a mask as if he was expecting a blow.

And her heart cracked further, aching so intensely she almost could not speak. He was *expecting* this. How?

She swallowed. "I cannot live with these lies any longer, and I do not have much time. Palmerton will be here very soon, when he finds I'm missing."

He glanced toward his study door before he drew in a quick breath.

"Rafe," she bit out, forcing herself to say it.

"I am not—"

"I know." He leaned back. "Explain it to me. Go on. I want to understand."

But his voice was cold, as if he was readying himself to have his heart ripped asunder.

He flinched. "I don't even know your name."

The air rushed out of her lungs. "I—"

"I'm accustomed to being lied to. But I thought you…" He winced, then steeled himself. "I will listen to your explanations. I'm not a monster. But Charlotte… Is your name even Charlotte?" he ground out.

"That is my name," she whispered, hating the separation darkening his eyes. "But it is not *Lady* Charlotte. It is just Charlotte. The house was my mother's, but she was not particularly important. My stepfather married her, and her fortune was not as great as he hoped. And I have lived in his house since my mother's death. He inherited it, of course, but I—"

He was looking at her as if she had transformed into an enemy. "Cease, Charlotte."

She squared her shoulders and kept going. "I have cleaned the rooms. I have cleaned the chimneys. I have baked bread. I have swept the floors—"

"Stop, Charlotte," he said more forcefully. "You make no sense. What do you mean? You are some sort of servant in his house?"

She gave a tight nod.

His gaze narrowed. "But you said he was your uncle, did you not?"

"He is not my uncle," she confessed as she realized that the tangle of her lies might be too hard to untie. "I am not Francesca's cousin. She is my stepsister. I lied to you."

"Why in God's name would you do that?" he rasped, his voice shaking, and for a moment the intensity of his emotion broke through. "Make me understand."

"Do you remember? When we met and when you first came to see Francesca?" she asked. "You would not stop. You kept insisting on knowing me when no one else wanted to know me, when no one else cared about me except Francesca and the other servants in the house."

His hands fell to his side as he stared at her. "That is why you didn't tell me?" He shook his head, clearly struggling to make sense of the muddy events. And then betrayal dawned in his eyes as he met her gaze. "You've lied to me. Almost from the first moment we met. At Vauxhall. When you showed me your mother's house. The hospital. And when we made—"

His voice broke and his shoulders sank before he said, "Did you think I would think so little of you? Did you think so little of me?"

A wave of horror crashed over her as he laid out her duplicity, a duplicity she had chosen to protect people, but he was not wrong. Her breath caught in her throat as she willed herself not to give up yet.

Boldly, she took his hands in hers and held on tightly. "No one cares about me, Rafe. No one loves me, save Francesca and Cook and Stevenson and Mary. I have lived in the servants' quarters of that house since my mother died when I was five, and I had never been to a party before. I did not learn to dance because I am not a lady," she rushed, letting all her fear and all her passion pour out before him. "I cannot sing an aria because I have not been raised to perform before the *ton*. I've never had a tutor. I have dressed Francesca for every outing she has ever had. I am virtually her lady's maid. I am a charity case, kept from the orphans' asylum through Palmerton's allowance."

His face creased with confusion. "How am I to believe…"

"I've been lying to you from the moment I met you, but not out of malice or manipulation. I've lied out of fear," she said bluntly. "I am not someone you can marry, Rafe. I never was."

And before she could say another word, the door jolted open and Palmerton strode in.

Her stepfather's eyes were wild as he

assessed them. But then he stopped and straightened. He lowered his head as if struck by tragedy.

"She's told you the truth, then?" Palmerton asked softly.

Rafe's gaze narrowed with fury. "She has told me that she is but a servant in your house, Palmerton, and certainly not the daughter of Faraday. Explain yourself."

Palmerton *tsk*ed. "She is lying, again, Your Grace. She is often muddled, and she is, unfortunately, a young lady who excels at lies. I had hoped she was improving. You see, even now, she does not have the courage to tell you the truth, and so she's making up some wild fabrication. A servant?" Palmerton scoffed.

Rafe's face darkened with his doubts, his betrayal palpable as he took in Palmerton and then Charlotte.

Charlotte felt her heart hammering against her ribs, still terrified by her stepfather and what he was capable of. His very presence awakened fear within her. Fear of his temper and what he might do.

Palmerton gave Charlotte a wounded look. "The very idea is ludicrous. Now, Charlotte, I will take you home. You've done enough."

"Charlotte," Rafe whispered, repeating, "I don't understand."

"I have come, and I have told you the truth," she declared. "But know this: what I felt has been no lie."

Rafe's tortured gaze met hers. "I—"

"Charlotte," Palmerton cut in abruptly as he stepped forward, silencing her. "I have Stevenson downstairs. Go to him."

Those simple words. They cut through the air like a knife. A warning. A clear warning that she must obey or the consequences would be dire.

He had Stevenson hostage. And no doubt, Stevenson would be harmed if she did not go with Palmerton now.

"It is enough," Rafe ground out. "Palmerton—"

"No, Your Grace," she whispered, even as the agony of having to let him go coursed through her. "He is right. I must go. I have misled you again and again. Please forgive me."

She curtsied to him, horrified that her stepfather had won. She'd been so certain she could defeat him this time. Defeat him with the truth.

But not when he held someone she loved in his clutches. And not when Rafe was caught up in the turmoil of the lies she had spun. If she could go back to the day he had called upon Francesca, she would. But there was no going back.

With that, she whirled around and stumbled out of the room.

. . .

"I will send you more information once a doctor has come and assessed her, Your Grace," Palmerton stated. "But I must go with her now. She's in no state to be alone."

Rafe stared blankly, his whole world crumbling around him.

She had left as swiftly as she had come.

"I should go after her," he ground out, trying to make sense of what had just unfolded.

"No, Your Grace," Palmerton said firmly. "She may become hysterical. She needs laudanum and rest."

"What?" he rasped. He could not get his balance.

She was a servant. That was why she had lied to him?

It had felt the utmost betrayal, receiving that letter. But he understood. He wasn't bloody well going to judge her for being afraid of a duke if she was a servant.

But now, Palmerton was suggesting she had lied about that, too?

"Explain," he bit out.

Palmerton's shoulders sagged. "I told you her mother was not well. Charlotte is often the same. She cannot help herself. It is why I've kept her away from society. It had seemed meeting you had a calming effect."

"But why did you accept her ruse?"

"Humiliation. I could not bear to humiliate my daughter. I planned on telling you. But if I am honest, I hoped you would see that Charlotte was not well, in time, and still consider Francesca. I was a fool. But I also wanted to protect my poor Charlotte. She begged me not to tell you. She swore she'd confess to you that she was not well, and I did not wish to take that from her. A fool again," Palmerton lamented.

"Please forgive my tenderhearted hope to save her from this sort of unpleasant night, Your Grace. I will have no choice now but to consider that she is a danger to herself," he said with a bow, then pivoted on his heel and made a swift exit.

Rafe's mind swung about as he desperately tried to make sense of Palmerton's explanation—that she was a liar, that perhaps she was even mad. That he had gone along with the lies to give Charlotte a chance to tell him the truth.

That certainly seemed to be the intimation.

But…she had not seemed mad. Ever.

There had been no hint that anything was wrong with her. She had seemed perfect in every way. Had he been tricked so easily, or had he simply wished to believe in her so much that he had failed to see that what he wanted to believe was a fantasy?

"My darling," a voice called from the door.

"Who was that?"

His mother had been upstairs with his grandmother, making plans for her ball. He wished she had not been here of all nights. But he had to tell her. It could not be avoided.

"Mama," he said, his heart hollow and his voice brittle. "There is to be no wedding."

"*What?*" she blurted, storming into the room. "What do you mean *no wedding*?"

CHAPTER TWENTY-EIGHT

Rain slashed against the coach as it raced into the countryside and away from London. The ferocity of the cruel weather mirrored the turmoil inside Charlotte's heart.

She had lost Rafe. She had lost it all. And the pain of it cut through her with such intensity she could scarce draw breath.

Anger slipped through her veins—anger that she'd had her entire life stolen from her, trying to protect her loved ones from a monster.

And she had failed, ultimately. None of them were safer, and she was in greater danger.

She swallowed the despair threatening to tighten her throat. Rafe thought she had betrayed him. That she had lied to him for what? No doubt, he assumed it was for baubles and a fortune or a duchess's coronet.

Nothing could be further from the truth.

How she loathed the fear that had driven her and kept her silent when she should have shouted the truth to all and sundry. But fear made people make the worst choices.

She stared at Palmerton and her stepbrother, Phillip, as she tried to fathom her stepfather's sudden actions.

She did not understand why Phillip was in this coach, and oddly, it appeared that Phillip did not know, either.

His brown eyes were wide, his sandy hair wild, and he sat in the corner, his shirt open at the neck as if he had been hauled into the coach from someplace where he had been about to do something disreputable.

Which, knowing his character, was extremely likely. He held a flask in his hand and drank from it deeply before he whined, "Papa, I am not marrying Charlotte."

Palmerton sat still for a single moment, wound his hand back—then slapped his son. "You will not argue with me, boy. You are indeed marrying her."

The gesture was no small thing, for Phillip was no child. He was a man of twenty-five years and over six feet tall. And yet, he did not retaliate. He sat wedged into the corner of the coach, a muscle ticking in his cheek.

She watched the exchange with growing horror as she realized that Phillip *would* do exactly as his father wished.

Palmerton held him, too, his own flesh and blood, in his metaphorical grip with an iron fist.

After all, he controlled the purse strings, and Phillip knew well enough that there was little for a young man of his few skills and expensive tastes to do but obey his father.

And be paid out his substantial allowance in exchange for obedience.

Palmerton's face tensed. "If you do not marry that girl, we will have nothing."

"What do you mean?" Phillip sneered. "Charlotte is but a servant. How can you have me marry a servant?" He tugged petulantly at his wrinkled shirt. "I can marry one of the rich city girls anytime I want."

His father snorted. "I have not encouraged you to wed one of those low city girls all these years for good reason, boy. Luckily, you've had no desire to wed, and you certainly haven't been foolish enough to fancy yourself in love."

Palmerton ground his teeth as he looked out into the dark night. It was as if years of holding on tight were finally wearing him down.

"I should have forced you two to wed as soon as you were of legal age," he said to himself. "But marrying you so young might have drawn notice."

Notice? What the blazes was he on about?

"You will have me marry Phillip to keep me away from the duke?" She leaned forward and locked gazes with him. "You just made certain that he would never marry me, because now he thinks I'm mad."

"I had to do something," Palmerton snapped, sweat beading his brow. "I could not let him think that I had been lying to him, too. I needed him to think that I was protecting you, that I was protecting *him*, that somehow, we would sort all of this out, that he had not been played for a total fool. But you *did* play him for a fool. Didn't you, my dear?"

"I did not," she countered, her stomach twisting.

"You lied to him. Again and again. And now you will pay the price." Palmerton sucked in a breath and smoothed his hands down the front of his waistcoat. "You will marry my son tonight. I have a special license. And none of us will ever need worry again." Palmerton nodded to himself. "The duke will not disdain us because you have scandalized him."

"I don't understand," she said, desperately trying to make sense of any of this.

"You don't need to understand," he ground out. "You simply need to walk down the aisle of the small church I have chosen and say 'I do.' And then everything will be sorted."

"How does my marrying Phillip solve *anything*?" she asked.

He stared at her tightly. "That is none of your affair. You will do as you are told, or I shall make your life a living hell."

"You have already made my life a living

hell!" she roared. "You have destroyed my life, and now you have ruined the duke's, too."

"Do not think so highly of yourself," he hissed before he cocked his head to the side and drawled: "He shall forget you tomorrow. And there's still a chance he might consider Francesca. She is far superior to you."

"Francesca has no desire to marry him," she snapped back, unwilling to cower before him any longer, no matter the stakes. "Francesca is in love with George, the Earl of Darrow."

"More fool she, if she can have a duke."

"*You* are the fool," she finally permitted herself to declare, "to think that people can give their hearts and take them back willy-nilly like that."

She squared her shoulders, lifted her chin, and stated, "Rafe loves me."

Palmerton stared at her...then laughed. That laugh filled the coach and boomed off the silk walls. He wiped at his eye.

"He loves an imaginary person, Charlotte. Which he has finally realized this night." His laughter dimmed. "He knows now that Lady Charlotte does not actually exist."

"No," she said, her voice sounding strangled, her throat tightening with her mounting grief for a lost dream. "Lady Charlotte does not exist. And I have lied to him, but all my life, I wanted more. All my life, I wanted to be loved."

"'I wanted to be loved,'" Palmerton mocked. He wiped a hand over his weary face. "Oh, my dear girl. No one can love someone like you. Alone, unwanted, cast aside. Why would anyone love you?"

Each word struck her like a blow.

The logical part of her brain was certain he was mistaken. But something deep in her soul... It screamed that he was right.

Palmerton shook his head. "Love is overrated. The only thing that is valuable in this life is *security*." He emphasized that word with a shake of his tightened fist. This man was fighting something deeper than she knew—something he kept hidden within *himself*.

"What made you like this?" she gasped. "What made you so cold and hard?"

Palmerton looked away, his voice rough. "I have seen true hell, and you know nothing of it. You have not suffered the way that I have seen poverty cause suffering. When I married your mother, I was only pulling myself and my children up out of hell, and I promised myself then that we would never go back."

She'd never seen him so angry and at the same time...sad. His eyes were charged, electric, yet covered with a glossy sheen. Charlotte knew anger, and she knew sadness, but she did not know one could be simultaneously consumed by both as her stepfather was in this moment.

Phillip, who had been silent, appeared just as confused as she. But whether she understood it or not wasn't important. Because no matter Palmerton's reason behind this, she knew it was wrong.

"You cannot make me marry him," she said at last, her voice hollow. "It is against the law."

"The law is what I say it is," he countered, his voice cracking like a whip. "I will pay the priest, and you will say yes. Phillip will say yes. And this will all be done. My threats have not changed, my dear. Stevenson rides atop this coach, and I can break him on the side of the road and no one will say a thing. I can still destroy all those you love if you do not do what I wish. I can destroy all the *things* you love as well. Or at least sell them off."

"What things?" She had no valuables—he'd made sure of it.

Palmerton lifted a brow. "Your family's home."

Her heart began to pound, and her stomach lurched up into her throat. She could take it no more. His taunts. His lies. His betrayals.

She could no longer live like this. She could no longer live at his mercy. Her mother... Her father... They would not have wanted such a life for her. And she would no longer allow herself to be treated thus.

"No," she said firmly as the coach rumbled into the darkness.

Palmerton grew very quiet as he studied her. Then evenly, he demanded, "What do you mean no?"

"Just what I said," she dared to say. "I refuse to marry Phillip, no matter what you do. No matter what you say, you cannot make me."

"Oh, sweet Charlotte." He grinned. "I can make you do anything."

CHAPTER TWENTY-NINE

"Charlotte has been lying to me, Mama," Rafe managed.

"I beg your pardon?"

He swallowed, blinking. "Charlotte is not who she claimed, at least not in the way that she has explained herself to you and me."

"You are speaking nonsense," his mother countered archly.

"I am not," he said, lifting his tortured gaze to hers. "Palmerton just escorted her out now. She was saying the strangest things, saying that she would have been sent to the orphans' asylum without Palmerton. But Palmerton insists she lies all of the time and that he will send me news of what is to transpire."

"Do you trust him?" she demanded.

"No," he said firmly. And he didn't. The man had pivoted so quickly to a new tale that he could only believe Palmerton's ability to lie was superior to Charlotte's.

That did not stop the deep ache ripping him asunder. He had been so certain that he had found love. Now, he felt as if he was facing a tangle of stories, not knowing what to believe.

But she had looked at him with such deep hope. Such pain…

"So, do not trust him," his mother declared.

"Certainly not over Charlotte."

He nodded tightly, uncertain how to proceed. "She was clearly shaken by the lies she said she told me. My God, Mama, she gave me a false name the day we met. How am I to believe her side, despite the lies? I have no idea who she truly is…"

"Yes, I understand you, my love, and you are deeply upset by what you've discovered. But would you abandon her?"

"No," he growled fiercely. For he could not deny the way his heart and soul responded to her presence. The lies? She'd seemed so frantic in her confession. He longed to believe she had not intended to betray him with words.

Did he dare to believe it?

His mother's face tensed. "Perhaps she's tricked us all. Perhaps what Palmerton says is true. But at present? Now, you must find out what is at the bottom of this before you make your decisions about her."

He nodded, his hands curling into fists as he glanced out to the foyer and into the dark night. "I do not want her in his house, Mama. I never should have let them leave together. I was shaken. I could not think. But I am going to go and get her. She seemed…afraid."

"Then go," his mother insisted.

But before he could head for the door, his grandmother strode in, leaning heavily on her silver-handled cane, a book in her free hand.

Though she was well over eighty, she was still immensely capable, and she crossed to him with the same authority she'd possessed when she had been the duchess. "My dears, whatever is going on? An old woman cannot take this sort of excitement at this hour of night. At least, not any longer. I heard shouting."

"Grandmama," he returned, "it is nothing to concern you."

"Ha!" she retorted. "What concerns you concerns me. It sounds as if there was a great deal of drama just now, and I wish to hear all about it. When one sits by the fire as often as I do, one needs to be regaled with the drama of the day, and one cannot experience it."

Rafe nodded, unwilling to fob her off. She'd been such a fixture in his childhood. Always daring him to do more, be more, and to enjoy what this life had to offer whilst it lasted. "That was the young lady whom I was going to marry," he said, taking her back toward the library.

"*Was* going to?" his grandmother asked, blinking up at him.

"*Was* going to," he affirmed. "There is something quite strange afoot. She claims she is beneath me and cannot marry a duke. Worse, Palmerton has made insinuations about her health."

"Devil take it," his grandmama said frankly. "That is not done by young ladies about to marry dukes."

"I agree," his own mother said.

Rafe felt both pressed to go and pressed to stay. His grandmother was a wise woman and might have answers. "She said that she could not lie to me any longer, that she was little better than a servant."

"A servant?" her grandmother gasped. "You have fallen in love with a servant, my boy? I could understand a merchant or someone not born to the *ton* as we discussed, but a servant? We shall have to help her adjust. It will take time."

"Grandmama," he began, stunned by her complete acceptance of it all.

She squeezed his hand, then smiled boldly. "The scandal of it is positively delicious. You *could* still marry her, you know. It has been done. Lords have married barmaids. It doesn't always work out very well for the young lady, but if you love her, my darling, do not let her go over such a thing. If we cannot do what we want, who can?"

His grandmother's sentiment rang through his head, and he blinked. "Grandmama, she has lied to me."

His grandmother *tsk*ed. "She was afraid, my dear. She was afraid. Wouldn't you be afraid to tell the king that you were merely a servant?"

"I am not the king," he pointed out.

"To a servant, you might as well be the

king, my dear. Did you not love her when you met her? Was she a servant when you met her? Were you fooled by your affinity for her, assuming that she was a lady?"

He thought back to that day on the pavement in Southwark. She had been dressed in an ill-fitting gown of good quality, and she'd had no lady's maid or chaperone. She'd also been desperately upset over the loss of what any member of the *ton* would consider a small sum. And then he thought back to her standing in the foyer after their surprising reunion, hiding her hands in her skirts.

"Yes, I think she was a servant," he breathed. "She was simply pretending to be a lady."

"Why?" his grandmother asked.

He closed his eyes as his heart tightened with sorrow and with admiration for Charlotte. "Because she was trying to save someone."

The older woman pounded her cane into the floor. "That sounds like a very noble reason to pretend to be a lady, my darling." His grandmother met his gaze. "Now, who is this young servant who has stolen your heart at great risk to herself?"

The dowager duchess was quiet for a long moment—the first moment that Rafe could recall.

"Her name is Charlotte," his mother said, and then she sighed.

"Charlotte?" his grandmother mused. Her eyes sharpened as if she sensed a mystery and could not wait to discover the scandal. "In whose house does she reside, that she was so able to trick you into believing that she was a lady?"

"Lord Palmerton," he said. "We were to introduce you at the ball. You did suggest he wasn't one with whom it was best to be associated."

His grandmother snorted. "Yes. I did mention that. He's a slick fish, but such lies to a duke are beyond the pale."

"Have you met him? Or is it all rumor?" Rafe asked, his insides twisting as his concern for Charlotte intensified.

His grandmother inclined her head. "He was on the tip of every tongue." She glanced to her daughter-in-law. "You and my son were traveling abroad at the time."

His grandmother pursed her lips as if recalling a particularly difficult story. "He married one of the greatest fortunes in the land." She lifted a gnarled finger to her lips, thinking. "Her name was Claire Rimbaux."

"Claire Rimbaux?" he echoed.

"Of the Rimbaux family?" his mother gasped.

"Quite right," his grandmother affirmed. "Her first marriage, a great love match, was to the son of the Prince de León. An exile from his small country. They both almost lost their heads in the revolution. Revolutions were rife those days, but they managed to come to Scotland with all of their money and his jewels. His title is ancient, my dear—one of the oldest princely lines in Europe. Claire and her prince had a single child. Her name was Charlotte. Tragically, the prince died not long after."

"What?" he breathed.

His grandmama nodded, her usual luster dim as she told the tale. "Palmerton married the young widow, who had a little girl. It greatly advanced him in society." Her eyes narrowed. "Many thought it odd that he should be able to achieve her affection."

His mother's eyes widened. "Do you mean to say that Charlotte is a *princess*?"

"If Claire, Palmerton's last wife, was Charlotte's mother? Then yes, she is one of the last of that line."

A shadow passed over his grandmother's face. "I visited their chateau many times—absolutely beautiful. The tragedy. The whole family met with Madame Guillotine, save her grandfather and her father, of course."

As the story sank in, Rafe reeled.

My God. It made sickening sense. Charlotte wasn't Faraday's daughter. That was clear.

So who were her parents? If she had lived in that house all of her life? If her name was Charlotte, and Palmerton had control over her, and now his seeming wish to keep her hidden away?

There seemed little question to the truth of her identity.

If it was true, one could argue that Charlotte outranked Rafe. For he was not a royal duke.

And all this time, she had been kept unaware. For she clearly had no idea who her father was, if she'd been but an infant when he died.

How the hell had Palmerton managed such a nefarious feat?

His grandmother shook her head. "It was a great loss that Claire's husband survived the revolution that followed, only to be taken by smallpox here in England. And then Claire died not long after marrying Palmerton."

"But how did Palmerton get away with hiding Charlotte?" he demanded.

His grandmother frowned as she struggled to remember. "We all thought that something had happened to the little girl the same summer her mother died. She disappeared from society, and no one saw her again. I think it was accepted that she, too, had been claimed by illness as so many children are. I never liked the man, which was why I advised against him. But to society? He has done nothing wrong. He has simply suffered the loss of his wife and stepdaughter. But it seems he is a fiend."

"Why would Palmerton do such a thing?" his mother exclaimed.

A sinking sensation grabbed hold of Rafe. "Her fortune, Mama. No doubt Charlotte, the Princess de León, has vast wealth and lands. And Palmerton has likely kept quiet control of it all these years."

Rafe turned to the dark windows, his soul crying out for the pain of the woman he loved.

Did he still love her? He felt as if she had slipped away from him. That she was a figment. A whisper. Who *was* Charlotte? Did he really know her at all?

At this moment? None of that mattered, even if he felt as if his soul had been crushed beneath the weight of loss.

The little girl had *disappeared*, and no one had seen her again.

Had no one questioned her quiet disappearance?

Of course not.

How many other girls had disappeared without a trace?

How many girls had been shunted off into houses without anyone thinking of or considering them again, even if they did come from great families?

He snapped his gaze to his mother as he thought of the way his great-aunt had been cast out. "The foundling hospital, Mama—" His voice broke.

"This all started because I forced your hand," she rushed. "And I pray you can forgive me. Of course it is yours," his mother declared, her gaze full of sorrow.

"I am grateful you took such action," he said truthfully. "If you had not, I wouldn't have pursued Charlotte. And she needs me. My God…"

His mother sucked in a harsh breath, nodding. Understanding.

It didn't matter that he might not know who Charlotte's true spirit was, or that she had lied to him again and again.

She had been the victim of the worst abuse, and she was no doubt only protecting herself.

He felt sick. "Palmerton is a villain, and he is so artful," Rafe ground out, "he would have had us blame Charlotte for *his* deceits and cruelty."

"Yes," his mother said. "And Charlotte is with him now."

"Not for long," Rafe vowed, before he bowed to the two women he admired so much, who had raised him to believe in love and hope.

Nothing was going to stop him from restoring Charlotte to her rightful place.

Whether she wished to marry him now or not.

CHAPTER THIRTY

Rafe raced across England as if the hounds of hell were on his heels.

The long night had been one of cavernous pain. Of discovering the woman he loved did not exist and that all his feelings were directed at an imagined person. But the fact was, Charlotte was very real and in very serious jeopardy.

It did not matter that she had lied about her lineage. She'd had good reason, and he could not leave her to Palmerton's machinations.

The man seemed bent on releasing hell this night.

Only the light from the moon spilling over the rolling hills outside the city illuminated the road before him.

The sound of his stallion's hooves eating up the earth thundered through the night.

He charged as fast as he could, trying to make up speed that no coach lumbering over grooved English roads could ever match.

Rafe was grateful for the stamina and power of his steed as he pursued Charlotte and the man determined to destroy her life.

If Rafe was honest? Palmerton had destroyed his life, too, stealing the future that he'd been so certain he had found.

But the fear of Charlotte in the clutches of a clearly desperate man hummed through him. If he did not help her, free her from such a man? Sleep would abandon him, and he would not know the light of happiness ever again.

Somewhere behind him, George and Matt were cutting up the road, following him after Charlotte.

Only moments after his grandmama had revealed Charlotte's true identity, George, Matt, and Lady Francesca had clamored into his house, shouting and making a ruckus as if rebellion threatened to tear down all he held dear.

They were not wrong.

It was a damn miracle they had arrived before he could leave in pursuit.

Lady Francesca had looked terrified as she'd grabbed his hands most rudely and rushed out her fears. She had been utterly panicked as she babbled.

She had gone first to George to seek help, but he had urged her to go straight to the duke.

He lamented that she had not come to him immediately. But he understood her need to go to the man she trusted most. The man she loved.

From her news, it seemed that Palmerton

had yanked his half-clothed and drunken son, Phillip, out of the house in a rage, ranting about the need for haste in pursuit of Charlotte.

His fury that Charlotte had managed to steal out of the house had sent him all but frothing that they could lose everything.

Lady Francesca, brave woman that she was, had not stayed at home and wrung her hands. No, she had understood the great danger Charlotte was in and had taken action. Apparently, she was no longer to be a victim of her father anymore.

And Lady Francesca had had a good idea of where her father might be taking Charlotte.

Lady Francesca had been certain he would take her north to the small country manor they kept for the hunting Season. There was a vicar there who loved his brandy and was known for clandestine marriages that did not always have the enthusiastic consent of the ladies.

And then she had revealed that Palmerton had been shouting about the special license in his pocket. Her brother, Phillip, had resisted, and Palmerton had shoved him into the coach like a parcel.

At that damning information, Rafe's body had gone cold, and he'd acted without hesitation.

Quickly, he'd dashed out notes to his friends in justice. And then, he, Matt, and George had taken to the North Road.

Palmerton had to be placed in custody. And they had to rescue Charlotte before she was married to the man's son, all her freedom lost.

Yes, the moment Lady Francesca had finished her tale, worthy of any drama by the great writers of the previous century, he had put into work the networks that he kept at the ready.

As a duke, he was in control of much information, and it had taken him barely minutes to see that at least Palmerton could not steal her out of the country through one of the ports.

At Rafe's written instruction, runners had gone off in multiple directions.

He could have sent toughs after her, or Bow Street Runners, but he needed to go himself. He needed to see her safe with his own eyes.

If he did not find her, she could be condemned to a lifelong hell.

As Rafe squeezed his knees and willed his stallion on, he focused on the road ahead, desperate to see a coach, desperate to see any sign of her at all.

And when at last he did spot a conveyance in the distance, rumbling over the deeply uneven mud, he prayed that it was her.

Rafe whispered to his stallion, who loved to run, determined to close the gap.

And just as his mount burst forward with renewed speed, the door of the coach swung open and a figure tumbled out. They rolled multiple times on the earth before rolling to a halt.

His heart wrenched into his mouth, and he felt ice-cold terror in his veins. Terror as he had never known before.

Could it be her? Was she alive? Had Palmerton killed her and thrown her out of the coach?

For he did not put it past Charlotte to defy the man. She might have lied to Rafe, but he was certain that her fierce strength had been no pretense. She was a glorious being; of that, he had no doubt.

Rafe did not dare take his gaze away from the small figure sprawled on the side of the road.

He had to believe that George and Matt were close behind him to provide assistance when he required it.

With every fiber of his being, he willed the small frame to be well. To be alive.

For in his heart, he knew it was her.

The figure beside the road stumbled to their feet.

A skirt swung about their body, and they staggered in the dim light.

It *was* a woman.

And by God, it *was* Charlotte.

Her blond hair shone in the moonlight like spun silver, tumbling down her back.

He bent down over his horse's neck, urging the stallion on to impossible speed.

Sensing his need, the animal obliged, kicking up clods from the earth, his chest pumping like a great forge.

And his beautiful, intelligent steed spotted Charlotte, and, sensing Rafe's intent, the horse angled in swiftly.

Charlotte's eyes flared as she spotted horse and rider coming out of the darkness, but she did not shrink.

Quite the contrary.

His bold Charlotte stood her ground, and when he raced up to her and held out his hand, she caught his gaze, took his hand, and used her own force to help him haul her up onto the stallion and sit behind him.

The coach stopped just a few feet ahead, and someone jumped down.

"Keep your hands off her!" Palmerton shouted, his eyes wild.

"I should say the same of you, but it seems that she has freed herself," Rafe snarled as he circled the coach.

"Are you well?" he asked Charlotte over his shoulder, savoring the feel of her body pressed against his.

She nodded tightly. "I am perfectly safe," she said, "but Palmerton is unhinged. And he is armed."

"To think he tried to insinuate that you are the one who has lost your wits," he growled, grasping her hand over his heart.

God, he wanted to keep her this close forever. His own heart, his own blood raged against his intellect. He *did* know her. He knew her to her core. And that inner knowing of his longed to feel her body aligned to his, her palm over his beating heart. To feel her thighs along his.

The stallion blew out a breath and pawed the earth furiously, as though taking on Rafe's anger.

Charlotte brought both of her hands to Rafe's hips, then slid them to his middle.

She held tightly to his waist, leaving not a breath between their bodies.

She pressed her cheek to his back for a single moment and said, "I have never been more glad to see anyone in my entire life than I am to see you. Thank you for not abandoning me."

And his heart... His damn heart bled in that moment. That he had ever given her cause to think he would not always come to her aid was a stain on his honor and a betrayal of his soul.

"How could I not, my love?" he said. "You

are my world."

She stilled at those words, and her breath hitched in her throat. "Rafe?"

"I will always come for you," he growled lowly, determined to make her understand the extent of his feelings. "I don't care how far I have to go, what I have to do, but I will never allow anyone to harm you. Not ever again."

Though he hated that she had lied and he loathed the confusion he had felt, she was his mirror, his other half, and he felt alive with her arms about him.

He whipped up the reins and trotted his horse to Palmerton, knowing what needed to be done.

And knowing that George and Matt were ready, should the need arise.

"You are a villain, sir," he said coldly. "I don't use that word often. It has an air of exaggeration, but in your case? It is the truth. What the devil has possessed you to behave thus? Did you truly think you could kidnap a princess?"

"What?" Charlotte gasped, her breath whooshing against his shoulder.

He knew he would have to explain in more detail, and perhaps it had been a poor decision to say such a thing, but he wanted Palmerton to have to writhe before her. To tell her what he had done.

Palmerton winced, but then he threw back his shoulders and drawled, "Now that you know she is the Princess de León, you are here to save her? Before, when she was only Charlotte the servant, you let her race into the night."

"I do not care if she is a princess or not," he roared, "but she needs to know the truth. And I certainly will not let a man like you take advantage of her. Her whole family has known tragedy, and you would heap more upon it."

Palmerton paled in the moonlight, as if Rafe had struck him with those words, but he did not look remorseful. No, his look was the look of a man who was cornered. "Her family is not the only one who has known tragedy," he snapped, a strange look twisting his features, as if an old wound had risen to the surface and opened. "My father died in poverty, and I will not allow such a thing to befall myself or my children."

"And so you would lie to her and force her to marry your son?" Rafe countered, disgusted by the selfishness of the man before her.

"Indeed," Palmerton replied easily. "That is how things are done. Girls are forced to marry men every day. I have raised Charlotte since she was little more than a babe. I have fed her. I have clothed her. I have given her shelter."

"All with *her* money," Rafe spat out, furious that the man refused to take responsibility for his crimes.

Palmerton shook his head. "That is not true."

"It *is* true," Rafe declared without relent.

"Rafe?" Charlotte gripped his linen shirt more tightly. "What are you talking about?"

"I will explain soon," he assured, "but know that Palmerton has been lying to you for your whole life."

"You're mistaken—"

"Point of fact, you did lie to me, Charlotte," he said. "'Lady' is not your correct form of address. Nor is 'Miss.'"

"I don't understand," she protested. "I'm not a lady, Rafe. I tried to explain it to you tonight. I am but a servant in his house, allowed to stay out of the charity of his good wishes."

"Out of the charity of his good wishes?" he growled, wishing he could jump down from his stallion and pound Palmerton into the earth. But he would not leave Charlotte for his own desire for blood.

"No, Charlotte," Rafe explained slowly. "This man, your stepfather, was able to stay in your house out of the charity of your solicitor, who thought that Palmerton was acting on your behalf."

Palmerton's mouth pressed into a slit, and his eyes flashed with hatred at this piece of news.

Phillip remained in the shadows of the coach, half drunk, clearly unwilling to provoke any sort of trouble, even as his father shook with rage.

Rafe did not miss the resentment in the old man as he continued, "Palmerton is quite a convincing fellow, you know."

"I do know," she breathed, "but I don't understand the rest of it. When my mother died, he inherited everything by law."

"He can't inherit it, Charlotte," Rafe replied gently but firmly. "There is an entail. It is all tied to *your* title, my love."

"My *title*?" she gasped. "Rafe, someone has fooled you. I do not have a title."

"Think back, love," he said softly. "Can you remember your father?"

"No," she said quietly. "I do not remember him."

Rafe nodded, wishing he could pull her onto his lap now and comfort her for all the pain she had suffered. For all the grief caused to her. All the pain she had never been allowed to express.

"Palmerton," he bit out instead. "You are despicable. You have let her live her entire life without knowing the importance of her lineage, without letting her have the history of her stories, without telling her the truth of her parents."

For the first time, Palmerton looked to the

night sky as if there might be answers in the stars shining overhead.

"You have denied her of her soul, her rights," Rafe gritted out. "I should kill you here."

Palmerton let out a beleaguered cry, like an animal that felt a mortal blow, before he wrenched a pistol from the small of his back. "I beg of you, Your Grace, try."

"Now, now, old man," Matt called from the distance. "You shall have to have remarkable aim, for I have had you in my sights these last five minutes."

Palmerton swung his gaze to Lord Matthew, who was riding up behind them.

The Earl of Darrow rode closely beside his twin brother, his own pistol drawn.

"You are outnumbered, sir," George drawled. "And I think it would be wise if you did not die here on the road like a dog, though we would happily arrange it for you."

"Tell her who she is," Matt challenged, brandishing his pistol with the panache of the highwaymen of old.

Palmerton swallowed. "She is my daughter by marriage."

"Tell her *more*," Rafe growled.

Palmerton licked his lips and glanced from man to man, a rat in a trap.

Charlotte's hands trembled as she held on to him, and he could feel their iciness through his shirt.

"My darling," he said, "you're going to have to be very brave. The news is good, but it will shock you to your core. It certainly shocked me tonight."

"How did this news find you?" she demanded.

"My grandmother," he replied. "She knew your mother and your father. She even visited your family's home on the Continent and in Scotland before your father died."

"Damned meddling old woman," Palmerton hissed.

"Keep mention of my grandmother out of your mouth," Rafe returned.

"The Continent?" she echoed. "Scotland? I am dreaming, Rafe, or I have completely lost my mind."

"I promise it is neither," he said, his heart so heavy for all that she had been through. "I want you to wake, Charlotte. I want you to wake from this nightmare that you've been living for years. Most of it made by him."

She shook her head against his back, her hair teasing over them as the wind began to gust.

"Now, I want you to confess," Rafe said, pulling his own pistol from his waistband. He cocked it, aiming it at Palmerton. "Three pistols against your one, sir, and I do not think your son is brave enough to come out of the coach to defend you."

CHAPTER THIRTY-ONE

The stallion, as if sensing Charlotte's distress, reared onto its hind legs and pawed the air with its massive hooves. Rafe reached back with one arm, holding her tight even as he skillfully kept his pistol trained on her guardian.

When the stallion's forehooves hit the ground, her teeth clapped together and she swallowed back her fear.

She could not be afraid any longer.

She had been afraid long enough.

Now? She needed answers. She raised her chin, looked at her stepfather, and insisted, "You will tell me what this means now. I am sure they would happily kill you if necessary, and though I would regret any man's death, I'm sure there is someone who can tell me the truth of my history without you alive on this earth."

Palmerton's eyes widened in shock at the veracity of her claim. He swallowed, then nodded, lowering his weapon.

"When your mother died," Palmerton began bitterly, "I was certain I would inherit a fortune. That *is* the law of England. Husbands absorb their wives' property and fortune."

Palmerton scowled, his lip curling with

anger. "But your father had been incredibly wise. I did not realize that a great deal of her assets were tied up and untouchable. All of his land and wealth were kept in trust by solicitors to ensure that you would inherit them upon your majority. I was simply allowed to ensure enough money was spent to keep you in the fashion in which you were supposed to live. The fashion of a princess. Much to my good fortune, they simply trusted you to my care."

She was not surprised by this. It was the way of the world for young girls to be entirely forgotten or entrusted to men who did not care for them.

He let out a hollow laugh. Whether it was at himself or fate, it was impossible to tell. Then he ground out, "But I kept you from society, Charlotte. I used the money for myself, my son, and my daughter. After all, it was supposed to be *mine*," he said with a glint of madness in his eyes. "I won your mother's hand; I took care of her when she was dying. I was supposed to inherit that money, not you."

Bile rose in her throat at his callous explanation of his cruelty, and she prayed that her mother had not known how truly awful he was.

"And what did you do to deserve those funds?" He snorted. "Nothing. You were simply born. I had the labor of convincing your mother to marry me." He repeatedly pointed a finger to his chest. "*Me*. I held her hand as she suffered from the grief of your father. I took care of her when she fell apart and grew ill."

He shook his head, shadows playing over his face, making his features appear sunken. "And then I was left with nothing. Do you think that I could allow that after all I had done, after all that I had spent to catch her eye? No."

Palmerton shrugged as if his choices were completely understandable. "So, I simply didn't speak about you to anyone the summer your mother died. Instead, I took you to the country and said that we were all mourning Claire, which we were. You were."

His face grew more serious as he thought back to that time so long ago when he had made choices that had altered their fates forever. "I fired all of the servants. I hired new ones."

She gasped, and suddenly she began to understand why she did not have memories of her youngest years.

There was no one and nothing to encourage her to remember them. She had thought perhaps that one of the servants had known her mother, but when she stopped and considered it now...

It was clear that Mary and Stevenson had

not known her mother. Nor had Cook.

No one had shared any stories of her mother when she'd been small. No one had known her father, either.

Palmerton had been able to tell anyone whatever he pleased about her, about her life. And that had been that she was simply Charlotte. With no fortune. No title. No importance.

"You would do this for money?" she marveled, horrified by his selfishness.

"You speak of money like it's nothing, when you know how important it is, Charlotte." Palmerton pinned her with a judging glare. "Look at you. You wanted a duke. You dared dream he could be yours, and when he wanted you, you could not say no. You lied to him. You didn't tell him you were a servant. You said you were *Lady* Charlotte. Now, imagine," he said, "my own fears. My father drove our family into the ground. He spent everything we had. He tortured my mother with debt. I swore that I would be wealthy, my children would be wealthy. When I was on the brink of losing everything, I took out a loan, I spent a great deal of money, and I convinced your mother that I was as wealthy as she. I was kind to her."

Much to her shock, this point seemed to matter to him. She didn't understand why. He had not been kind to Francesca or herself.

"I was kind to her," he insisted again. "I promise you, until the end. I hid the fact that it was all for security. *My* family's security. I lied, just as you did, Charlotte, when you hid the fact that you were a servant from the duke."

She sucked in a sharp breath as she realized what he was doing.

"You and I are nothing alike," she countered.

"We are both liars to gain advantage," he stated, his eyes hard. "Do not mistake that. You will always be a liar, Charlotte. Do not fool yourself."

The bitterness of his words crept through her like acid.

"Do not listen to him," Rafe growled. Then, to Palmerton: "I should kill you here and now."

"So you've threatened," Palmerton retorted, "but I do not think you are willing to answer to the magistrates."

Matt shot his pistol, and a lead ball lodged in the ground next to Palmerton's feet.

Palmerton jumped, a scream tearing from his throat.

Matt whipped his other pistol from his belt and took aim again. "The duke might not be willing, but I certainly am," he said merrily. "I've always fancied a stint in a prison. I quite like the idea of having to escape. I think I'd be good at it."

Matt waggled his brows as he gave the appearance of weighing his options. "Or perhaps I'd simply run. I fancy the life of a pirate—can't you see me as a privateer? I think I'd be excellent at it." A hard glint replaced the mischievous sheen in Matt's gaze. "So don't tempt me, Palmerton; I'd happily kill you. My brother and the duke can stay in England and be good men. I will take you down, if necessary, because someone like you deserves to die for actions like this."

George shook his head, mirroring his brother's disgust. "She has been nothing but a kind person to everyone she has met. While you are foul. I understand that your childhood has caused you to act in the most nefarious of ways, but you are not a child, sir. You are a grown man, and you should have learned by now that you cannot hurt others to get whatever you want."

Palmerton lifted his chin, unwilling to face his role. "So you say, but look at the *ton*. Look at all of you, living off the backs of the poor, willing to do whatever it takes to keep the money that you have and keep your hands clean."

The duke blew out a heavy breath and began, "You are not wrong, Palmerton. It is why I spend most of my life trying to make right the wrongs done to the people of England. It is why I spend almost every waking hour at work. But you? You gamble, you whore, and you steal. You may speak a good game, sir, about the way society is, but unlike me, you have no intention of doing anything about it except using those who are innocent."

Palmerton said nothing to this, at last having run out of artful replies.

"Tell her the most important part," Rafe demanded. "Tell her exactly who she is. I want her to hear it from you."

Palmerton's hands curled into fists, and each word came out of his mouth as if it were a tooth being pulled by a surgeon. "Your father was the Prince de León," he admitted. "One of the last men of his house. You are an aristocrat. When your grandfather and father fled for their lives during the revolution, they came over in a boat with trunks of coin and jewels. They'd transferred most of their money in the years before the revolution, sensing that trouble was at hand. Of course, you have lost the chateaus on the Continent, the thousands of acres, the vineyards, but you have an estate in Scotland; you have land in the Americas." Palmerton swallowed as if he felt sick. "And you have a fortune worthy of any king."

Charlotte's head spun. "I-it's not possible," she stuttered.

Rafe glanced back over his shoulder at her, his eyes soft. "Charlotte, you likely have more money than me."

She stared at the duke, completely flummoxed. "How is any of this real? I can't believe that this is happening."

"Believe it," he soothed. "It is true. You are a princess, Charlotte. *You* are the happy ending."

"This does not feel like a happy ending," she protested. "My mother, my father, my grandfather—I shall never know any of them, and I have been kept away from their memory my whole life."

Rafe nodded, his face a mask of sorrow for her. "But you are no longer a prisoner of Palmerton. He can do nothing more to hurt you. Everything that he has threatened you with? That is done. You are free," he declared.

She studied Rafe, the man she loved, the duke she had dreamed of marrying but had believed could never be hers.

As a *princess*, though, she could be his, and no one would question it. But would that be the only reason he would take her now? Because she was not a servant but a princess?

The doubt cut through any burgeoning hope. How could she ever know if he truly *loved and wanted* her? She couldn't. She sucked in a sharp breath as she tried to keep the agony of it in check.

"Rafe," she began. "Thank you for unveiling all of this to me."

"Don't thank me," he said softly. "You must thank my grandmama, for she put the pieces of your history together. And I think that she would like to meet you, if you will allow it."

Palmerton let out a disgusted laugh. "Oh, a happy reunion, is it? Is that how it's to be?"

"Yes," Rafe said, swinging his gaze back to him. "And you, sir, will be spending the night in jail. The rest of your nights, I think."

Palmerton took a step back, but Matt shook his head and pointed his pistol to the spot he had just abdicated.

"I would send you to some colony somewhere," Rafe drawled. "But I would not like to do that to another nation of people. They do not deserve someone as ill as you."

Rafe arched a brow at Matt and George. "What do you think? A particularly damp cell somewhere in the north of Scotland?"

"A prison on an island, surely," replied George.

Matt nodded. "How terribly exclusive for you, Palmerton."

Rafe leaned forward. "I will not kill you now, though I should. You'll never be able to leave, and you'll never be able to pay your way out. It will be just what you always wanted. A castle for you and you alone."

Palmerton let out a murderous cry and started forward.

Rafe took aim, exhaled, and pulled the trigger.

The bullet went through Palmerton's arm. Dark blood bloomed against the older man's coat.

Palmerton cursed and stared at the spreading stain. "I thought you weren't going to shoot me."

"I didn't say I wouldn't shoot you," Rafe said. "I just said that I wouldn't kill you. There's a great deal of difference. Now, we must get you to a doctor, sir, so I can keep my promise."

Charlotte took in Rafe, stunned by this man. This kind, strong man who had offered her his hand and who now defended her with pistol and brutal word.

CHAPTER THIRTY-TWO

They said little on the ride back to London.

At his orders, Matt and George took Palmerton and his son away.

Phillip was three sheets to the wind and unwilling to defend his father. In fact, he'd seemed quite happy to throw his father into the proverbial clink.

Palmerton would be locked up.

Matt and George would not let him escape, or they'd kill him if he tried to get away.

The law would be on the side of the Earl of Darrow and his brother, given what Palmerton had done.

Frankly, Rafe did not mind either outcome. He did not wish to kill the man or for his friends to have to shoot Palmerton, but Palmerton had brutalized his family and Charlotte. He felt little sympathy for him, given the misery he'd caused.

Now, Lady Francesca and Charlotte were free of him. More than free.

For George was going to take Lady Francesca in hand and make certain she was taken care of. If she wished to marry the Earl of Darrow, he would make certain she had a dowry and money of her own so that she might never be at the mercy of a man again.

And Rafe was going to take care of Charlotte for the rest of her days, if she would but let him.

It was true she might not wish to marry him, now, after he'd watched her walk out... and then followed once he knew her true lineage. He wouldn't blame her for thinking it was her title that made him come to her and nothing else.

Perhaps they would choose to part. The thought made his gut tighten.

But he was still going to ensure that nothing ever harmed her. Because still, that voice deep inside him growled like an awakened beast: *Mine.*

He was glad she had her freedom now, a true freedom to choose her own path, but that would never stop this feeling—that urge to be one with her, to hold her, to show her how very loved she was.

As they returned through the city, winding through the new parks and wide lanes lined with beautiful new brick and stone homes, he guided his stallion up to his townhouse.

Rafe swung his leg over the horse's neck, then jumped down, not needing a mounting block. He turned back to Charlotte, slid her from the stallion's back, and took her into his arms, cradling her against his chest.

A footman rushed out to take the stallion for a cooldown and to the stables.

Rafe carried Charlotte up the wide steps and under the portico.

"Rafe," she said softly, placing a hand on his chest. "Put me down."

How he loved the feel of her palm on his chest. But he did not want to relinquish his hold on her. Not yet. Not ever.

"Let me take care of you," he whispered.

"You have taken very good care of me," she replied, then glanced at the closed door, pride filling her eyes. "But I wish to enter your house on my own two feet."

"Whatever my princess requires," he said, inclining his head. And he understood her sense of dignity. It was something he'd never want to see taken from her—even if he would have smoothed every difficulty before her, if she but allowed him.

She looked up at him, tears in her eyes. "I do not know what to say to that. You have given me a whole new life, Rafe."

"No, my love, I have not," he replied honestly. As he led her back into his house under very different circumstances than she had entered earlier that night, he fought the urge to remonstrate himself.

How could he not have seen that she was in such dire straits this last week? How could he not see that the distance she was putting between them had been forced by Palmerton's hand? But he could not go back.

He could not give himself better clarity. No. All he could do was go forward with the knowledge he had now.

Gently, he took her hand, and they walked into the candle glow in the foyer.

"Your new life, Charlotte? It was always yours. Always," he declared. "No one could ever truly take it away from you. They could only try to hide it. Now, you know exactly who you are."

"Yes… No." She shook her head, then lifted her gaze to his. "I don't know. Do you still believe you don't know me? Are we strangers?"

He studied her face—the face that had etched itself on his heart. He longed to wipe away her doubts, her suffering…

Before he could think further, before he could let logic overrule his mind, he cupped her beloved face in his palms, took her mouth, and stole a kiss.

He bent her back, then, his hands weaving into her hair, and he devoured her mouth with a possessive kiss that burned through him like fire through a field.

She held on tightly to his waist, kissing him back with as much fervor as he showed her.

Then she pulled back and whispered, "I want you. I want you more than anything in the whole world."

"And I you," he breathed against her cheek.

He did not question or hesitate. He'd almost lost her for good.

Rafe swept her into his arms again.

Perhaps she wished to enter on her own two feet, but he would carry her to his chamber. He took the many stairs quickly, ignoring anything but her.

All he wanted in this moment was to feel her against him.

This night had terrified him. He hadn't known real fear before. Not truly.

He had been so shaken, and now he needed the steadying feel of her body against his to make him feel alive again, to make him feel as if the world was no longer shaking with loss.

No, he wanted it to shake with their passion instead.

So, when he crossed into his chamber and kicked the door shut behind them, he took her to the bed without pause and placed her down upon the counterpane, ready to make love to her all night long.

He wanted to brand himself with her body during this night of passion. To mark her in turn with his adoration of her curves.

She looked up at him from beneath half-hooded lids, stunned by his abandon. "Rafe, whatever are you doing?"

"I am showing you that you are mine," he said.

"Yours?" she asked before she teased, "I thought you said I was free."

"You *are* free," he announced, winding his hands with hers. "You can go through my door and leave forever. I won't stop you, if that is what you truly want. But in my heart of hearts, you will always be mine, Charlotte."

"You wish to marry me still?" she breathed, her eyes wide with astonishment.

He leaned over her and gently kissed her mouth before whispering against her ear, "I will marry you tonight. I will marry you tomorrow. I will marry you any day you choose."

At last, a growl rumbled out of his throat as he pulled her into his arms and tilted her head back so that he might study the planes of her beautiful face. "But know this, my love. You do not have to marry me out of duty or obligation."

"I never thought I could have you at all," she confessed. Her brow furrowed, and she traced her fingertips over his jawline as she explained, "I did not think that my dream of loving you could be fulfilled, that I could be your duchess."

Charlotte drew in a shuddering breath. "I did not think that love could ever be mine. I was not so foolish as to believe that a fairy-tale ending would befall me. I never thought that I would get to the ending of my story and have the prince."

He smiled ruefully. "I am not a prince, my darling."

"You might as well be," she said, "and you are mine as much as I am yours. Now, Rafe," she breathed, "I have fallen in love with you."

"And I you, Charlotte," he admitted without hesitation, elated that she would finally say the words he had been longing to hear.

"I do not care that you're a duke," she declared passionately. "I have seen you and the kindness you have bestowed on me, the choices you tried to give me, and the love you wanted to shower upon me."

Her lips pressed together for a long moment. "Rafe, I couldn't want more than what you offered me. I want *you*." She propped herself up on her arm and kissed him gently, then whispered against his lips, "I have lived my whole life without a fortune. I have lived my whole life without a title. I do not need one. The only thing it does now is make me worthy of you."

He blinked, shocked by her last statement.

As it rattled through him, he yanked her against his chest, and he stroked her hair back from her brow.

"You have always been worthy of me, Charlotte. It is I who am lucky to be worthy of you. It is *you* who is worthy, and I… I am happy to kneel before you, my princess."

And he did.

Rafe climbed off the side of the bed and knelt before her.

"Let me worship you," he whispered, pulling her legs to the side of the bed. Gently, he pushed them apart and kissed the inside of her thigh. "Marry me. Be mine. Be my princess."

She reached forward and stroked the hair away from his face. "Yes," she said. "Whatever the risk, now, always, forever, I am yours."

As a duke, Rafe knew his power—everyone bowed and scraped to him—but he was ready to bow to her.

Kneeling before her, her hips on the edge of the bed, he fisted her skirts and slid them upward until he saw the edge of her silk stockings tied above her knee.

He kissed the line where the silk met her flesh. And then he dragged his lips slowly, teasing with his teeth and tongue until he came to the spot for which he hungered so.

She propped herself up on her elbows, her brows rising. "Whatever are you doing?"

He gave her a wicked smile. "I'm about to kiss you."

"How the devil do you think you can kiss me when you're—"

And without waiting another moment, he *showed* her what he meant. As he'd dreamt of, over and over again, he pressed his face between her thighs and stroked his tongue into her wet folds, taking her into his mouth.

Her amazed cry filled the chamber, and that was all the encouragement he needed. Rafe licked and sucked and devoured every bit of her sweet, sensitive cunny, devouring her as if she was his last meal.

He listened for her sounds of delight. What gave her the most pleasure, which stroke pushed her the furthest along the path toward oblivion.

He wanted that blissful oblivion for her. He wanted it for her again and again.

Rafe circled his tongue over her sensitive sex, kissing until her legs were trembling with anticipation.

Then slowly he took his forefinger and inserted where he longed to thrust his cock.

But for now?

For now, he wanted her to feel his desire, his love for her and her body.

Deliberately, he stroked her inside as he stroked out, building a slow, deliberate rhythm.

He curved his finger, and she gasped with astonishment as he found a particular spot.

Damned satisfied at how he was pleasing her, Rafe smiled to himself.

As she tossed her head back and forth on the counterpane, he continued his kiss, then added another finger to her wet, hot core.

She wound her hands in his hair, her body arched against him.

"Oh, Rafe," she moaned, her voice light and full of amazement.

Slowly, he raised himself up, his smile one of pure satisfaction at the knowledge that he had given her such bliss.

Rafe climbed up the bed and quickly divested himself of his garments.

She watched his movements with a half-hooded gaze, still drunk on pleasure.

"My ribbon," she breathed, her eyes widening with astonishment.

He glanced to his wrist, his heart beating wildly. The blue ribbon was tied there, as it had been since he picked it up after their dance at Vauxhall. "Yes. I should have returned—"

"You have no idea how glad I am that it was you who found it."

"I have kept it close."

"I had to pawn the jewel…"

"For Stevenson," he said, realization dawning on him.

She nodded.

He began to untie it, to return it, but she shook her head fiercely. "I want you to wear it. Never take it off. It is the only thing I have that is truly mine. And I want to give it you."

His heart… Damnation. How his heart

filled with love and wonder for her. All that she had gone through. He was a duke who owned gold, jewels, and estates, but in all his life, he'd never been given something so powerful as her ribbon and this moment.

He leaned over her, his mouth just above hers as he whispered, "It will never leave me. Never leave me, Charlotte. Never again."

She reached up and pulled his mouth back down to hers, taking his lips in a wild kiss as if she was determined to drive out everything but them and their bodies intertwined.

The kiss set his blood ablaze with renewed need. He had to see her. All of her. And so as soon as he had slid his breeches down his body, he worked at her garments, quickly untying strings and shimmying fabric over her body.

When she was naked, save for her silk stockings, he gazed at her curves with wonder.

Every bit of her. Every beautiful part was home to him. A place where he felt complete.

He took her in his arms, lay down beside her, and rolled her onto her side.

She let out a gasp of surprise as he hooked her leg up over his hip.

Staring deeply into her eyes, he thrust into her body.

Eyes wide, lips parted, she grabbed onto his shoulders.

Damnation, she was so wet and hot and ready for him.

Rafe nearly came at the feel of it, but he wanted this to last.

He wanted this moment to go on and on.

He wanted to forget the world and be here, just with her.

And so, determined for them to be lost in this, he thrust slowly, deliberately into her body.

Charlotte let out a low moan as he moved in her.

And then, much to his amazement, she placed her hand on his cheek. Her eyes filled with emotion as she leaned in, then kissed him.

That kiss sent him over the edge.

He angled his body so that it stroked her most sensitive spot.

And it seemed that she, too, could no longer wait.

The intimacy, the pleasure, the closeness between them, and all that had nearly been stolen away from them this night was replaced by sheer bliss.

Charlotte's body tightened around his, and he came in a shattering wave of ecstasy. Just as she joined him there, their arms entwined about each other. As one.

EPILOGUE

Rafe's grandmama carefully placed the coronet of diamonds upon Charlotte's head.

The older woman easily arranged it, tucking and pinning it into Charlotte's beautifully curled hair.

She stared at herself in the mirror, then looked to Rafe's grandmother, who was positively beaming.

The room was lit by the glow of candlelight, and it was still hard to believe that this beautiful chamber was hers.

She no longer slept on a hard bed in a drafty room with no furniture to speak of.

Now, she was Rafe's guest, and this bedchamber surely rivaled any princess's throughout the world.

The water-blue silk hangings shone a gentle cloud color, and the ivory furnishings filled her heart with delight.

But the thing that had touched her above all? The bookshelves that had been brought in that morning, lined with dozens of the latest novels and old favorites from the last twenty years.

It had been a gesture from Rafe to make the room feel as if it was her home. She had been tempted to return to her mother's home, *her* home, but given the tumult, it had been deemed best by all if she did not live alone at present.

One day, she'd return. One day soon, no doubt. For she would always love that place with all her heart.

But it was her past. She could see that after all that had transpired. She knew her family story and had more than just a few rooms to remind her of her parents.

Now she stood wearing family jewels.

"My dear girl," the older woman said, "you have been a princess all your life. You have always been a princess, but now you are dressed like one."

Charlotte's heart squeezed, and she turned to the older woman and took her hands. "Thank you," she said, emotion threatening to overwhelm her once again.

It seemed to be her general state of affairs now. There was so much to feel. Gratitude, wonder, passion, and yes...grief.

But in this moment, her heart was alight, for she had never been cared for so thoroughly by someone who could have been *her* grandmother.

"No," Rafe's grandmama said, her voice shaking ever so slightly. "It is I who must thank you. You have brought my grandson so much happiness by simply being in his life. You are not required to marry him, my dear.

You are not even required to love him, but know that we all care about you very much, and we hope that you shall let us be in your life always. I know that you have little family with you—just your stepsister—but sometimes, we can find family and make it our own."

Charlotte bit down on her lower lip, determined not to cry. It was not sorrow that sent the tears to her eyes or tightened her throat. It was wonder at the kindness she had discovered in this house.

Rafe's grandmama patted Charlotte's hand. "I know what it is like to lose people." She sighed, her silver coiffure bobbing. "Someone of my age always knows what it is like to lose people. Most of my friends are gone. Almost everyone that I have loved is gone, except for my grandson, of course, and my daughter-in-law. I hope that you will let me come to love you, and that you might come to love me, too. It would be a great joy for an old woman."

She squeezed the older woman's beringed hands, touched beyond words. "It would be my honor."

And then, the dowager duchess gave her a curtsy. "No, Princess de León, it would be my honor." She took a step back and picked up her cane from where it rested against the full-length mirror. "Now, might I take you down to the ball?"

Charlotte could scarce draw breath as she contemplated how her life had changed.

She had been alone so long, save Francesca, Stevenson, Mary, and Cook, that she did not know how to behave with so many people who cared for her. The very idea that she might have a family, not out of obligation but out of desire?

It was almost too much for her to bear.

But she nodded at the older woman, picked up her long train, and allowed herself to be swept out of the room.

Despite holding the strap in her hand, the elaborate train of silk and jewels followed behind her, dancing over the beautiful carpets.

It took skill to manage it, and she had been practicing all afternoon.

Her ball gown was more elaborate than the one she had been wearing when she had her fitting. This one looked as if it had been embroidered with silver and gold thread.

Jewels had been sewn into the flowers embroidered along the hem, and the chiffon that barely skimmed her breasts and shoulders looked like whispers of air over her pale skin.

Diamonds clung to her throat and spilled over her wrists and down from her ears. And of course, there was her coronet, a veritable crown of jewels that had been worn by generations of duchesses. But none of them touched the beautiful sapphire ring that Rafe had presented her with. It shone now on her finger, glinting in the light, a constant and beloved reminder of his devotion to her.

Charlotte knew that she was one glittering picture of luxury and elegance. And in all her life, she had never felt so out of sorts.

She *looked* like a princess now. She *was* a princess, but she did not know what to do. Or how to feel.

She still felt like…well, just Charlotte.

The truth was, she loved Rafe. There was no question. That was all that mattered.

And as his grandmother led her into the ballroom, the entire crowd of important guests turned in her direction. The gilded *ton* of London were now fully aware of exactly who she was.

The scandal had traveled through the city like wildfire after Palmerton was imprisoned.

They all remembered the unknown Lady Charlotte who had sung a country ballad at her first party.

Now earls, countesses, viscounts and their wives, marquesses and barons alike curtsied when she came into the room.

Her title was one that could not be sniffed at, after all. Watching hundreds of gentlemen and ladies in silks and jewels from all over the world bow to her was enough to startle anyone.

Surely such homage could shake anyone to their core?

Her insides began to quake. And for one brief moment, her legs turned to jelly.

She had no idea how to act the grand princess. She longed for the quiet of a small room and the escape of her stories.

But when she turned, half ready to run, she spotted Francesca, who was also curtsying to her.

Francesca lifted her head and beamed. Her stepsister raised herself up and ran to her, damning decorum, and Charlotte was so very glad.

"My darling sister," Francesca gushed, "I cannot tell you how happy I am for you tonight."

Charlotte shook her head. "I… I don't deserve—"

Francesca took her gloved hand and leaned in. "I am not happy for you because of all these peacocks paying you court," she whispered. "I am happy because you are so loved. I love you. Rafe loves you. His family loves you. And it is all because you have been so unwavering in your sense of self, Charlotte. You would not back down."

Francesca pressed a small kiss to her cheek. "Do not back down now."

Those words were exactly what she needed to hear, and she hugged her stepsister to her, ignoring the surprised stares of several of the English nobility.

They all needed more embraces, in her opinion.

At last, she drew in a breath and strode forward into the ballroom, which was decorated as if it was a night of enchantment.

Lanterns of every hue hung from the ceilings, and flowers festooned the walls and columns.

It was a beautiful sight to behold. And it, in many ways, was all for her.

She caught sight of Rafe's mother, who gazed on her with approval.

Charlotte returned her smile, but she did not yet feel content.

No, there was someone she needed to see. Someone for whom her heart longed.

Finally, she spotted the duke, who stood in the center of the dance floor.

Slowly, everyone backed away from him, clearing the long area meant for dancers.

His elaborate black coat clung tightly to his broad frame. His dark hair was styled playfully back from his strong face, and he waited silently for her to arrive.

Rafe said nothing. He did not have to.

His dark gaze met hers, and the power of it nearly undid her. In the very best way. She was home, with him, here.

And then to her utter delight, he held out

his hand to her. Just as he had done that night in Vauxhall Gardens, when she had told him she did not know how to dance.

She'd never forget the way he had offered her his hand that night, leading her down the garden path to teach her the steps of the waltz.

There, under the bows of the tree, the soft music in the air and his affinity for her shown without hesitation, her life had changed utterly.

He'd kissed her. And their passion had proclaimed itself. Undeniable and true.

Rafe had been so kind then, showing her that she could have what she wanted, promising her that she could be anyone she wanted.

And now she was a princess.

She did not care about being a princess, per se. Oh, she cared that she had found out the truth about her family and that she had independence and wealth.

But what she truly cared about now was that she could actually be his.

It was there in his eyes. His loyalty and his love. He would weather any storm to have her. And her heart thrilled, knowing it to be so.

Without hesitation, she strode across the dance floor and stood before him.

"I have something for you," he said softly.

She stilled, surprised. "I do not need gifts—"

"It is not a gift," he said as he slipped his

hand into his pocket.

Her heart began to beat wildly against her ribs. Whatever could it be?

He held his closed fist out to her, then slowly opened it.

No…could it really be…?

Her mother's pearl had been laced onto the blue silk ribbon that Rafe had found. It rested in his palm, safe, at home, beckoning her.

She gasped, and tears rushed into her eyes. "How?"

"The day we met," he began, "I did not understand how you could be so upset about the loss of those coins. But once I understood that you had to pawn the only thing you had of your mother? The pain of it must have been immense, and yet… Your only thought was of Stevenson. Of saving him. I scoured the shops these last days until I found it had been sold, and then I found the man who had bought it. After I told him the tale, he relinquished your mother's pearl to you with a free heart and easy hand."

Charlotte couldn't speak as he carefully traced the ribbon around her throat and tied it carefully. "It was always coming home to you, my love. As was I."

A tear slipped down her cheek, and oh so gently, he caught it with his thumb and wiped it away. "I did not mean to make you cry."

"Out of happiness, Rafe," she declared. "I had no idea I could be so happy. I had no idea...I could still come home."

His eyes widened, and love heated his gaze.

He gave her a deep bow. "Will you dance with me, Princess?"

She lowered herself into a perfect curtsy before him, then lifted her gaze to his and said, "Yes, Your Grace, I will."

His chest expanded, and he breathed a sigh of relief.

"Did you think I might say no?" she allowed herself to tease as the music began playing a romantic and whimsical waltz.

"You've told me no before," he pointed out gently.

She smiled up at him. "I will likely tell you no again someday."

"And if I *ask* you now?" he said, slipping his palm to her back.

"Ask me what?"

He helped her to take up her train with her hand, the blue sapphire ring on her finger sparkling. And then, he began to lead them about the room, lilting, turning, twirling, and dipping as the crowd watched.

They were no longer simply walking, as they had started doing upon their first attempt in Vauxhall. No. Now their bodies had met and melded and known bliss.

Just as he had promised.

And now, in the waltz, as he took her down the dance floor, she felt the bliss that only he could bring her rising up again as she waited for him to speak.

"Charlotte," he asked, "my love, the one who bashed me with a brick, who told me what was what, and who explained the challenges of society to me, will you go throughout this life by my side? Will you be my partner and my lover, not only my wife? Will you walk with me, tell me when I'm being a fool, teach me when I'm being an ass, and spend the rest of my days with me?"

He paused, drew in a breath, then asked, his voice deep with emotion: "Will you dance with me every night by the fire?"

It did not matter that they waltzed before hundreds; now, at last, she truly let tears slip down her face. She gasped for breath as he twirled her around, then turned her under his arms.

"I have made you cry again," he said, his voice shaking.

"Yes, you have," she affirmed before she smiled up at him, unable to hide her happiness. "Oh, Rafe, these tears of joy are long overdue, for I am full of so much bliss I do not think I can contain it."

"Is that a yes?" he queried, his eyes searching her face.

"Yes, my love, yes. A thousand times yes."

And with that, he turned her gently under his arm, pulled her into him, and slowly spun them about.

"To our happily ever after?" he asked.

"No," she said.

"No?" he queried, his eyebrows raising.

"No happily ever after," she mused. "To our happily ever *beginning*."

ACKNOWLEDGMENTS

A huge thank you to Lydia, Curtis, Liz, Jessica, Bree, and the entire Entangled team! I also must thank Patricia D., Louisa C., Meghan, and Lisa who cheered me on!